Wondering Life 迷茫人生

I0681917

Young Dai-Shan

小代山

Mu Tong 牧童(Herd boy)

Acknowledgement 致谢(*zhixie*)

Without the encouragement and support of my family and friends, this book would not be possible. Thanks to my children for editing and providing feedback.

ISBN: 978-0-9948791-7-2 (paperback)

Wondering Life - *Young Dai-shan* by *Mu Tong*

Printed and distributed on Amazon.

Disclaimer:
While all care is taken to ensure the story is purely for entertainment, the author and the publisher have no intention to offend or undermine anyone or any organization and shall not be liable for any consequence because of the information contained herein.

To my parents and all parents who dedicated their lives to unconditionally raising their children, Thank you!

To those children who grew up in rural China in the 1950s – 1970s, may you all have been successful in your lives.

Notice to Readers 敬告读者*(jing-gao duzhe)*

The story is based on real people, real events, and personal memories of 60 years ago from an old scholar whose life crossed oceans and continents. However, the main events, incidents, details and timelines have been changed through artistic process for dramatic purposes; The characters, locations and storyline are purely fabricated. They do not represent anything in real life.

The presented events are just an ordinary person's observations at the time. The author has no opinion or comments, nor implication of what really occurred in real life. The story is purely for entertainment. How much to believe is completely at the reader's discretion.

这个故事以真人真事为题材，根据一位跨洋过州老者对 60 多年前的回忆构思而成。而主要事件，时间，地点和故事情节(剧情)通过艺术加工编辑而成。人物，地名，以及很多细节纯属艺术构造，不可当真。所涉及到的事和物只是一个普通人对其生活环境的观察而已，别无任何见解或评论，更无其他涵义。只供业余欣赏，信多信少，全由读者(听众)自己定夺。

Readers are further reminded that the story is from the view of a child. Many things may not have a rationale, and many descriptions may not have a clearly stated meaning. Often, the meaning of what is said is what a reader understood and there is no exact interpretation. Readers need to interpret what in the story based their own experience and knowledge of the culture, the society and the political environment.

进一步提醒读者：故事是从一个小孩的角度出发而写。很多事情似乎没有明显的理由，或确切的含义。通常，一句话的含义得由读者自己去理解。请读者根据自己的经历和对社会，文化及政治环境的了解去解读。

Preface 序言 (*xu yan*)

This book is intended for Chinese descendants born after the 1970s, particularly those born outside of China, to help them understand their roots and culture, as a mirror reflecting a corner of life in their parent's and grandparents' generations from the 1950s, particularly in rural China. It's also suitable for other Chinese immigrants and descendants who had little or no life experience prior to and during the cultural revolution in China. It can be useful for people of other nationalities who are interested in Chinese culture to learn what life was like in rural China during the 2nd half of the 20th century.

这本书以 1970 以后出生的，特别在中国大陆以外出生的华裔后代读者为主要对象，以帮助他们了解自己的根和文化及其父母一代的生活大环境中的一个角落.同时也适合其他华人和爱好中华文化的其他民族了解一些 20 世纪后半时期的中国农村人口当时的生活环境，尤其是文革期间。

The story starts with a legend and witnesses the birth of the main character, his childhood, juvenile and youth in a small mountain village, and his experience during the unprecedented Cultural Revolution in rural China.

故事从一个民间传说开始，迎来了主人公的诞生，伴随他在一个小山村度过了幼年，少年和青年时代，并经历了前所未有的乡村文革。

During his growing path life was hard, and people were always worried about food and clothing, despite of working hard year-round. At his young age, he had no idea why. He witnessed the occurrence of many things and first thought that was the way things were, but he still wanted to figure out the reason behind it. He grew up in the wondering era. Sometimes, the result for something seemed inevitable, but he didn't know how many other factors could affect it.

在主人公的成长过程中，生活是艰苦的。 尽管终年劳累，人们常为温饱发愁。他小小年纪，不知那为什么。他见证了很多事情的发生，本以为事情就应该那样，但还是想知道为什么。他在迷茫中成长。很多事情的发展，看似必然的，但却不知受多少因素的影响。

He was exploring life on his own; he was striving for a better outcome with limited or no resources, and he was determined to change his future. Sometimes, he seemed to be lucky. However, he didn't realize that was not because of his fate or his striving efforts alone, but the comprehensive result of many complex factors. That was the way it was. The year 1977 arrived and he happened to catch the opportunity to take the first Gaokao (university entrance exams), which was cancelled at the start of the cultural revolution. However, his ancestors for many generations were lifelong peasants, and his parents had merely any education. What would be his chance to pass that extremely competitive Gaokao, as a boy from a small poor mountain village?

他在独自探索人生，他在徒手奋斗，他立志要改变自己的命运。有时侯看来他也是幸运的，但他不知那其实不是命运所定或单凭自己努力所致，而是复杂因数的综合结果。那就是当时的社会状况。1977 年到了，他赶上了文革后的第一次高考。但他祖上世代务农，父母几乎就是文盲，在那次竞争激励的高考中他又有多少胜算呢？

Prologue 序篇 (*xu pian*)

This happened a few hundred years ago.
故事发生在几百多年以前.

According to the elders: A long, long time ago, in South-Western China (the *Duotong* 多通 Basin), there was a huge rainstorm disaster: water rose very high, submerging all buildings and turning the land into an ocean. All houses collapsed, and numerous people drowned. After the stormwater retreated, pandemic swept through the land. Hunger, disease, lack of shelter and medication altogether wiped out all of humankind. On this vast land, there was barely any trace of human life. The disaster destroyed all civilization. As a result, there is no record of the disaster in history books.

据老人们说：在很久很久以前，在西南的一块土地上（如今的多通盆地）发生了一场特大洪灾。洪水蹬天，冲垮了所有的房屋，淹没了整个大地，死人无数。随之而来的是一场瘟疫。饥荒，疫情遍天下，民不僚生，无衣无药，人几乎都死光了。 苍茫大地渺无人烟…。 这场灾难毁灭了这块大地上所有文明，当然也没留下历史记载。

Many years later, the land gradually returned to habitable conditions, vegetation started growing and evidence of small wild animals became visible here and there.

很多年以后，大地慢慢地复苏，逐渐出现了生机。草木重生，还出现了活跃的小动物。

Not sure how many more years past again and not sure exactly when, at some point the Imperial Court decided to

1

reclaim this once-rich land through mandatory migration from neighboring provinces, including Hunan and Guangdong. That was forced migration by the armed soldiers. No matter how unwilling they were, the migrants had to leave their homeland under the threat of the armed soldiers and the order "to kill anyone who disobeyed".

不知又过了多少年。 据传说，朝廷官府决定从外地（包括湖南和广东地区）强行移民来填补这块曾经富饶的平原，重耕这块土地。那是强制移民。这批百姓无论多么不愿意，在"违者斩首"的官令和手持屠刀的官兵威逼下，离开了自己的家园.

There was a village called "Wagon Garden 车子园 (*Che-zi-yuan*)" in the then Guangdong province. In the village, there once lived the Yao family with grandparents, two brothers and their spouses and children. One day, a group of armed soldiers showed up at the Yao's residence. A man wearing an Imperial officer hat thrust an Imperial Court order at the residents and arrogantly announced. "Your family have been chosen to relocate to a beautiful land, and you must leave this place by the deadline. Otherwise…". The officer made a swift gesture with his right hand at his neck, meaning "chop your head off" and then walked away with his head up high without acknowledging anyone around.

在广东省曾有一个名叫"车子园"的地方，住着一家姓姚的兄弟俩，还有他们的父母，妻子和孩子。一天，一个朝廷官员在手持屠刀的官兵陪同下来到了姚家住宅，仍给他们一道官令， 并傲慢地说道"*你们家已被选上，要搬迁到一个美好的地方，你们必须在截至日期以前离开这里。否则…*" 他用右手在自己脖子上做了一个手势，意思是"斩首"，然后趾高气扬地离开了。

Like many other families, the Yao family had lived on that land for many generations and was reluctant to leave their own home. They were not rich but could manage to survive over the years.

与其他家庭一样，姚家在此已生活了若干代人，很不愿意离开。他们虽然不富裕，但也能维持生活。

The deadline was approaching. The Yao family became worried. A neighbor passed by and cried out, "*ai-ya 哎呀, Bu-dei-liao la 不得了啦* [1]. Why are you still here? Some people in the neighboring village have already been prosecuted by the soldiers because they remained past the deadline. The officers chopped their heads off. It's horrible. You'd better get moving, hurry."

预定的期限就快到了，姚家开始有些担忧。一个邻居路过，一见他们就惊叫了起来，"*哎呀，不得了啦。你们为什么还在这里？邻村有的人已经被处死了，就因为他们过了期限。官兵把他们的头砍了。太可怕了。你们还是快走吧。快点！*"

A long line of migrants walked along a trail, old and young, men and women, in their straw hats, carrying their simple belongings on their backs, shoulders, and in their hands: bamboo baskets, bags. At the end of the line were the armed soldiers. The migrants walked thousands of miles to their destinations and finally settled in their new homeland.

"This is the legendary Hu-Guang migration to fill the *Duotong* basin", the elders said, "not many people are aware of this anymore today". It is no longer possible to verify the Yao family's old address since there was no historical record. This legendary place had become a mystery. However, the story passed on from generation to

---

[1] Ai-ya 哎呀 *Bu-dei-liao la* 不得了啦 – an expression of being surprised and worried, claiming something big, often disastrous is happening.

generation by word of mouth. It has been over a few hundred years since then.

长长的一行移民，头带草帽，沿着小路，带上全家老小，背上，肩上，手上带着简陋的家档，后面还有手持屠刀的官兵。他们徒步千里，终于来到了目的地。并从此在这块土地上繁衍生息。"这就是'湖-广填多通'的民间传说"，老人们说，"至今已没有多少人知晓喽"。因无文字记载，姚家原来的住址现也无法考证。但故事已在民间流传了下来。至今大约已有好几百年了。

The elders also said, under the threat of the armed soldiers, the two brothers of the Yao family brought their family and followed the migration trail. Since they started late, they lagged far behind the others. What happened on the way made their journey more difficult. They arrived at a remote place confronting a river. Suddenly there was a heavy rainstorm. Storm water roared down the river and made it difficult for everyone to cross, particularly the young and elders. Under the threat of the armed merciless soldiers behind, the family had to make a tough decision: one brother with his immediate family would depart first to cross the river to reach the destination as soon as possible with a hope to find a piece of land. Another with the elders and the rest would wait until the water level retreated. To avoid execution by the armed soldiers, those left behind must change their surname from Yao 姚 to Duan 段 (meaning: being cut off). They told their children: The Yao and Duan families were from the same ancestor and their descendants would not be allowed to marry each other.

老人们还说，在官兵的强制威胁下，姚氏兄弟已到了最后期限才带上家人离开家园。因动身晚，他们远远地掉在了后面。但途中还未入境又碰上一场大爆雨，河里滚滚洪水，拦住了去路，还有老的，小的，很难过河。为了避免官兵的追杀，他们不得已将

4

一家人分开：一个姚氏兄弟带上自己的妻子和孩子先过河，希望能占一块地。另一个兄弟和其他人留下等河水退了再过河。由于官兵的驱赶，未过河的人只好改姓为"段"。因此，后来祖先规定姚姓和段姓为本家人，不能通婚。

Those who crossed the river had to hurry to reach the destination. When the others eventually crossed the river later, there was no way for them to find out where the rest of the family went. Post service was out of reach for ordinary people in that chaotic situation. The two Yao brothers were thus separated forever.

话说已过河的这家姚姓人只好冲冲赶路。后来过河的人已无法找到他们的行踪。对普通人来说通讯是不可能的。兄弟俩从此永远地分开了。

Let us find out what happened to the brother who crossed the river earlier. His name was *Yao, Yin-Dru* 姚印祖[2]. He and his family had to catch up with the migration crowd. Long journey, fatigue and hunger exhausted them along the way. They eventually arrived at the new land, but they were too late. All inhabitable land had been claimed by those who arrived earlier. They searched various places but could not find a place to settle down.

再来看看那位已过河的姚家兄弟，他名叫姚印祖。过河以后他带着全家冲忙赶路。长途疲劳，饥饿让全家筋疲力尽。他们终于到达了目的地，但太晚了。 当时的土地都已被先到的人们全部分光。到处奔波，几经周转，却无身存之地。

To survive, the *Yin-Dru* family had to come up with a

---

[2] Yao 姚 - surname, Yin 印 - predetermined generation rank, middle name, Dru 祖 - given name. This name was the only thing on record in Yao family shrine.

plan. A seemingly kind settler saw the situation of this family and told them that one settler at a hill nearby might be willing to share part of his land, but he wanted some compensation. The *Yin-Dru* family's possessions were not worth anything, with no silver coins[3] left and what they had available was only their family members. The children were too young[4]. *Yin-Dru* was the backbone to support the family. No matter how unwilling and how hurtful, he couldn't find a solution to save the family without breaking up the family.

为了生存，他们必须寻找一条生路。一个看似善良的人得知他们的困境，告诉他们，附近小山上有一个早到的人可能有一些土地出让，但他们希望有报酬。印祖一家已没有什么有价值的了，银子已花光。他们所剩的就只有这家人了。孩子们又还小，姚印祖是支持全家的支柱。他们又面临着一个前所未有的困境，无论如何也无法保全这个家。

Yin-Dru discussed the situation and all feasible options with his wife. By the end, this couple who built a family together and suffered so much on their journey made a very tough decision, a decision no one should have to make. They had to break up the family. The kind wife agreed to go to live with another man in exchange for some silver coins to help her family and own children survive.

印祖和妻子商量，但始终想不出一个办法。最终做出了一个让人听了撕心裂肺的决定，一个如何人都不应该面临的决定：拆散这个家，他们俩共同建立的，历经千辛万苦的这个家。为了让她

---

[3] Coin of real silver was used to buy stuff at that time.

[4] In human history, adults were making efforts to feed their young. However, children helping parents doing chores at home or in the field as a young labor was also common, particularly in rural areas. It is reasonable to say this is still the practice in rural families.

自己的家和孩子有机会生存下去，这位善良的妻子同意了去跟另外的一个男人生活以换得一些银子。

The couple hugged each other, and both started crying, loudly and heartbreakingly. That made their children worried: "*Ah-ba* 阿爸, *Ah-niang* 阿娘[5], why are you both crying, what happened?", the older child asked. "Your mother has to go to a far-away place to help our family and you children may not be able to see her for a long time." Their father told them. "Children, you should remember it is your mother who sacrificed herself to save our family", he continued.

The mother hugged each child tearfully but couldn't say a single word. She then went away with a stranger and turned back to look at her children one last time until she disappeared in the far distance. No one knew her whereabouts and how well her life was thereafter.

夫妻俩拥抱在一起，失声痛苦。孩子们见了感到不安，忙问，"阿爸，阿娘，你们哭什么？发生了什么事？"

"为了帮助我们这个家，你们的妈妈要去一个很远的地方。你们可能很久都难见到她了"，父亲告诉他们。"你们要记住，是你们的妈妈拯救了我们这个家。"

妈妈拥抱了每一个孩子，但说不出一句话，含着泪水，一步一回头地跟一个陌生的男人走了，直到她消失在远方。后来谁也不知道她的下落，她是否过的幸福。

Eventually, the Yin-Dru finally had a piece of land on the upper portion of a small mountain for his remaining family. They settled down on this not-rich but habitable land, which was approximately 50 kilometers away from

---

[5] Based on Cantonese custom, a pre-fix "ah" is added when calling someone, ex., ah-ba (father), ah-niang (mother), etc.

Zhongdu-fu 中都府 (city) in the South-East direction and now called Yao'sville 姚家梁子 (*Yao-Jia LiangZi*)[6]. The Yao family has lived there ever since. Their descendants continued living on that land for a few hundred years. The elders always used the story to educate their descendants to love and take care of the land. However, no one could verify the whereabouts of that land today. By the mid 20th century, the 12th generation of the *Yin-Dru* family were born and lived on the same land[7].

　　印祖拿着以自己老婆为代价换来的银子，买下了一小块坡地，终于为家人建立了一个生存的基地。此活听了让人心酸。此地就是如今的"姚家梁子"，位于中都府东南方大约50公里。后来老人们常用这个故事来教育后生们要珍惜这块土地。但这块地今天在哪里实在无法考证。据推算，从姚氏祖先进入多通地区到20世纪中期大概已经历了十二代人了。

棚子弯

姚家梁子 Yao'sville - 2025

---

[6] Yao'sville 姚家梁子 (*Yao-Jia LiangZi*) - a place adopted from a local village, which has a low mountain terrain, named after the first settler of Yao's ancestor.

[7] As of today, in the 21st century, the 14th generation of the *Yin-Dru* family has arrived. 21世纪的早期已迎来了姚家的第十四代曾孙。

A few hundred years have past. The Yao descendants have lost their heritage and no longer speak cantonese. The only thing they have kept is the prefix "ah". The total population in Yao'sville has reached 80 including other families. People in a neighbouring village seem to speak a cantonese dialect but they do not sound like what you hear in Guangzhou or Hongkong.

几百年过去了。姚家梁子的人们已经失去了他们的广东文化，也不再会说广东话。他们唯一保存下来的是对家人的称呼"阿".包括其他外姓人，村子里的人口已达到了80。邻村的人好像保留了他们的广东语言，但他们说的与你在广州或香港听到的却不一样。

Chapter 1

The Infancy Time
牛儿的出生和幼年时代
(*Niu-er de chu sheng he you-nian shidai*)

1. Yao'sville 姚家梁子 (*Yao-Jia LiangZi*)

Yao'sville 姚家梁子 was a poor mountain village, located on the edge of *Zhongdu* 中都 *plain* 平原 (*ping-yuan*), within *Duotong* 多通 *basin* 盆地 (*pen-di*), in South-West China. The general terrain in the region is very hilly with a series of mountain ridges, some being a few hundred meters high here and there.

The village is situated at the upper portion of a small mountain. Its terrain is hilly, overall sloping to the south. The north and west sides are steep slopes. The east side is on a higher elevation creating a peak, over 300 meters high, sloping east more than 40°. A few zig-zag foot paths exist through the hilly terrain.

Due to the landform condition, there is no adequate water supply in the village because the land is isolated from others around. The only water sources are the rainwater and a small spring seeping out of the ground at the lower part. In drought seasons, the spring becomes dripping and nearly dry out. Severe water shortage occurs often in spring and early summer. At these times, villagers had to go down the hill to the neighboring village to carry water on shoulders with a pair of pails for their daily use and irrigation. That is a strength-demanding work.

The village did not have a big forest resource but with plenty of healthy woods mostly small cedar trees. The soil on this land is not rich in comparison with that in the valley below. The inhabitants live on growing corn, wheat, and sweet potato as the primary crops for many generations. They couldn't grow rice because of the water shortage. Yao'sville is a typical poor mountain village, although it is less than 50 kilometers away from *Zhongdu-fu*, the capital of *Duotong* 多通 Province 省 (*sheng*).

Since the Yao's ancestor, *Yin-Dru* 印祖 settled here, a few hundred years had passed, and his descendants had lived on this land for ten generations by the 1900's. It was a poor land, but it was their homeland. By that time, the Yin-Dru's descendants wouldn't know which piece of land their ancestor originally acquired at the cost of breaking up the family and many didn't even know what had happened.

After ten generations, *Yin-Dru's* descendants had grown and split into six families and there was now a total of 11 families living in this village including a few other families (Xie 谢, *Ye* 叶, Wu 吴, Zhang 张 and Zhou 周) who migrated here some years ago along the way. Among the six Yao descendant families, three were direct brothers: Wang-da, the eldest, Wang-er, the second and Wang-san, the third plus a younger sister who married into the Zhou family in the same village. It was said their father was married at a very young age of 16 and raised a family with four children.

The other three Yao families were distant cousins, traced back a few generations. Based on the old tradition, boys and their descendants would carry the family name, with each generation rank being predetermined. Siblings would normally live together with parents until the parents passed away. Therefore, it could be speculated that: for the previous ten generations, the *Yin-Dru*'s descendants had at least split six times leading to the six families at this time; several generations would only have raised one boy who became an adult and continued the family line.

One thing worth mentioning is that in the old days, the survival rate of children was low due to the lack of health services and adequate medication. If a family had no boy to raise up to continue the family name, the family line would eventually disappear.

Within the next 30 to 40 years, out of the six Yao families, except for Wang-san, each had two boys who grew up to adulthoods and *Yin-Dru*'s descendants had grown and evolved to 10 families by the 11th generation.

The Wang-da family had three siblings. The eldest was a girl who was "married" to her future husband at a very young age as a child bride. In the old days, when a family could not afford to raise all children, a girl would usually be sent to her future husband home as a child bride, and she would formally get married when grown up. In those times, marriage was pre-arranged by parents when children were still very young. The two younger children of the Wang-da family were boys, one named *Shi-qing* 世青 and the youngest named *Shi-dan* 世单. They lived together in a relatively large family even after they got married.

The Wang-er family had four siblings. The two younger ones were boys, and they lived in a house right behind the Wang-da family's two brothers.

Wang-san suffered from metal illness, never married and lived by himself in a room just next to Wang-da's families.

Over the years, some more families with other surnames had moved to this village and increased the total number of families to 19 and the population reached 100[8].

Although the village was only approximately 50 kilometers away from *Zhongdu-fu*, it felt far away at that time. Because of the hilly terrain and its geographical location, no major transportation infrastructure existed

---

[8] The population reached its peak of 120 in the 1970's but dropped to below 40 by the beginning of the 21st century due to mass migration to cities during China's further economic reform.

in the mountainous area. There was a main road passing the village at half a kilometer away down the valley, which connected *Zhongdu-fu* to other cities in that direction. The road had a gravel surface[9], that followed the valley and gradually ascended to the top of the mountain before descending to *Zhongdu Plain*.

There was little public transportation. Few buses passed by everyday on the road, connecting neighboring major towns. There was no bus stop close to the village and the buses generally did not stop on the road to pick up passengers. It was difficult to get on a bus unless you walked to a nearby town 3 kilometers away in the mountain terrain. Ordinary people did not have spare money for taking a bus anyway. Villagers went to the surrounding markets usually on foot, despite some being as far as 5 to 10 kilometers away, to sell their produce and surplus and then buy necessities: salt, cooking oil, soy sauce, meat, etc. The primary and the only method to transport their stuff was on their shoulders and backs. That needed physical strength. If someone took a bus to a nearby place, neighbors would make a joke "Here is the rich guy."

2. Land Reform and Creation of Family-Class 土地改革和阶级成分的产生 (*tudi gaige he jieji chengfen de chansheng*)

Time went fast and the year 1949 arrived. China had a huge change: the old government fled to Taiwan, a new government was setup by the Chinese Communist Party (CP) and the People's Republic of China was established. Everything belonged to "peoples" and the citizens were supposed to live better lives.

---

[9] Today the road has a concrete surface and is a secondary highway.

In 1950, the year after the establishment of the People's Republic of China, the whole nation went through tremendous changes and reforms. The new government implemented *Land Reform*[10] 土地改革(*tu-di gai-ge*) on land ownership and simultaneously created family classes, with a new term: *Cheng-Feng* 成分 for every family based on their wealth and possession. The creation of *Cheng-Feng* touched every citizen and affected their lives for many decades.

During the land reform, the vast amount of farmland, which were previously owned by the Landlords (landowners), were confiscated by the new government, and re-allocated to individual poor peasants who had no land before. The task was usually performed by a land-reform-team, which was made of one or two CP delegates together with a few activists in a village. To better control its citizens, the government divided adults and their families in rural area into the following five classes, called *"class composition"* 阶级成分 (*jieji cheng-feng*).

I. *Di-Dru* 地主: Those landowners who owned farmlands, but the family themselves did not do farm work, and they lived on collecting land rent or hiring others to farm. In this case, their farmlands were completely confiscated, or in some cases a portion of their lands were left for their own use based on the average per person in the village.

They were the class to be knocked down by the CP-led revolution. In many cases, they were prosecuted at the discretion of the land-reform-team if they were believed to be *"guilty"* of something. Their children

---

[10] Land reform was the first most drastic change made by the government which had huge impact on ordinary citizens.

were deprived of all privileges.

II. *Rich-Peasant* 富农(*fu-nong*): Those peasants who also owned some land, collected land rent, and hired others to help. However, the family engaged in farm work too. In this case, their surplus land was confiscated, and they were often treated in the same way as *Di-zhu*.

III. *Middle-Peasant* 中农(*zhong-nong*): Those peasants who owned little land, did farm work by themselves, and could manage to make ends meet but did not collect land rent.

If they hired others to help during busy season, they would be labeled as the Upper-Middle-Peasant 上中农 (*shang zhong-nong*). If their own land was not sufficient for their living and they needed to work for others to earn extra to meet their family needs, they were labeled as the Lower-Middle-Peasant 下中农 (*xia zhong-nong*).

IV. *Poor-Peasant* 贫农(*pin-nong*): Those peasants who owned very little land but primarily relied on working for others for a living.

V. *Peasant-for-Hire* 雇农(*gu-nong*): Those peasants who had no land and their livelihood completely relied on working for others.

After the land reform, peasants in the rural areas were initially farming on their own land. The family classification has since divided people for many decades. Classes I and II were considered as the enemy and Classes IV and V as well as Class III-lower were the primary groups of people the CP relied upon in the rural area.

Children of all classes would bear similar designations, labeled Birth-Family class 家庭出身 (*jia-ting-chu-shen*) (basically the same as family class). For example, "his

16

Birth-Family class is Middle-Peasant". Their future advancement and careers could be significantly impacted depending on one's birth-family class. If one were born to a family in Classes I or II, they would never have a future. If one were born to a family in Class III, their future may also be impacted with limited access to the privileges which were mostly reserved for people in Classes IV and V.

In urban areas, Cheng-Feng designation was also created in a similar process. People who worked in a factory but did not own anything were called "workers" - the laborer-for-hire, whom the CP relied upon.

With no exception, land reform was implemented in Yao'sville too. It was said, when the land-reform-team completed their analysis, they found that all peasants in this village were in Classes IV and V and no one was qualified for Di-Dru (class I) nor Rich-Peasant (Class II). In order for them to demonstrate to their superiors that they did a thorough and good job, they thought they needed to designate at least one family in Class III.

Then they did a micro-analysis and approached the two brothers, *Shi-qing* and *Shi-dan* and intended to "promote" them to the class of Middle-Peasant, citing that they had a piece of land and hired helpers during the previous busy season but ignored the fact that they also helped others in the same season. As you may remember that piece of land they had in passion was most likely inherited partially from their ancestor who acquired it at the cost of selling his wife. The two brothers had no knowledge and no clue what the Class III meant to them. They did not even know what questions to ask and went along. They have bore Middle-Peasant class ever since.

17

3. Parents-Arranged Marriage 父母包办婚姻 (*fumu baoban hunyin*)

About 4 kilometers away down the hilly terrain from Yao'sville, the landscape changed to flat with rich soil and water resources to grow rice. There is a village called Lin'sville 林家坝子 (*Lin-Jia BaZi*[11]), where most residents had the same surname *Lin* 林. In such areas, the population was denser, and spare land was scarcer than in the mountainous areas. They grew rice, wheat, corn and other crops. Although some farmers had own cows or buffaloes to plow their farms, others would need to "borrow" neighbor's resources or "hire" someone with some compensation, such as manual labor, harvesting crops, etc.

At Lin'sville, one Lin family had four siblings - three daughters and a son. The youngest daughter was named *Min-fei*. Two older daughters were married as child brides, one of them to a Yi family in Yao'sville and another one to a family in a neighboring commune.

In that year, the Lin family didn't have the necessary livestock to plow the farm and was in need for assistance to prepare the farm in the spring. They hired a neighbor to plow the land but due to some reason the work was not finished, half the land waiting to be plowed. The family was looking for help. The news traveled to Yao'sville by words.

The *Shi-qing* and *Shi-dan* family happened to have a cow and agreed to send *Shi-dan, the* younger brother, to help. He took plowing equipment and went there with their cow and completed plowing the remaining half of the Lin's farm. He did the work thoroughly without taking any shortcuts.

---

[11] BaZi: a flat terrain, in contrast to hilly terrain.

18

Half a year later, it was harvesting time. *Min-fei*'s father was surprised to see the crops in the field: the crops in the part of the land plowed by *Shi-dan* grew much better than those in the other part. He was impressed with *Shi-dan's* work and thought: This young man was a good farmer and could be relied upon.

Min-fei had reached marriageable age. It was reasonable to assume that her sister who married the Ye's family in Yao'sville many years ago played a role in her marriage arrangement. One day, a match maker approached her father to propose a marriage with *Shi-dan*. He agreed, probably with consent of his wife, but it was unlikely he discussed the matter with their daughter. Apparently, he believed he made the right decision for his daughter's future happiness.

According to tradition, marriage would normally be arranged through a match maker by parents. Marriage agreed by two people themselves without a match maker would be considered morally unacceptable in society at that time. That was the way marriage was done for many generations. In general, children just had to follow whatever their parents had arranged for them.

After the new government came to power, it promoted 自由恋爱(*ziyou lian-ai*): the freedom for a couple to fall in love and get married on a mutual and voluntary basis. Even in such cases where the two people agreed on their own, a match maker was still needed for formality.

With the arrangement of a match maker, the parents of each side would first have an opportunity to see and/or meet the future son-in-law/daughter-in-law. If the parents on both sides agreed, the man's family would prepare one package of *Cai-li* 彩礼 (marriage proposal present) based on what was acceptable at the time, usually including some valuable goods, such as crops, new fabric, money, even livestock. Richer families would give more to show their status and generosity. Then the young man with his parents, accompanied by the match maker, took *Cai-li* to the girl's family to make a proposal. From that day, this young couple would be formally engaged.

A few weeks, months or years later depending on their agreement and the family situation, a wedding ceremony would be held to complete the marriage with a mass banquet and by witness of family elders, relatives and neighbors. Registration could be done in a local government office to get a marriage certificate in advance. In some cases, no registration was done but just witness by local authorities. In many cases, the couple might have not seen each other until the wedding day.

Although a new marriage law was proclaimed in 1950 in China which was supposed to stop arranged marriage and promote free marriage, the tradition dies hard and parent-arranged marriages continued for a long time, particularly in rural areas. At that time and many years thereafter, physically forced marriage may not be common but morally obligated marriage would not be unusual in many cases.

Now back to *Min-fei*, she did not know much about her future husband. Although she might have seen him when he was there to help her family plow the farm, she had no idea he was the man she would live with in her life. Before the wedding, she most likely didn't have much of a chance to talk to him, not to mention like him as a person or fall in love with him. She married her husband *Shi-dan* under the arrangement of a match maker with her parents' consent. It was hard to tell if she was happy or if she had just agreed to it. One thing that was sure was that she obeyed her parents' arrangement.

4. Arrival of the Little Calf 牛儿的出生 (*Niu-er de chusheng*)

The year 1955 arrived. It was in the middle of January, the deep winter; the temperature was in the single digit on the thermometer, often below zero Celsius. The villagers in Yao'sville had just celebrated the Spring Festival a couple of weeks ago and they were still somewhat in a festive mood. They greeted each other by saying happy Spring Festival 过年好 (*guo nian hao*) or 春节快乐(*chun-jie-kuai-le*).

At that time, *Min-fei* and her husband *Shi-dan* had just started living separately from his older brother Shi-qing's family not long ago. Family separation in many cases was a big domestic problem those days, especially when there was family property to split. Siblings became enemies and some never talked to each other thereafter, mostly due to dispute in property sharing. For the Yao brothers, it was actually very simple. Their original home was a three-room bungalow made of clay walls and straw roof. A few years ago, just after *Shi-dan* got married, they added three larger rooms to the old building, making an L-shaped building. His brother *Shi-qing*'s family lived in the new section ever since and Shi-dan with his wife remained in the old section, using two rooms with the middle room as a main room 堂屋 (*tangwu*) for common purposes.

After the land reform, the government started a series of organizational reforms in the rural areas, which we will get back to later with more detail. This time, basically, all land were put back together in a collective farm group, peasants then worked together and got their shares of allotted harvests from the farming group. There was not much personal property left except their homes. Under that circumstance, it did not seem to make much sense to have a big family eating together and it was more appropriate for them just to make own food to avoid complaint of who did more house chores and who ate more food, etc. So, the two brother families collected their own share of harvests from the group and started cooking on their own. That seemed fairer to all.

One small concern was about the rooms. *Shi-qing*'s family had five people and *Shi-dan*'s family had only two with one expected new arrival. However, property sharing in family separation was not necessarily based on the number of people but on the number of siblings. The old section of the home was sandwiched between buildings with no room to expand, while the new section was larger and had more space to expand in the future. *Shi-dan* didn't know what to say but *Min-fei* insisted they should keep the three rooms. Then they did.

It was a day in January on the lunar calendar (February on the solar calendar), a very special day for the *Shi-dan* family. In the morning, it was partially sunny. As usual, the first thing the villagers did was to go to the field to do one hour or so work in the farm before returning home for breakfast. After eating, everyone went to the field again. Villagers lived their everyday life like that year after year, and by the end they managed to make their ends meet for most of them, but some ended up in the debt.

Min-fei, in her late pregnancy, did the same as the others that morning. However, she returned home before the lunch break, saying she was not feeling well. She went to rest in her bedroom by herself.

The bedroom was one of the three rooms in a simple bungalow, the other two rooms being the kitchen and living room. The bungalow walls were built manually by compacting moistened clay in a wooden mould, one section at a time, from the ground all the way up. The wall was reinforced inside with inter-locked bamboo strips and loops.

Dai-shan's birth home

The floor was simply dry compacted soil. The roof was made of a few logs as the load carrier at the bottom across the room, regularly spaced wooden boards or bamboo strips in the middle layer, and curved clay tiles[12] on the top. The building was generally not airtight, and there was no insulation, heating, tap water, nor sewer line. The condition is similar to but no better than a simple cabin you see today.

outdoor lamp

indoor lamp

Kerosene Lamps

Electric power was far beyond the reach of rural residents because it was not available. Lighting depended on Kerosene

---

[12] Clay tile is a curved squarish plate, approximately ½" x 8" x 8", made through drying and kilning, a similar process as making brick.

lamps. This was the type of primitive housing they and every other nearby family lived in.

Min-fei had been resting in her room for over one hour, without much comfort or care of close ones. A neighbor happened to pass by her house and heard something unusual. She went in and noticed that *Min-fei* was in labor and needed help. She went out of the house and shouted to the field to inform her husband to return home immediately. He rushed back from the field upon the news and was instructed to get a midwife.

In the neighboring village about 0.5 kilometer down the hill, there was a clinic, which was not something you can imagine by today's standards. There was no trained doctor. Often there was one or sometimes two staff on duty. They were similar to nurses who were trained on simple first aid procedures. They had some western medicine for first aid, fever, diarrhea, etc. A Chinese medicine doctor often came to the clinic if anyone needed attention, and he/she would give a prescription for them to buy herb medicine from a specialty herb store.

In that clinic, there was one nurse who was trained to deliver babies, and she came as quickly as she could. She got there just in time. She told the father-to-be to boil some water and soak a pair of scissors in the boiling water. He did not understand why but just followed instructions. He was then told to leave the room and to prepare a *Hong-long* 烘笼[13] (a hot ash

烘笼 Hong Long

portable heating cage

---

[13] A portable heating cage with a ceramic bowl inside which is filled with hot charcoal or ashes of burned wood sticks and hays.

heater). More about the *Hong-long* and the earth-stove will be explained a little later.

For now, let's focus on the progress in that room. The father to be left the room and waited anxiously outside. Suddenly "Ng-aah, Ng-aah, ···", the crying voice of a newborn baby was heard from her room. Another member of the 12th generation of the *Yao* family had arrived. *Min-fei* gave birth to her first child, a boy. She was brave and a great mother! The nurse told the new father "You have a son".

The new father rushed into the room and saw *Min-fei* holding the baby, bundled with old clothes, in her arms trying to keep the baby warm. Very excited with their first child, the new father didn't know what to do. He picked up the Hong-long on the floor, gently stirred the warm ash inside and brought it closer to the bed, trying to keep the new mother and baby warm. The arrival of the little boy brought great joy to the family.

At that time, the Wang-da family already had three grand children from his uncle Shi-qing, and the Wang-er family had five grand children from the two other uncles. Counting them all together, the newborn boy would be the 9th member of the 12th generation in the Yao family. He would be the No. 9. The number would be different if all children from his aunts in the "*Shi*" generation were counted.

Coincidentally, on that same day in the afternoon, the family's brown cow also gave birth to a calf. The calf tried to stand on its own knees first, tumbled, attempted a few more times and eventually managed to stand up on its own feet. Before you could even notice, the little calf

Niu-er 牛儿

could walk around and start begging for milk from her mother. You may be wondering about the cow. It was the cow of the two brothers, and it became the property of the collective farming group when they joined the group. It was however still under their care, mostly by his cousin.

In local rural area, it was a custom for parents to name their newborn child after some sort of animal. It was believed: the child would be as strong and as tough as the animal in growing up and in resisting illness. During those times, due to lack of access to health care, children who caught any disease or became seriously ill might not have much chance of survival. As you may have guessed, this newborn boy, the No. 9, was named *Niu-er* 牛 儿 (*little calf*) by his parents, sharing the same name as the little calf. Niu-er and the *little calf* started growing together.

The Yao ancestry

When *Niu-er* was born, he had several cousins already as shown in the chart where he was in the family tree.

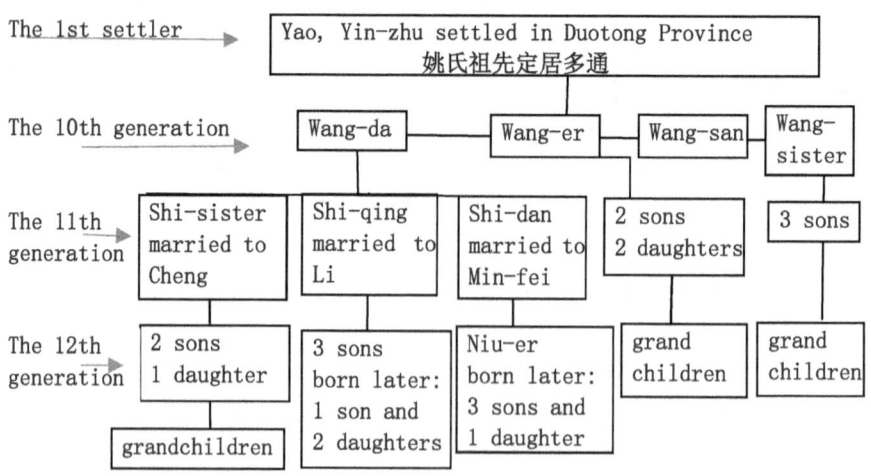

Cooking on earth stove by burning hay / brushes

Now let us see how to cook and how to keep warm in rural areas in those days. Usually, a kitchen would have a water tank made of 5 slabs of stone or ceramic or chiseled in a large stone; an earth-stove made of earth blocks and a place to store fuel materials like sticks, hays and wood.

To make an earth-stove, first clay was mixed with some chopped hay as reinforcement and water added to make a paste. The paste was poured into a rectangular wooden mold (approximately 6" x 8" x 12"). The mold was removed shortly to let it dry as earth blocks.

Earth stove

Then the dried earth blocks were stacked together to the proper height and size, the joints being filled with clay mud. On the top surface a large hole was left at the center, just the size of a wok (2' to 3' in diameter), hollow underneath, with an opening on the side for adding fuel material. The outside surface was covered with mud to make it smooth in most cases and may be coated with paint or covered with ceramic tiles sometimes.

Often, there would be two woks side by side, one for cooking food and another for making pig food. Sometimes, a *Feng-xiang* 风箱 (a manually operated wooden pump) may be installed on the side to help with burning. In a more advanced construction, the lower portion was also made hollow to clear ash and a chimney was added on the top to allow air circulation and increase the efficiency.

The burned charcoal or hot ash can be put into a *Hong-long* as a portable heater in a room or even on the bed. A

Hong-long filled with hot charcoal could last a few hours.

5. *Niu-er* and His Grandparents 牛儿和他的外祖父母 (*Niu-er he ta-de wai zu-fu-mu*)

A couple of months after birth, *Niu-er* grew stronger and his mother recovered as well. One day, she decided to take *Niu-er* to see her parents, *"Wai-gong* 外公 " (grandfather) and *"Wai-po* 外婆" (grandmother on his mother's side). She carried her infant on her back in a baby carrier backpack made of fabric, held a Ti-dou 提兜 (a hand-held bamboo basket) in one hand, which was filled with a bundle of noodle (1.0 kg), 10 chicken eggs plus a strip of pork meat, all covered with a towel; and grabbed a live rooster in another hand, a typical style for a young mother returning home to visit her parents for the first time with a new baby.

Ti-dou

Min-fei kept her maiden last name "Lin" after marriage[14]. She was also the youngest among four siblings. Her two older sisters were "married" to their future-to-be husbands many years ago as child brides. Her brother, *Min-guang*, married some years ago and already had a son and lived with her parents. In the old days, a married woman was supposed to live with her husband's family after marriage and the man was supposed to stay home carrying the responsibility of taking care of his own parents, particularly when they become old. There was exception if it was clearly intended at the beginning for the man to live with the woman's family and taking responsibility in that family. That was called *dao-cha-men* 倒插门 (literally

[14] In old China, a woman would adopt her husband's surname after marriage. After 1949, they kept their maiden names.

means inverted door, implying a man living with his wife's family after marriage).

You can imagine how much welcome *Min-fei* and her new baby received from her parents and brother. The boy was particularly favored by his *Wai-po* 外婆, a woman who had no schooling but was well respected by others in the surrounding areas due to her passion and skills in helping women with their health, particularly about pregnancy.

Wai-po, people called her *Lin-Tang's*[15], trembled to the yard on her two tiny wrapped-feet (包小脚 *bao-xiao-jiao*) to meet them. In old Chinese culture, a woman was supposed to stay home and not to go out. Their feet were wrapped tight from childhood to prevent them from growing, a very painful endeavor. A pair of tiny feet made it difficult for them to walk and even to keep balance. The way she walked made you think she might fall at anytime.

"Quick, let me see my little *wai-sun-er* 外孙儿 (grandson of a daughter)", as *Wai-po* was talking she took over the baby to hold him. The mother and the new baby brought great joy to the whole family. *Niu-er* was too young to remember anything from those days, although he stayed often with *Wai-po* later when he was in elementary school.

A couple of years later, the little calf grew to an adult cow and became a mother herself, while *Niu-er* had just learned the basics of walking and talking. But he came along.

Niu-er's father was the youngest among the three siblings, at least 16 years younger than his older sister. Ever since he was born, *Niu-er* never saw his *Ah-gong* 阿公

---

[15] In old China, a woman might not have a given name and was usually referred by her husband's surname + her surname, e.g., *Lin-Tang's*.

(grandfather on his father side). Later his mother told him: before his *Ah-po* 阿婆 (grandmother on his father side) passed away, he was old enough to grab food from his *Ah-po*'s hands. However, *Niu-er* was less than two years old and had no memory of his *Ah-po* either.

With no grandparents nearby to help look after the child, his mother had to take care of him herself while managing to do a huge amount of house chores and help with farm work in the field in all seasons.

Did anyone think of kindergarten? That type of thing was never heard of in the rural area. You must be crazy to keep your young baby in a play pin or a room, like a bunch of piglets. Often a mother would take the baby to the field at work so she could keep an eye on the baby.

Before he could walk, *Niu-er* would sit in a bamboo cradle and play by himself while his mother was doing her chores. When she went to do farm work, she would carry him on her back in a baby carrier, called *Bei-dou* 背篼[16], weaved with bamboo strips by his father, who was not good at bamboo weaving but could make it work.

When *Niu-er* learned to walk, he went

Bei-dou

outdoors like his same aged "sister", the little calf. He followed his mother in the field and picked up things to play with by himself: grass, small pebbles, or sometimes grasshoppers or butterflies. It was fun to chase them.

6. The Changing Years 变换的年代 (*bian huan de nian-dai*)

From 1950 to 1962 before *Niu-er* started school, the new

---

[16] *Bei-dou*, made of bamboo strips, specifically for carrying babe on the back.

government initiated many unprecedented changes on the land, which had a huge impact on society and affected the daily life of every citizen. There were many things *Niuer* did not understand and they were the reasons why this little boy saw so many hard-to-explain things as he grew up. The following is a brief description of a few events to give you some background.

Mutual-Aid Group 互助组 *(huzhu-zu)*／ *Cooperative* 合作社 *(hezuo-she)*

After the Land Reform, farmers had their own land to work on initially. They were very happy no doubt. However, there was a big problem: in those days and in tradition, farming was very labor intensive and many of the chores in the field required considerable physical strength.

As an example, a pair of wooden pails were used as the primary containers to carry water or liquid waste on shoulders to the field to water crops. It may weigh 90 - 110 lbs. It is not easy if you must do it all day long continuously, and it was more difficult in mountainous areas to climb up the terrace with a heavy load.

Wooden pails

If a family had male laborers (a boy, a man, etc.), the heavy work would rest on them. If a family did not have a male labor, there would be a big problem in getting farming done in time during the busy seasons. That was the primary reason why a peasant family favored having a boy because he could help with the farming when he grew up. On the other hand, a girl would by tradition leave her parents to live with her husband's family after marriage.

As a solution to the problem, the government first encouraged peasants to form a *Mutual-Aid Group* 互助组

(*huzhu-zu*) on a voluntary basis to help each other out when needed. This format later further evolved into a more formal organization as *Cooperative* 合作社(*hezuo-she*). The idea seemed good. However, a family with strong laborers would not be interested and often the most in need family might not be able to join a group.

The People's Commune 人民公社 (*ren-min gongshe*)

It was around 1958 when the government made another historical change: formally establishing a township organization in rural areas, called People's Commune 人民公社 (*ren-min Gongshe*)[17], on the basis of the previous *Cooperatives*. From then on, all resources belonged to the the collective organizations, not individuals. As you may have noticed, many organizations had a name with a prefix "People's", which was often dropped for short.

The establishment of the People's Commune was expected to solve the aforementioned problems and to help those in need. It was also said, another major reason was to learn the style of the former Union of Soviet Socialist Republics (USSR), and to enter the idealistic communist society as early as possible, a society where people would work on a voluntary basis but could take whatever they need for their lives. Isn't that nice?

At this point, it seems necessary to pause for a second for a briefing on communism. It all started from a German-born philosopher, named Karl Marx, who had several other titles including political theorist and economist. Marx received his doctorate in philosophy in 1841 and spent a

---

[17] This system was dismantled around 1984, and all farmlands were then contracted to individual peasants.

few years developing his ideology and a programme for a revolution. He was expelled from German and moved to London in 1849.

He and Freidrich Engels, another philosopher, published a pamphlet titled "*The communist Manifesto* 共产党宣言 (*gongchan-dang xuanyan*)" and a three volume *Das Kapital* 知本论 (*zhiben-lun*) with lengthy discussions on capitalism and the surplus values 剩余价值 (*shengyu jiazhi*) of work, which in simple plain language, is the difference between the amount of value produced by a worker and the amount of cost (all necessary costs plus what is paid to the worker). Marx believed, it was the surplus values that the employers exploited the workers upon, and the working class should take the surplus values back, by force if necessary. He expected that the working-class movement would eventually conquer political power and establish a classless, communist society, in which all people are equal, no oppression, no exploitation and everyone is free. That was probably the seduction to so many followers during the communist ideological movement in those days.

His ideology was eventually developed into Marxism-Leninism. Chairman Mao of China once said that all in all, the Marxism could be summarised by a single sentence: "Rebellion was justified 造反有理 (*zaofan youli*)". That was the principle for the Chinese revolution. The communist movement spread to many countries and there was an organization called Communist International, which coached all followers around the world, including the Chinese CP on how to carry out a revolution and overthrow the ruling governments. During the communist movement, many working-class people followed and millions of them sacrificed their lives helping in forceful fights to achieve the goal.

33

The movement succeeded in overthrowing older governments in many countries. However, the idealistic communist society never came. Instead, a socialist society was established as a "transition". That is what you know today in those countries. What life is like and how the wealth is distributed in socialist countries will not be explored further here.

From a scholastic point of view, Marx appeared to have done a good job in analysing the subject. But as a political idealism to guide society, it is highly arguable. Marx's detrimental error was that he either forgot or intentionally ignored the fact that humans are selfish and greedy. When there are no rules to restrict one's action, the more wealth and the power one person has, the more the person wants, and this person will never be satisfied with what he has and will never give up what is his possession. Marx failed to explore effective means of controlling the problem to ensure the movement stay in the right course.

Interested readers are encouraged to find other sources on the communist movement and the status of existing socialist countries.

Now let's get back to Yao'sville. Under this organizational system, the commune was under the administration of County and had two more levels below: *Gongshe* 公社, *Dadui* 大队, and the farming group 生产队 (*sheng-chan dui*) which was also called *xiao-dui* 小队. All resources in a farming group were pooled together and belonged to the collective group. Each farming group was also fiscally self-responsible.

Yao'sville was the then 4th farming group, of the *Alliance Dadui*, in the *Hongxing* 红 *Gongshe* 公社 (Red flag commune). The chart below illustrates the organizational structure at that time.

Administrative organization chart
(Before cultural revolution)

There was a CP committee in the Commune headed by a leader called "*Shuji* 书记" and there was a CP Branch in each *Dadui* with a leader called "*Zhishu* 支书". The *Shuji* and *Zhishu* held the highest power in the respective organization.

From then on, everything was under the control of the *Shuji* in the Commune; the *Zhishu* in a *Dadui* was responsible for implementing policies; and the farming group with a leader, called *Group Captain* 生产队长 (*sheng-chan dui-zhang*), simply followed the upper-level instructions.

Under the commune system, each person was entitled to 2 *fen* 分 (approximately 1430 square feet) farmland, called *Ziliu-di* 自留地 (land reserved for private use), for a family to keep and to grow their own vegetables. The rest of the land and other resources were all pooled together in each farming group; all peasants in the group worked together and everything was managed by the *Group Captain*. Families were not supposed to have their own livestock

35

(cow, goat, pig, etc.) and poultry in the early days of the commune system.

It should be noted that the allotted *Ziliu-di* was not changed for a family thereafter, either with new additions or death. Whatever they had then stayed like that.

At same time, most families were also allotted a small piece of non-farmland on the hill, called *Ziliu-shan* 自留山, which was not for farming but for grass and trees. A couple of families did not receive it for unknown reasons, most likely they didn't have it when they joined the commune. Maybe they came from outside the village later. The users of the *Ziliu-shan* were not allowed to cut any trees but free to harvest the grass, which was usually left grown up and harvested as hay and used either as cooking fuel or for making roof.

All peasants in a farming group worked together in the same farm, at the same time, doing the same thing under the deployment of the group captain. At the end of each season, they all shared the harvest based on the number of people in the family (children received less).

Individual contribution in farming to the group was recorded as earned points, called *Gong-fen* 工分. There were usually three levels of labor designations: full labor (a man who must engage in heavy physical work), woman labor and child labor. Typically, a man working a whole day could earn 10 points *gong-fen*; a woman 7 to 8 points and a child (younger than 15) 3 to 5 points depending on the age. A full day of work normally had three shifts: morning shift (before breakfast for one hour or so), mid-day and afternoon shifts.

All earned points in a family were added together by the end of the year. All points in the whole group were summed up and 10% of the sum was the total number of the equivalent full-labor-days

The total harvest in the group was added together for the whole year. After making contributions to the government, it was the total worth in the group for the year. The total worth divided by the total number of full-labor-days in the whole group determined the worth of a full labor (10 points of *gong-fen)* earned in one day. The total gong-fen earned in a family was then compared with the total crops which had been allocated to the family during the year.

In many cases, a family was just about to make ends meet. Families with male laborers may get extra cash. Families without full male labor or having not earned enough points would often have to repay back to the group.

Under this system, to earn more points of gong-fen, a family needed to have more people working on the farm. Young *Niu-er* with his mother visited his Wai-po often and sometimes stayed a couple of weeks. He gradually learned to talk like kids there and he called his mother *Mama* 妈妈 (tradition of Hunan descendants). According to the tradition of the Yao family, he should call his mother *Yao-niang* 幺娘 (*yao* - the youngest sibling, a tradition of Guangdong descendants). It was said, Niu-er's father went to bring them back home and wanted his mother to work in the commune farm to earn some points to help support the family. His father even thought that *Niu-er* picked-up the language of his *wai-po*'s family because he had stayed there for too long.

At that time, China had a planned economy 计划经济 (*jihua jingji*), under which production and distribution of almost everything was planned by the governments. Unlike in the market economy, everything was controlled by one or a few people, rather than the market.

As you may have noticed by this point, the commune system created a hidden problem, a huge problem in fact. When people worked together like that, with no differentiation made between an individual's performance and actual contribution, at the end of the day everyone earns approximately the same points. That is the popular phenomenon called *eating-free-buffet* 吃大锅饭 (*chi-daguo fan*), meaning sharing food in a big wok. It was observed that in such a situation, it was difficult to motivate everyone to increase productivity and some individuals would just be lazy.

The Great Leap Forward 大跃进 (*da yuejin*) – The Great Famine 大饥荒 (*da ji-huang*)

The People's Republic of China was established after eight years of anti-Japanese invasion and three years of civil war between the previous government ruled by the *Guo-Ming-Dang* 国民党 party and the force led by the CP party. The previous government lost the fight, retreated to Taiwan 台湾 in 1949, and reportedly took a vast amount of treasure with them, leaving a war-torn country behind and nearly 400 million people in poverty.

The new government tried a few ways to stimulate the economy, but the challenge remained. Rebuilding a nation from the war-torn land was not an easy task. The backbone of a nation would greatly depend on its industry. The new China had very little industry to start with at that time. Very basic raw material, iron and steel, were scarce.

In an attempt to speed up re-building the industry, the government mobilized the whole nation to engage in "steelmaking" 炼钢 (*lian-gang*). The *Great Leap Forward* 大跃进 (*da yuejin*) started.

At the beginning of the People's Commune time, all people in a farming group were not only working together but also eating together. Individual families were not supposed to cook their own food[18]. Therefore, all cooking utensils would not be needed. Every family was persuaded to donate everything made of metal in their possession. Everywhere in the whole nation people started making steel!

Like in other places, they cut down trees on the hills in *Yao'sville,* destroying the healthy forestry and leaving an open ground. Structures were demolished whatever was deemed not useful. they dug holes in the ground and started making steel.

Yes, peasants were engaged in steelmaking too!

Well, you can imagine the outcome – failure. Steelmaking was a very specialized industrial process, and it was not something anybody could do. You needed the necessary knowledge, facility and special training.

Niu-er remembered, his mother told him later that she had hidden some of their useful metal items (wok, cooking utensils), which came in handy later when they were allowed to cook their own food again.

During those years, in addition to steel making, another mass movement was to increase yield in the farm, to help the reconstruction of the nation. The upper-level governments would send officials to lower levels to inspect the results. The ones who claimed to have produced high yield got huge praise, while the ones who did not would be criticized, or even be punished.

As a result, some of the people in charge of an organization tried to reach their goals by any means. False reporting became popular. This happened from the

---

[18] That was very short-lived. Families cooked own food shortly after.

bottom at the farming group to the very top of the government. For example, if someone reported a production of 200 lbs wheat on one *Mu* 亩 (1 Mu 亩 = 1/6 acre) farm, another would report 400 lbs. Then the next one would make it to 800 lbs, and so on. The more the better, the more revolutionary, the more supportive to the government, and the more praise they would receive. That was the famous phenomenon of *"false-reporting and irresponsible praise"* 虚报胡夸 (*xu-bao hu-kua*). The economy was suddenly blown up, like a balloon.

In many cases, inspecting officials would set the commune which reported the highest production as a model and call for others to learn. There would usually be an on-site mass meeting 现场会 (*xian-chang-hui*) for other communes to see and learn. Anyone with a common sense would know that that kind of production was not true at that time. To hide the truth, some people were very sneaky and tried all means to cover up their false report. Before the meeting date, they would tell peasants to cut down wheat from other farms and replant them on a small land. See, "they grew so well, guaranteed high yield".

Niu-er was too young to understand much of what happened around him. But there was one thing he remembered well: a "banquet night". Usually during the on-site meeting, the host group would make a banquet and prepare lots of good food to treat all guests with hospitality (or a venue to flatter higher level officials). *Niu-er* and a few other families lived in houses surrounding a courtyard 四合院 (*sihe yuan*). One night, he noticed that many people in the village came to that courtyard and started making so much delicious looking food, the type of food he had never seen before but looked yummy and smelled good. They used all the cooking utensils in every family there including those in his family. They all seemed very busy. Some were cutting vegetables, some slicing meat. Yes, they slaughtered the only pig the farming group had. They shredded carrots and sweet potatoes and deep fried them too. He was just told not to disturb the other's work and to behave on his own.

They seemed to have worked very late that night. *Niu-er* went to sleep at some point and couldn't remember what happened thereafter. When he woke up the next day, he never saw any food and wondered for a long time what happened to it. His parents might not have a chance to eat it either.

Based on the false reporting, the upper government asked local governments to contribute more than before to support the nation's reconstruction. As you can imagine, they did not actually produce that much but had to contribute more. The result was much less left for the peasants themselves.

Due to various reasons, from 1959 to 1962, great famine 大饥荒 (*da ji-huang*) spread over the entire nation, leading people to starve to death. The exact death toll was unknown. *Niu-er* did not know what was going on around him but only hoped to have more food. It was around those years, he lost his *Ah-po* and *yao Ah-gong* 幺阿公 (*Wang-san*), the youngest brother of his grandfather. For both of them, he barely had any memory, but he remembered the day when his oldest cousin found *Wang-san*'s body on the loft above the stable, where who lived alone.

The government reported later in the 1990's that it was the combined result of human errors in policy making and natural disasters in the "*three difficult years*" [19] but

---

[19] This can be found online in many sources today.

did not acknowledge it as famine. What really happened will be up to the readers to interpret with historical reports and facts from other sources.

Free speech/expression 大鸣大放 *(da-ming da-fang)* **and** *Anti-Rightist Movement* 反右运动 *(fan-you yun-dong)*

While *Niu-er* and the little calf were growing up at their own paces, some other things happened in their homeland over the years may also make people feel afraid.

Starting in 1957, the government called for input from citizens on its policies, saying "everyone is free to speak and free to express their opinions 大鸣大放 *(da-ming da-fang)*". Many people, particularly intellectuals, did express their opinions, some made suggestions, and some criticized the wrongdoings. Shortly after, those who criticized or said things against the policies or some CP leaders, were classified as "the Rightist" 右派 *(you-pai)* - a new class of people's enemy was created. This was followed by an "Anti - the Rightist Movement 反右运动 *(fan-you yun-dong)*" across the country.

During the movement, the rightists would be criticized in mass meetings. Often, they were forced to carry a large (2' - 3' dimension) plate, labeled with their name *XXX - the Rightist*, hung on their necks with a thin string or to hold something high in their hands above their heads. That was the physical punishment in addition to verbal abuse.

As *Niu-er* grew older, he followed his mother wherever she went. When she needed to go to the market to exchange some necessities, she would tell him to stay home, "be good 乖阿 *(guai, ah?)*, I will buy candy for you when I come back". Then she would buy him a piece of rice-made candy for one *Fen* 1分钱 *(yi-fen-qian,* ¥0.01*)*. Sometimes he would insist on going with her. One day, *Niu-er* went to the market with his mother and saw a big crowd. In the center of the crowd was a man holding a large yam, about 1.0 kg, over his head. He looked exhausted. Some people were shouting at him and pointing fingers at him.

"Mama why does that man hold a sweet potato over his head?", "Why are the people angry at him?", the little boy asked. His mother quickly pulled him aside and walked away, then whispered to him "he is a rightist, he complained there's not enough food."

Creation of the Rightist made the fifth category of enemy, together with the other four categories, they were collectively called "The *Five Categories* 五类份子 (*wu-lei fenzi*)", the enemies of people. They included:

1) *Di-Dru* 地主,
2) *Rich-Peasant* 富农 (*fu-nong*),
3) Counter revolutionaries 反革命 (*fan-ge-ming*), those who hold different views openly against CP and its policies,
4) Criminals 坏分子 (*huai fen-zi*), those who committee crimes or do bad things to society,
5) Rightists 右派 (*you-pai*), those who had different opinions from the CP government.

People in the five categories were deemed "in opposition of people" and were often the target for criticism in mass meetings whenever there was a political event. Their children would face an uncertain future and were deprived of many rights[20].

---

[20] They were collectively further labelled as the Black Five categories 黑五类 (*hei wu-lei*) during the Cultural Revolution. Their categorized titles were finally removed around 1978, and their children were then supposed to be treated equally as others.

Chapter 2

Dai-Shan's Childhood
代山的童年 *(Daishan de tong-nian)*

Niu-er lived through his childhood in the hungry years. People were poor and food was scarce across the nation. His parents were busy and worked hard doing farm work and earned very little, hardly enough to make ends meet. *Niu-er* grew in the difficult time together with many other young kids like him.

For a child like Niu-er, there were no snacks to eat except the three meals a day. Even the three meals were very unbalanced in nutrition. In the winter and spring, there was nothing much edible in the field. In the late summer and fall when crops became ripe, people might be able to find something to eat in secret when they were very hungry. For example, when yam was ready, they could dig one up to eat raw without others seeing. If they worked in a corn field in late summer when corn was ready for harvest, people would look for the "sweet corn-cane" (the ones with no corn cobs) to chew like sugar cane. Niu-er remembered well the times he went to the corn field after harvesting to look for the sweet corn-canes.

Often, after work, Niu-er's mother would go to the field to pick grass to feed rabbits at home. When she found any wild fruits, such as raspberries in the bushes she would keep it and bring home for Niu-er and his two siblings (one brother and one sister). His favorite wild fruit was the thorny plum 刺李子 (*ci li-zi*), which grew on low thorny bushes.

7. Need a School Name 需要一个上学的名字 (*xuyao yi-ge shangxue de ming-zi*)

Soon, *Niu-er* became six and half years old and reached school age. That was 1961, late in the summer, and school would start soon in September. In those days, children would start school at the age of seven because there was no kindergarten in the rural area. One day, he heard other kids talking about going to school, but there was no school nearby. "Hmm, that might be fun", he thought, and he went to ask his mother about schooling, "Mama, what is school? I want to go to school too".

Niu-er's mother never went to school and couldn't read at all. However, she managed to recognize her own name and learned to do mental math by herself because it was not convenient to ask someone else to help with calculations to sell or buy something at the market. His father had attended classes in a night school for peasant 农民夜校 (*nongmin yexiao*) for a few months just after the new China was established. The night school was specifically opened for peasants who had no education to help them read some common words and do simple calculations. That was part of the government's attempt to eliminate illiteracy in rural area. His father could read some simple words and manage to read simple stories in newspapers on surface of the words (not the implication) but could not be able to write a (mail) letter.

His mother thought, they couldn't rely on others all the time to read and write, at least her children should be able to do calculations on their own at the market. She was convinced that the family should have someone who would be able to read and write. After discussing with his father, she was determined to send *Niu-er* to school. She told the little boy he could go. You can imagine how excited he was.

Then he remembered how other kids teased him about his name sometimes and was embarrassed. His mother noticed and asked, "what is it now?" He said to his mother "I need a school name". Yes, of course. Mother didn't forget that.

Everyone got an adult name when they grew a little older. She intended to ask his father.

Based on tradition, everyone in his generation had a middle name for the generation rank. *Niu-er* was in the Dai 代 generation and just needed to add a given name at the end. The origin of the generational rank will be explored later.

His father thought a second and said, "Hmm, his enfant name is *Niu-er. Dai-niu* 代牛 sounds just good to me".

"What?" The boy was not happy. His mother thought about it. Since he was born in a mountain village, she said "*Dai-shan* 代山 would sound better". So, *Dai-shan* 代山 he was. Thus, the little boy had a full name as: *Yao, Dai-shan* 姚代山. From then, when anyone called him by his infant name, Niu-er, he would just turn his head away, pretending having not heard it.

8. Walking to Elementary School in a Neighboring County
走路到邻县上小学 (*zoulu dao lin xian shang xiao-xue*)

There were no schools in the surrounding villages. The closest school was located about 2.5 kilometers away in the neighboring county – *Zhongxin* 中新 county 县 (*xian*), across the county border, on another side of the hill, in a place called *Shuwan* 书湾 (school bay. *Wan* 湾 a geographical bay). The school was named *Shuwan* 书湾 Elementary school 小学 (*xiao-xue*), located near a small town. For a place with such a name, it would mean that it had some history as a school, dated long before the new China.

There was a trail from *Yao'sville* to the school. Over half of it was on the hill. It started from the village, gradually ascending the hill, then joined an old trail,

47

called *lao malu* 老马路 (Old Horse Road). The trail passed-by a small village about halfway and went through the town market, called *Longsheng Chang* 隆盛场, before reaching the school.

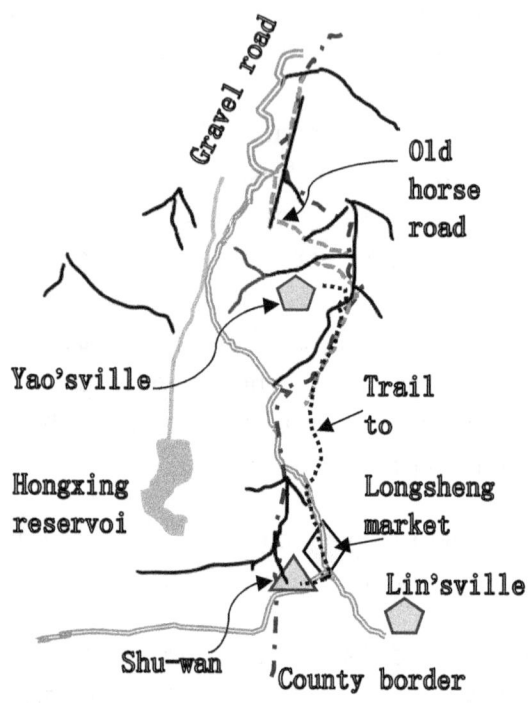

The Old Horse Road was a dirt road with no gravels. It was built along the ridge of the hills many decades ago by the then government. It basically cut through the hills, passed Yao'sville, descended behind the village and ascended again. It was wide enough for two wagons in some places. There was no automobile then and the main transportation was wagon pulled by horses, and sometimes by cows. That was why it was called horse road. However, villagers said there had never been any wagon on the road ever since it was built. Most likely, the reason the old road was not used much was due to the steep slope behind

48

Yao'sville and a horse was just not strong enough to pull a wagon up the road. There was one exception, a few years before 1949 when the army passed-by, which elapsed for three days and three nights continuously. Prior to that time, Duotong province was ruled by several warlords, who were eventually incorporated into the national army by the former government of the Republic of China 民国政府 (*min-guo zhengfu*). The army passed *Yao'sville* was likely going towards *Zhongdu-fu* on some sort of missions.

The main gravel road down the hill was built many years later. It followed the gulley beside Yao'sville before ascending the hill for a gentle road gradient.

The *Longsheng* market had only one street with buildings side-by-side on both sides, stretching more than 500 meters long. The market street was very busy and very crowded during the "open market days 赶场 (*gan-chang*)" [21]. During the peak hours, you would have to squeeze through the crowd. Apparently, it would be a challenge for a little boy to walk that far to the school and to overcome those hurdles by himself. His mother had some concerns.

Fortunately, about five other children in the same village also planned to go to that school. They were all older than Dai-shan and the two oldest were teenagers. One of them was a mid-teen girl. She was a distant-aunt, and her grandfather was one of the siblings of *Dai-shan*'s great grandfather. Based on their generational ranks, he would call her *yao-gu* 幺姑[22] (the youngest aunt among her siblings). Dai-shan's mother asked her if she could help by walking with him on the way to and from school and

---

[21] The local government specified to open the market every 2 or 3 days when all people can go there to sell and buy their stuff.
[22] Yao 幺 – the youngest siblings, Gu 姑 – aunt, father's sister.

keeping an eye on him. She kindly agreed. He then followed her and other kids to school every Monday to Saturday. At that time, Saturday was a half day for school.

In those days, it was a real challenge for kids to go to school, not only because of the distance and the mountain trail, but also a lack of facilities. First, there was no facility serving food in the school. Although there was one or two restaurants near the marketplace, most of the kids would have no money to buy food nor time to go.

During summertime when the daytime was long, there were fewer problems. But in the winter when daytime was short, they had to get up early in the morning and walk to school before the sun rose and walk home at or after sun set. Rainy days posed another problem.

On the first day in the first week of September in 1961, Dai-shan started school. His mother got up early and prepared his school things for him, a home-made book bag, and a *Fan-zhong* 饭盅 (a food container) . The book

book bag
书包

Fan zhong 饭盅

bag was made by sewing two pieces of fabric together with two long cloth straps, pretty much like a popular lady's handbag today.

At the beginning, the book bag was pretty much empty except for a pencil and a notebook to write on. School would provide two textbooks: Chinese language 语文 (*yu-wen*) and elementary math 算数 (*suan-su*). Plus, exercise notebooks to be purchased.

The fan-zhong would contain cooked food but the lid was loose just like that on a teacup. No one had ever heard of sandwiches in those days. typical food would be *Momo*

馍馍 (a thick pan cake, steamed or cooked in a wok with other food), which was easier to take, *Xi-fan* 稀饭 (rice porridge) or *Bao-gu kaokao* 包谷烤烤 (also called 包谷粥—cornmeal porridge). The porridge was often mixed with sweet potato in season from August to February. Apparently, the Fan-zhong with a loose lid was not easy to take with porridge in it. Dai-shan would have to hold it with both hands while walking and watching the road.

With a book bag hung across his neck on one side of his shoulder and a Fan-zhong in two little hands, Dai-shan followed the other kids, walking 2.5 kilometers each way, 6 days a week. Often, he had to walk fast to catch up with others while keeping an eye on the mountain trail. Sometimes, he had to run to keep up.

Not sure how many times he cried when he was a little late to leave home or school, or when he couldn't keep up with others. Often the older ones would wait for him. This lasted at least two years until he got familiar with the routine and became a little older.

Once in school, the first thing he had to do was to drop off his Fan-zhong on the counter in the school's *Shi-tang* 食堂 (similar to a canteen), where food was made for teachers and staff. Almost all the pupils brought their own home-cooked food in a Fan-zhong to school. The Shi-tang also had two very large woks, which were used to steam and warm up the pupil's food on multiple layers. The cooking staff would put these food containers on bamboo racks in multiple layers and steam them in the woks, just in time for lunch. At lunch time, the pupils rushed to the shi-tang to fetch their own Fan-zhongs, which would already be back on the counter again just waiting to be picked up. There was a charge for the service, 1.0 fen 一分 (*yi-fen*, ¥0.01) each time.

After lunch, *Dai-shan* would go to the classroom and wait for class to start or take a nap in the summertime. Often there was a little spare time before the class, and he would join other kids to play in the school yard.

The Shuwan Elementary school had quite a formal school setting. It had two courtyards connected side-by-side sharing a row of building in the center, with a total of 7 sections of buildings. The larger courtyard was large enough for gatherings and events of the whole school. There were also two large fields outside, which were used for mass events of the school, for example, the outdoor radio-led gymnastics 广播体操 (*guang-bo ti-cao*)[23] in mid morning and physical education classes 体育课(*ti-yu ke*). There were also a few huge, hundred-year-old cedar trees[24] in the courtyards and outside. They really made the school standout, an ideal place for students to study.

The school included grade one to grade six. Each grade had two classes, maximum 30 pupils in each class. There would be around 300 pupils in school usually. It attracted kids from 10 kilometers away or further.

Dai-shan and three other kids (distant cousins) from his village were in the same class and the other two older ones in a higher grade. They had to walk by a village on the way to and from school twice a day. The village itself was not a problem. What made the little boy and his small friends uncomfortable were these two reasons: A family had a dog, which was normal in rural areas, and it barked every time someone passed by. That made the little kids worried, although it was kept inside the yard most of the

---

[23] In those days, all schools would have standardized physical exercise in mid-morning exactly at the same time for 15 to 20 minutes, following a loudspeaker or radio, to stretch limbs and body.
[24] Unfortunately, those trees are no longer in sight today.

time. Another reason was that there were also a few school-aged kids in that village. Some were not in school and just played around and sometimes would bully others. Occasionally they would shout at small kids passing by or even throw small stones to scare them. Dai-shan would usually pass there in a group or together with the older ones.

In addition to those kids in his own village, there were two other kids from a village more than one kilometer behind *Yao'sville* that were in the same class as Dai-shan. They often walked together too.

On rainy days, it would not be pleasant to walk. Although part of the road was natural stone, which was not a problem when wet, the rest of the road was muddy, and it was messy to walk through. When it was raining, his mother would usually want him to wear *Dou-peng* 斗篷 (also called *Dou-li* 斗笠. It was a large hat (2' to 3' in diameter) made of bamboo strips and lined with large strong leaves. It was too big for him and not very effective when it was windy. As a result, on rainy days he would most likely be soaked with both feet full of mud. That was not a problem in the summer because he could just walk on bare feet, but winter was really unpleasant.

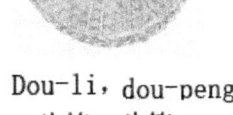

Dou-li, dou-peng
斗笠、斗篷

Going to Wai-po's home for overnight 去外婆家过夜 *(qu wai-pao jia guoye)*

Dai-shan had two cousins, the two sons of his *Jiu-jiu* 舅舅 (uncle, his mother's brother), one was the same age as him and another was about 2 years older. They were all in the same class. His mother often worried about him a lot when the weather was not good. When his Wai-po and his Jiu-jiu heard this, they both insisted on Dai-shan going to their home with his two cousins if he wanted to.

The school was a little more than one kilometer away from his *Wai-po* 外婆's home. The road was flat and there were also a bunch of kids from that village going to the same school, some in his class too. It was surely safer for him to go there than coming back to his home. Therefore, in the first two years of his schooling, he often went with his two cousins to *Wai-po*'s home whenever it was rainy, or it was too late to go home, particularly in the wintertime. They often walked together with other kids from that village.

After some time, he got along well with his cousins and other kids, and they often played together. Their favored games were marbles and folded papers.

They had no money to buy glass or real marbles. Instead, they used bodhi seeds 菩提子(*putizi*)[25] and a large piece of round stone. Sometimes, they played with folded paper instead of marbles.

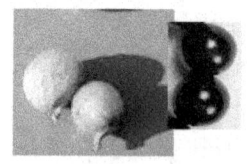
Play marbles

When he was small, he couldn't help with many chores. But when he grew bigger, there were a few times, he went with his cousins to take a buffalo from their village to feed along the roadsides and the field edges. It was more fun to look after a buffalo than a cow. The buffalo was

---

[25] Bodhi seeds 菩提子(*putizi*), grew on a type of tree. The shell was used to replace soap.

big and had a flat back. Kids often sat on the back of a buffalo while on an outing. It was not possible with a cow.

When he was at his Wai-po's home, he would share a room with his two cousins. Because they lived not far from the school, they normally did not bring food to school. Instead, they would go home for lunch during the two-hour lunch break.

He remembered, during those days, his *Wai-gong* 外公 (the grandfather of his two cousins) was often ill because of age. The best thing they had for an ill older person was simply some brown sugar made of sugar cane and egg from their own hens. Once in a while, some chicken meat. Dai-shan remembered that his *Wai-po* would give him a tiny piece of brown sugar sometimes and told him to eat inside their room, not to let the others see him.

9. The Years with Scarce Food 饥荒年代 (*jīhuang niándài*)

Dai-shan's mother tried to make different foods for him to take to school on different days, such as *Momo*, cornmeal porridge with and without sweet potato, or sweet potato only, often with some home-made pickle and occasionally with cooked fresh vegetables, which were produced from their own *Ziliu-di* 自留地. That was all they had from the farm. There was not much else to think of. They couldn't grow rice because of the lack of water resources and rice porridge was not on the list. They seldom ate Gan-fan 干饭 (rice cooked with just enough water).

His mother was from a rice growing family and occasionally she would buy a little freshly harvested raw rice on the market and make some rice porridge when she really missed it. Oh my, the food made of that fresh rice was unbelievably tasty. Dai-Shan remembered how delicious it was to eat and smell the fresh rice his mother cooked. He could smell it when some family was cooking it. There was no way to describe it unless you had personally eaten some. The rice purchased in stores was probably quite a few years after it was harvested and it never tasted as good.

Money was a very rare thing. His mother would normally have to sell something, like wheat, corn, sweet potato and then use the money to buy some rice. In fact, they had to do this sort of trade for all other necessary supplies: oil, salt, etc. They barely had money to buy soy sauce and vinegar, except on very special occasions. A 200 ml bottle of soy sauce would last for a few months. Instead, they used pickle juice in place of vinegar.

Meat was even more scarce. They could only afford to eat meat on special occasions, like festivals and birthdays. Even in those events, they were only able to buy 1.0 *Jin* 斤 (0.5 kg) of pork, which would cost ¥0.67.

The Spring Festival was an exception. Every family would try, by all means, to prepare as much meat and other good foods as they could afford to let the family have a feast. They often made more than they could eat in one meal, better with some leftovers, which would mean every year with a surplus (harvest more than needed): *nian-nian you-yu* 年年有余（余 *yu*, sounded like 鱼-fish）. Yes, fish should be on the table too. Unfortunately, they seldom had money to buy fish.

Other times, they might have meat once every two or three weeks. That was called *Da-yaji* 打牙祭 (treat yourself with meat and good food in non-special occasions).

Chicken[26] and other poultry were too expensive for them and for many families. Although they raised poultry, they had to sell them to buy other necessities. In most cases, chicken was reserved for very special occasions such as for a woman after giving birth or for elders. Oh, the home raised chicken, which had the freedom to run around, was completely different and tasted much better than the ones bought in the supermarket today, which never had a chance to walk out of its cage.

Teacher exchanged lunch with him 老师和他交换了午餐
(laoshi he tao Jiāohuàn le Wǔcān)

Dai-shan's mother thought he was at a growing age and needed enough nutrition (adequate and balanced nutrition was too luxurious for ordinary families to even think of). Home-grown vegetables were often added to supplement the family. One day, she made one *momo* with wheat flour and cooked vegetables for his lunch. The *momo* was about 3" to 4" diameter, larger than a moon cake sold in stores today. It was simply ordinary food. Young *Dai-Shan* was reluctant to take it because it was dry and not easy to swallow without soup or water. Oh, bottled water was a joke those days. They normally either drank boiled water or just spring water[27]. What he didn't know was that the *momo* was a meal millions of people dreamed of in those days. It was the *momo* that gave him the following historical memory, whether you believe it or not.

At this time, it was a few years after the formation

---

[26] Not the type of chicken you buy at the supermarket. These chickens were raised in a natural setting for 6 month or longer.
[27] Spring water from a well was free and tasted better than bottled water these days.

of the People's Commune, the time after the Great Leap Forward and False Reporting. Duotong province was one of the five provinces most stricken by the reported famine. Young *Dai-Shan* did not know much about what was going on around him,
but he knew there was not enough food to eat.

One morning, the young boy put his Fan-zhong on the counter to warm up, just as he did on other days. At lunch time, he fetched his Fan-zhong and walked down the courtyard to his classroom where he and his classmates usually had lunch. On one side of the courtyard was a row of teachers' *Qin-shi* 寝室 (bedrooms). When he was just about to pass his teacher's room, a very kind older lady, whom all the children called teacher granny Cheng, opened her door, smiled to him, and said gently "Come in for a second, Dai-Shan". He liked this teacher who smiled all the time at the class and taught them how to read and sing.

So, he walked into her room after her without hesitation. She closed the door seemingly to avoid others from seeing them, offered to let him sit on a wooden bench (there was no sofa or chair in her room), and then took out her food, a bowl of watery *xi-fan* 稀饭 (rice porridge). It was still warm with steam coming out and it looked so delicious. He stared at it. The teacher asked, "do you like xi-fan?", he nodded but his eyes were still on the rice. The teacher then said, "We can exchange food, you eat my xi-fan, and I will eat your *momo*. Do you like that?" He agreed and took the bowl and ate the xi-fan in no time.

When he got home that day, he was excited to tell his mother what happened at lunch. His mother tried a few times but couldn't find a proper word to say, and finally said, "Silly son, that *momo* was the food for your father for the day as a full laborer. A bowl of xi-fan would not last as long". But she couldn't say anything more as she remembered the family didn't have money to buy rice to eat.

You may wonder why the teacher exchanged her xi-fan for his *momo*. She simply did not have enough food to eat then. You can appreciate more after reading the following.

The ticket era 票证时代 *(piao zheng shidai)*

It was probably around that time when China started a quota system to control the supply and demand, as part of the planned economy.

Basically, all essential supplies required government-issued tickets to buy in government-run stores. You couldn't buy more than what you were allocated. Selling grains 粮食(*liang-shi*) on the market was prohibited. If anyone was caught selling, the grains would be confiscated, and the seller be punished.

In general, you would need:
- *Liang-piao* 粮票 for food/grain,
- *You-piao* 油票 for vegetable oil,
- *Rou-piao* 肉票 for meat/pork,
- *Bu-piao* 布票 for fabric, etc.

According to the government plan in those days, everyone had a quota of approximately 1.1 lb (500 grams) of *Zhu-liang* 主粮 (grains) per day, or 15 kilograms per month. The *Zhu-liang* was further classified into *Cu-liang* 粗粮 (coarse grains, including corn, oats, and sweet potato) and *Xi-liang* 细粮 (fine grains, including rice and wheat flour).

By today's diet, 1.1 lb of grain a day seems sufficient because it only makes up a small portion of the meal and there is meat and other components in the meal. However, in those days very little other ingredients were available, and people normally relied on the quota for food. Daily essentials were commonly in short supply.

The quota system made everyone's life difficult. For people in rural areas, they did not receive *Liang-piao* 粮票 because they were supposed to produce food for themselves with a limit to an equivalent quota. However, they got Bu-piao 布票 (5 meters per person per year) to buy fabrics[28] to make clothes but if they had a surplus, they would be expected to sell to the government at a fixed price. Unfortunately, farmers in many places couldn't produce everything needed for their daily lives and without tickets they would have to buy them on the black market at a higher price.

However, sweet potato was not considered the same as grains. 1.0 kilogram of sweet potato was counted as a fraction of a kilogram in the quota. Sweet potato was perishable, and the government normally would not accept it because of the difficulty in storage.

Farmers grew sweet potatoes basically for their own consumption. They stored it in a *Di-gao* 地窖 – an underground pit accessible from the top, either inside or outside a house. It was covered with hay if outside to avoid frost. It could keep sweet potatoes good for a few months if handled properly. Temperature and moisture must be suitable. Otherwise, the whole pit of sweet potatoes could become rotten. Many families relied on sweet potatoes as their main food source. If someone was eating sweet

Di-gao 地窖

---

[28] Fabric came in standard width and sold by length. Those days, it was common to buy fabric to make own clothes for much less cost.

potatoes three meals a day, it would be an indication of a poor family.

In addition, peasants each had 2 分 (*liang fen*) *Ziliu-di* 自留地 farmland[29] where they could grow vegetables to supplement food. Peasants were mostly focused on their *Ziliu-di* after working in the collective farm field. They grew vegetables, seeds, etc. and relied on the *Ziliu-di* to supplement the family income for buying various supplies.

Before the harvesting time, they would use the young leaves and vine tips of sweet potatoes to supplement their food. Dai-Shan remembered helping his mother pick some in the farm. Often, they could also dig up wild-grown edible vegetables 野菜 (*yei-cai*, e.g., dandelion and many others).

For people who lived in the urban areas, they received tickets for all supplies. That was all they would have without much else to supplement their food. Most likely there was no or very little chance for them to find a place to dig up *yei-cai* 野菜 in the cities. From that point of view, the lives of peasants seemed to be a little better than those people living in the cities during that "difficult period". However, the latter usually enjoyed more privileged treatment overall, as you can see later.

Now you may have better understanding why Dai-shan's teacher wanted to exchange food with him. How could an adult survive with 500 grams of food a day with very little supplementary food? She was not alone. The whole nation was in the same situation, including his father who had to do heavy manual labor work in the field.

---

[29] There was a cutoff date and those born after that date never had it.

61

Hu-kou 户口 (the registered residence)

At this point, it is important to clarify a concept: The registered residence, called *Hu-kou* 户口: People who lived in rural areas were called *Nong-min* 农民 (peasants, or farmers), while those who lived in urban areas were designated as *Ju-min* 居民 (specifically those who did not farm and resided in urban areas) by the government. Everyone's status of residence was registered on the family's residence registration booklet, called *Hu-kou Ben* 户口本, which was issued by the local police department, and is still in effect today.

There was a huge difference in supplies provided to people in the two types of residences. The *Ju-min* 居民 enjoyed lots of government designated privileges in supplies while the *Nong-min* 农民 did not. This lasted many decades until the end of the 20th century[30].

Hu-kou 户口 was just like an invisible chain which anchored a person in a fixed location. For many years, people could only find a job, buy the government-controlled items, and go to elementary and high schools in the place of their registered residence, where the *Hu-kou* is. Without a registered *Hu-kou*, they couldn't do anything[31] outside their registered residence areas. The above differential treatment of people separated ordinary citizens into two distinct classes. *Ju-min* received special privileges over *Nong-min*. It was extremely difficult for anyone with a *Nong-min* status to change to Ju-min status without a specific approved reason. One's

---

[30] This seems to have changed, and the difference still existed but less today.

[31] At a later time, it became possible to send kids to a school outside their own registered residence areas at a levied extra fee.

registered residence could be changed without difficulty only if he / she was admitted to a university, recruited to a factory / government agency, joined the army, etc.

It was almost impossible for a boy with a *Nong-min* status to marry a girl with a *Ju-min* status. Often, a boy couldn't marry his sweetheart simply because she was a *Nong-min*. If a girl did marry someone with a Ju-min status, she would be considered to have reached the end of her poor life and started her good life.

A crime of "buying and selling with an intention to make a profit" 投机倒把 (*touji-daoba*)

Because of the quota system, some people were speculating and engaged in buying and selling all kinds of goods and even tickets. In those days, it was illegal to buy something and sell it at a higher price, either at the same place or different places, with an intention to make a profit. People who engaged in this type of activity had to do it in secret. Peasants selling produce from their own Ziliudi 自留地 was an exception. The market management staff was trained to tell the difference.

This concept is very strange and difficult to understand today for people who were born outside of China. In normal situations, buying and selling something, hoping to make a profit is business, the activities many businesspeople are engaged in today. Without it, the economy would not be the way it is. In those days, the government on that land dictated what you could do and what you could not do. There were very complicated definitions. For ordinary people, buying something including the tickets and selling it for a profit was not allowed. Anyone found guilty of illegally buying and selling something would have committed a crime of *Touji-*

63

daoba 投机倒把, which had a significant political meaning and punishment. They might be treated the same way as those people in *The Five Categories* 五类份子.

There was one young man in *Yao*'sville who seemed not willing to stay home and work in the farm to earn Gong-fen and often went to different markets buying something here and selling it there. He was labeled as a *Touji-daoba* person and often criticized in the farmers' group meetings. Working in a Farming Group would earn less than ¥0.1 a day while he could make ¥1.0 or more profit each time. Young people were told to be a good peasant, to listen to the CP party and not to learn from him.

10. Excels in School 成绩优秀 (*cheng ji you-xiu*)

At a young age, *Dai-Shan* was very quiet, an introvert and did not have much to say to his peers. He was struggling to try to understand the difficult lives of his parents, uncles, and everyone around him in the village. They were poor. Many of them couldn't read, couldn't write and some even did not know how to use a steelyard on the market, which was the scale used those days to weigh produce.

Steelyard 秆秤

Why? because they didn't have education? or, because they lived on this poor barren land?

He had no answer to those questions. But one thing was sure, he knew he had to do well in school as that seemed to be the only hope for him.

At their young ages, the pupils in schools were educated: They were the lucky generation, being born in the new China and growing up under the red flags. They should "Cherish their happy lives which came not easy and be the good children of Chairman Mao. " They were told to study hard 好好学习 (*haohao xuexi*) and make progress everyday 天天向上 (*tian-tian xiang-shang*) and be prepared to be the successors of the revolutionary cause. They were also reminded that there were 2/3 population in the world who were still striving for their lives in a situation like "in deep water and hot fire" 水深火热之中 (*shui-shen huo-re zhi-zhong*) and were waiting for them to liberate.

Dai-Shan actually loved school, reading words and counting. He paid close attention to what his teachers said in the class and did all his homework in time. He wouldn't leave any questions un-answered overnight. He knew he could not ask his mother for any help related to schoolwork because she did not go to school. He could not ask his father either because he was busy all day long every day and probably could not help much either. He understood he had to get it done right, all by himself. If there was a question he couldn't answer, he would go to the teacher to ask the next school day. Not surprisingly, teachers normally loved pupils like Dai-shan who were keen to learn and tried to help when asked.

At home, after helping with house chores and whenever he had free time, he would read books. At night, there was no electric power, so he would read books beside a small kerosene lamp which had a 10 mm tall flame. His parents never needed to check on him for his schoolwork.

Through his hard work in school, he achieved very good results. In Grade two, he got the highest overall mark in final exams in his class. Those days, the grade was recorded solely based on results of the final exams.

On the last day of school in a semester, the whole school was assembled in the courtyard. There was a temporary stage. In the front of the stage was a desk covered with a large red cloth and at the rear of the stage, five portraits of Marx, Engels, Lenin, Starlin and Mao[32] were hung in sequence from left to right.

As part of the school-end ceremony, those pupils who made on the achievement list would receive their certificate and award prizes. When *Dai-Shan*'s name was called, he walked up to the stage. In front of the desk there was a small bench below the stage for the recipient to stand on. The school Principal was on the other side of the desk to hand over the certificate and prize to the recipient. Dai-Shan was a little short and couldn't reach the table. He intended to hold on to the red cloth which merely hung on the side, and he nearly tripped off the bench. Laughter broke out in the audience, and he was embarrassed. The principal walked to the side of the desk and gave him a large envelope.

Dai-shan took the envelope and walked back to his seat. Inside the envelope, there was an award certificate of first prize, a piece of paper stating that he was rewarded ¥2.50 and real cash of that amount. That was the total amount of fees his mother paid to the school for the whole semester. He was so happy and gave them to his mother as soon as he got home. His mother was so proud of him. His father didn't say anything but had a smile on his face.

He continued to excel throughout the years until he completed grade 5 in that school, just one year before graduation when the Great Cultural Revolution started. We will get to that in more detail a little later but for now we will talk more about Dai-shan in the school.

---

[32] It was common to see the portraits of the four communist ancestors plus Chairman Mao on the rear wall of a meeting room of an organization.

Temptation of an apricot 一个杏的诱惑 (yige xingde youhuo)

Due to his outstanding achievements in school, he was selected as the class leader that year. The duties included helping brush off the blackboard after each class, leading pupils to sweep classroom floors and windows sometimes, etc.

It was routine in the summer that after lunch, from 1:00pm until 2:00pm, all pupils were supposed to take a nap, sitting on their own benches, with their arms on the desk and heads in their arms. To ensure all pupils obeyed the rule, there would be two pupil representatives patrolling all classrooms and monitoring their activities.

One day it was *Dai-Shan*'s turn, partnering with another pupil in grade 5 to patrol together. They wore a red sleeve band labeled 值日 (zhiri) – on duty. They patrolled every classroom, usually standing at the door and glancing through the room, just to make sure everyone was napping. When he got to the door of a 6 classroom by himself, he looked around, and everyone seemed to be napping. He was just about to walk away when he suddenly spotted two apricots inside the desk near the door, right in front of him. He ate apricot before, and it was very delicious. Today he had not had lunch yet before he came on duty. The fruit made him feel hungry. It looked so tempting and he felt like eating. But he hesitated and looked around. No one was looking and the pupil sitting beside the table seemed to be napping too. The hunger Tempted him to do something. He couldn't help but picking one up and put it quickly in his pocket and walked away, his heart beating fast.

Well, that pupil wasn't really napping. He was awake and saw *Dai-Shan*'s hand. He, a boy as big as an adult,

67

rose up from his seat and followed Dai-shan as he walked down the hallway. He whispered to him: "did you just take one of my apricots?" *Dai-shan* was so ashamed, with his head down and flushed face, he nodded. "I was so hungry", he replied. That pupil looked at this little boy, and then said with a softer tone, "You shouldn't take anything from others without asking for permission first". Looking at this little boy in front of him, he added "It's OK, you can keep it, but don't do that again" and then went back to his seat. That pupil never reported the incident.

Although no one saw what happed, it was a lesson Dai-shan learned and remembered after he grew up many years later. He learned to respect others and their stuff, especially from the way that pupil treated him. He often picked up wild edible fruits when he was out in the field, and he would share with other kids.

Dai-shan couldn't remember at what time his mother planted two apricot trees in their yard, and they had fruit for many years until the trees became old and died. His mother was always doing her best for her children and she later planted two walnut trees in the yard after the apricot trees died. On the other hand, his father, either because he was too busy to do such thing or just didn't have a vision, did not intend to plant any tree as he thought it would take too long for the tree to grow up.

11. Young Helper 小帮手 (*xiao bang-shou*)

After Dai-shan came home from school, he usually tried to help his parents with house chores. When he was little, he would feed the chickens and make sure they were back in the chicken coop, called *Ji-juan* 鸡圈 (like a doghouse against the front wall of the house).

When he grew older, he would pick grass on the way home to feed the rabbits and go to the field to fetch goats and bring them home. This was at a later time when the government allowed peasants to raise their own poultry and small livestock. A baby rabbit would grow up in a few months and could sell for ¥2 to ¥3. Rabbits reproduce quickly, and the kits could be sold at ¥0.5 or more for a pair in one to two months.

For reference, a goat at one year old could sell for ¥10 to ¥20, depending on its weight. A pig, once a year, would be worth a lot more, ¥40 to ¥90. This type of side work was called *Fu-ye* 副业 and would be the main income source for peasants in those days, which was usually worth more than the Gong-fen they earned from everyday farming.

Shepherd boy and playful goats 放羊娃和调皮的山羊 (fang yang wa he tiao-pi de shan-yang)

When he grew up more, Dai-shan would help by going to the field to cut green grass with *Lian-dao* 镰刀 and *Bei-dou* 背篼 to feed the goats at night and on rainy days, and sometimes for the pigs as well. During the weekends and summertime when he was off school, he would tend the goats and take them to the hill while collecting grass at the same time.

As a shepherd boy, he learned how to handle a herd of up to four goats. Only a string was needed to attach to the mother goat's neck and the other goats would follow along. Every goat would wear a mouth cover (like a mask made of bamboo) to prevent them from eating crops along the way out and back home,

and the covers be removed once in the pasture field or at home. When they got used to it, no string was needed even for the mother goat.

Goats are very playful, particularly when they are young. After they eat enough grass, they often fight with each other, head-to-head pushing back and forth. Once in a while, Dai-shan would "fight" with them too. They seemed to know how much force to use and didn't push as hard as with the other goats.

One day, they were at the peak ridge 尖梁子 (*jian liang zi*) in the village. Dai-sha was kneeling at the edge of a cliff to cut some long green grass. A big adolescent male goat saw him and came close. They played with each other often. The posture Dai-shan was cutting grass in made the goat think that it was an invitation to play. He got close to Dai-shan and started pushing with his head.

Dai-shan played with goats on the ridge

Wow, that was close! It sent a chill down his spine. Dai-shan was almost pushed off the edge down the steep cliff! He quickly grabbed the horn of the goat to catch his balance. He shouted at the goat "Don't you do that again!". The goat seemed to know what trouble he made, he sniffed his nose and walked away quietly.

Another time, Dai-shan was with some friends on the highest hill cutting grass using a *Lian-dao* 镰刀. When a

Lian-dao was sharp enough, you only needed to pull it to cut grass. When it was dull, you would need to raise it up and drop it down on the grass while pulling it. Perhaps he was still learning that skill. At one time when he was not paying attention to what he was doing, or he was distracted by something else. Instead of the grass, his Lian-dao landed on the front of the tibia bone of his right leg because he was right-handed. He suddenly burst out crying loudly from the pain and the bleeding. The whole village could hear him crying.

There were no bandages and disinfection that sort of thing available. His little friends looked around quickly and found a type of grass, called *Suo-cao* 蓑草 (a type of grass with very thin leaves like chive, but 2' to 3' long) . The root of the grass was furry, like a cattail and was effective at stopping bleeding. They put some on his wound, pressed on it and eased bleeding. 20 minutes later his mother arrived and helped him get home. She was relieved that it didn't hurt his leg bone. That incident however left a scar on his leg for ever.

Picking up cattle poop 捡牛粪 (jian niu fen)

When he grew a little older, Dai-shan tried to help a little more. However, he was still too small to work with adults in the farming group. The only way he could help his parents earn some *Gong-fen* 工分 was to pick up 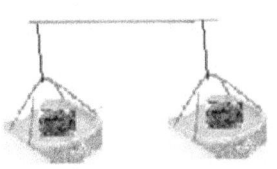 cattle poop somewhere out in the field or on the animal marketplace and submit to the Group as natural fertilizer.

One kilogram of cattle poop would earn 1.0 point of *Gong-fen*. He usually would be able to earn 2 to 3 points a day when he was lucky. That was quite good considering his father as a full laborer could only earn 10 points and his mother only 8 points in a whole day. However, sometimes he came home with empty buckets.

In those days, Dai-shan was often barefoot during the summer, like his father who was on barefoot most of the time. When he had to go to the field or walk far, he would wear *Cao-xie* 草鞋 made by his father with wheat/rice straw, or *suo-cao*.

 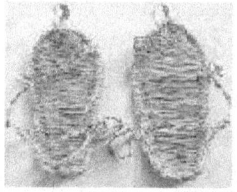 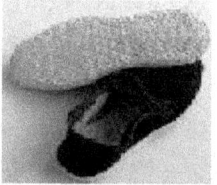

cao-mao 草帽　　cao-xie 草鞋　bu-xie 布鞋

In the wintertime, he would wear cloth shoes hand-made by his mother from old clothing. He never saw his mother sitting idle doing nothing. Whenever she had time to sit in group meetings or chat with others, she was sewing, making shoe bottom patches, one needle at a time. In the summertime, it sometimes got very hot. Like everyone else, Dai-shan would wear a *Cao-mao* 草帽 (wheat straw hat, 1.5' to 2' in diameter) on a sunny day to shade himself from the hot sunlight.

Dai-shan often went cattle-poop hunting with his two cousins, *Dong-wu* and *Dai-er*, both of whom were older than him. As you may have thought, a cattle boy would normally pick up after his own cattle to help his own parents earn some *Gong-fen*. Therefore, they would have to search for other sources and going to far away places.

The nearby free market had lots of buying and selling during the "open market" days, including livestock:

cattle, goats, pigs, etc. Old cattle that could no longer work in the farm would be sold to butchers for meat.

Some butchers came from far away, like *Zhongdu-fu* and neighboring counties. There were no trucks to transport the cattle, and so the cattle would have to walk to the destination before being slaughtered. The same for farmers from out of town. All these cattle would need grass to eat and would poop too. The livestock market and the road were where Dai-shan could find cattle poop. Well, he and his buddies were not the only ones with this idea. There were other kids doing the same thing. Sometimes, he and his buddies would go over 5 to 10 kilometers away down the road to find cattle poop.

Livestock negotiator 牛经纪 *(niu jing-ji)*

One day, Dai-shan went to the market with his father to sell their goat. He saw one distant uncle from his village approach his father and try to hold his father's hand. But his father seemed reluctant to "shake hands", and said "too early, I don't need help yet. May be later". Dai-shan asked "what did he want, *yao-ba*?". "He wanted to help me sell the goat, I think I can do it myself", his father answered.

At this point, it seems necessary to explain a bit about how the livestock market worked in the old days. It was a free market. Cattle were sold and bought by Farming Groups. Goats and pigs were sold and bought by individuals. No price was set or posted. A buyer and a seller always had different evaluations on the price.

For small animals (poultry, rabbits, etc.), the negotiation was open, and everyone nearby could hear it.

"How much do you want to sell it for?"

"¥4",

"Too expensive, how about ¥2[33]?"

The negotiation would go on and on until both sides agreed on a final price.

However, for goats, pigs and cattle, the negotiation often seemed to be silent, and no one could hear them talk at all.

Here was where a livestock negotiator came in. He would normally stand by, watching for a while. When he saw a potential deal could be reached, he would approach the seller and the buyer separately to ask their interests verbally. Once he had some idea he would negotiate secretly with each side. From that moment, it was a silent

Cattle market

negotiation. They started discussing price with their hands in the negotiator's large sleeves. No one else knew what numbers were being discussed. The negotiator was very persuasive, and they could often reach a deal. Once both sides settled, he would ask each side for a fee. That could be ¥1 to ¥2 or more, depending on the size of the deal.

Cattle slaughtering open field 露天宰牛场 *(lu-tian zai niu chang)*

There were a couple of times when Dai-shan saw something he had never seen before near that market. One day, he and other pupils were passing by the market on

---

[33] It was a normal to start bargaining by cutting the price by half.

the way home from school. There was a big crowd in an open ground surrounding and watching something. When he got into the crowd, he saw many cattle in the middle on leashes by their noses, some standing and some lying down on the ground.

Cattle were big and strong. If a leash were to be on its neck, no one would be able to control it. Therefore, a hole is pierced through its nose and a string is attached through the hole. This way, even a small boy would be able to pull large cattle.

It was an open slaughtering place, and these cattle were to be slaughtered right there. Dai-shan had seen a butcher slaughtering pigs in a slaughtering store before. The butcher would stab a short (approximately 10") sharp knife into the pig's chest to reach its heart making a quick kill while keeping the pig still on a stone step with two helpers holding its four legs. He had not seen how they slaughter cattle. Cattle were big and the technique for slaughtering pigs seemed not suitable.

While he watched with others in the crowd, a man pulled a rope suddenly which was tied to the four feet of a cattle. causing the cattle to fall immediately to the ground. The cattle struggled and tried to stand up but failed with its four feet tied together. It could only move its head but nothing else. Another man with a long knife, like sword, approached the cattle. With the assistance of another person, he grabbed the horn of the cattle, twisted the head to its side, and while keeping it still, quickly sliced the cattle's head off with his long knife. Someone immediately brought a big basin to catch the blood pouring out the cattle's neck. This was not a quick kill since the knife did not reach the heart. Dai-shan unconsciously stepped back and hid behind an adult, frightened. After a few minutes, the cattle stopped moving, having bled to death[34].

Dai-shan noticed some other cattle nearby, who had witnessed the process, with tears in their eyes. "That cow is crying", he couldn't help speaking out to himself. "Yes, they are like humans and have feelings", a person nearby responded "Perhaps, they knew it was their turn next".

Dai-shan often heard people saying "Cattle had the most miserable life. They worked the hardest in the farming field for their entire lives to serve humans, but in the end their heads were cut off and their flesh ended up on the table as food for humans". Kids were also taught to be honest, to be fair to others, not to cheat, and not to owe anyone anything. If someone did not pay back their debt while alive, he or she would repay their debt in their next lives by becoming working cattle for that person they were indebted to. That is what this saying is about: repay debt by becoming a working cattle or horse 当牛做马来还债 (*dangniu zuoma lai huanzhai*).

12. Memories of Some Childhood Events 童年的一些往事 (*tong-nian de yixie wang-shi*)

As Dai-shan grew older, he started asking his mother questions. He knew his grandparents on his mother's side well but had no memory of his grandfather Wang-da. When he saw other children with their grandparents, he wondered where his grandfather on his father's side was. His mother told him "*Ah-po* 阿婆(grandmother) passed away when you were about two. You probably don't remember. But you could

---

[34] This type of practice is believed to have been stopped.

grab food from her hands already. You have to ask your father about *Ah-gong* 阿公 (grandfather)". His father then told him "*Ah-gong* passed away a long time ago. That was before the liberation" (meaning before 1949).

It was a custom for relatives to visit each other, particularly on birthdays of elders, wedding ceremonies and the week after the Spring Festival. This type of mutual visit was very common among relatives of the three consecutive generations: grandparents, parents and grandchildren. Once grandparents passed away, visit to their families became less frequent and nearly disappeared in the generation of great grandchildren.

Dai-shan remembered visiting his aunt, *Da-gu* 大姑 (his father's older sister) a couple of times on her birthday in the neighboring county.

Dai-shan had also visited his other older aunt *Da-yi-niang* 大姨娘 (his mother's oldest sister) in the neighboring commune and had often visited the home of his *Er-yi-niang* 二姨娘, *Min-zhen (his mother's second sister)*, who lived in the same village, married to the Ye family. The 2nd child *of Er-yi-niang* was a boy, Cousin *Dong-wu* about 3 years older than Dai-shan. They grew up together and often did things together as described before.

His uncle Shi-qing (his father's older brother) had four sons and two daughters. The second child was also a boy, Cousin *Dai-er*, and was in similar age as *Dong-wu*. Dai-shan and the two cousins did many things together, such as collecting grass, shepherding goats and cows, picking up cattle poop, digging herbs in the field, swimming behind their parents' back in dug ponds (water storage pits built to collect rainwater in the field) and sometimes just having fun. They even swore to each other that by all means they would get out of their poor village to search for a better life somewhere[35].

Solving a riddle 解谜语 (jie miyu)

Dai-shan's grand uncle Wang-er had two daughters and two sons. One was Uncle Chang, and both uncles lived just behind Dai-shan's home. He didn't remember much official visit to them probably because they lived so close to each other and each family had their new relatives, except in very special occasions, such as when Uncle Chang's first son got married. Uncle Chang's third son, older than Dai-shan, was in the same class in school with Dai-shan. Sometimes they played together.

One of Uncle Chang's sisters had two sons in a village not far from Dai-shan's Wai-po's home. The older son: *Guang-da*, who had some education, traveled often, and was considered knowledgeable about the outside world, came to visit his two uncles often. He appeared to know a lot of things and have learned a bit of Chinese medicine too. Sometimes he would see some patients and prescribe Chinese medicine as well. Some patients believed him. However, the others called him *jianghu langzhong* 江湖郎中 (a charlatan, or a medicine doctor with no formal training).

Every time when Cousin *Guang-da* came, he would give advice to his uncles and make a speech to educate his young cousins as requested by his uncle. The structure of Uncle Chang's home was similar to Dai-shan's home, with a

---

[35] Cousin *Dai-er* was the first one to have a temporary job as a railway construction worker out of the county but then returned home to continue farming, married with two children. Cousin *Dong-wu* had many temporary construction jobs in nearby areas, then became a small contractor working near Zhongdu-fu and eventually settled in the suburb area with his wife.

wide-open front porch all along the front wall. During his visit, there were usually a large group of children including Dai-shan gathered in the courtyard and the front porch to listen to his speech about new things outside the village.

One day, *Guang-da* visited his uncle on his birthday. After the dinner, he started his speech to his younger cousins. Dai-shan gathered around too. In the middle of his speech, he decided to challenge his younger cousins. "Here is a riddle. I want to see if any of you can solve it", he said.

"There are three people, a mother tiger and two cubs. They are going to cross a river, but there is only one boat which only has the capacity for two.

"The constraints are: no one can swim, the people and the mother tiger are able to paddle the boat but the two cubs cannot, and whenever and anywhere the tigers outnumber the people, they will eat the people.

How can they all safely cross the river with the boat?"

He said, "I will give you 30 minutes to think over". All children started thinking and trying very hard. After a few minutes, some shook their head, and some seemed lost. Dai-shan was among them and was thinking too.

"15 minutes has passed; does anyone have any idea yet?" *Guang-da* asked.

"I think I got it", Dai-shan replied. *Guang-da* wasn't expecting that and asked Dai-shan to explain it step-by-step. After Dai-shan explained the procedure in sequence, he was very surprised and said, "well done, little cousin!" He then explained that there was only one way to cross the river and Dai-shan did it. Even then, some of his close cousins still didn't get it.

A little later, Dai-shan's mother came to fetch him for dinner. Guang-da told her "*yao jiu-niang* 幺舅娘 (aunt), Cousin Dai-shan is very smart and solved a difficult riddle. He will have a promising future if you let him continue his schooling". Dai-shan's mother, who had never gone to school, had a smile on her face and probably felt warm in her heart. Perhaps she believed it.

That certainly increased Dai-shan's confidence, but made his other cousins feel bad. The purpose of Guang-da's was to teach his cousins but none of them showed talent. Instead, a distance cousin shone. Their fathers often blamed them for not being able to learn.

On the Rich Land 在富饶之都 (*zai fu-rao zhi-du*)

When people talk about Duotong Province, they inevitably think of Zhongdu Plain. This is the area primarily called the Land of Abundance 富饶之都. The name came from the rich land, its geographic and weather conditions, where a large variety of crops and vegetables grow in abundance.

The capital of *Jingdian* 京甸 county 县 (*xian*) was *Jingdian-zhen* 京甸镇, located near the edge of Zhongdu Plain, just on the other side of the mountains from Yao'sville, about 20 kilometers away. This place was the richest place in the surrounding areas: It was simply flat with fertile soil, three rivers merged here to form a main branch river, which flows to the Yongzhi river 长江 down stream. In those days, peasants here could earn up to ¥1.00 a day while Dai-shan's father could only earn approximately ¥0.10 a day in Yao'sville. The two places were geographically so close to each other while the difference in the end product was so big.

Uncle Chang, who lived in the rear courtyard, had his second son Dai-qi adopted at a young age by a grand uncle who lived near *Jingdian-zhen*. Distant cousin Dai-qi grew up with his two grandparents and was doing well. His father was proud of him and often spoke of him at home to encourage other children to learn from him. Dai-qi had recently been recruited to the army and needed to get married before leaving home. His parents and grandparents decided to invite all their close relatives including Dai-shan's family to the wedding.

Dai-shan's father was busy as usual and couldn't go. They decided to let Dai-shan and his mother go to represent the family. Dai-shan had never been far from his home village and was excited to go and see this new place. Together there were a total of at least 10 people from the four Yao's families going.

The gravel road near their village was the primary route to *Zhongdu-fu* and 2 to 3 buses from other counties passed by everyday. They brought with them prepared presents and walked to the marketplace to wait for the bus. Dai-shan did not know how they paid for the bus tickets which would cost ¥0.5 per person. The bus climbed the mountain to the top and then descended on the other side before traveling on the flat terrain. The bus passed a bridge, then the center of *Jingdian-zhen* and another bridge shortly. After a few minutes, they got off the bus at a stop somewhere in a large, flat, farm field with endless rice crops.

"Wah, so wide and flat. What is this place, Mama?", Dai-shan asked. "This is called *Shi-li Ba* 十里坝" (a flat terrain of 5 kilometers long), his mother responded.

He stood high on his feet trying to see the edge of the field, but he couldn't. The field was filled with rice crops stretching more than 5 kilometers away[36]. Looking at this place and thinking of his home village, he couldn't believe the difference. This was the place that many peasants could only dream of. These two places were so close to each other but were so different. Although it was only about 20 kilometers away, he felt as if he were in a far away place.

"We have to walk now to get to your cousin's home", mother called to him. He followed others and walked for another half a kilometer before arriving at the destination, where his cousin, cousin's fiancée and two grandparents were waiting in the front yard. With that many people, there would not be a bed for everyone. They split into groups with some staying in neighbors' homes. Several kids were placed in one large room and slept on the floor. The next day was the wedding ceremony, followed by a banquet. Dai-shan couldn't remember much detail from the wedding but there was plenty of good food to eat. However, he was most impressed by the landscape and couldn't stop thinking of why his home village was so poor.

Gravel road maintenance 公路养护 (*gonglu yanghu*)

After the establishment of the new China, lack of machinery and technology was the biggest challenge during the rebuilding of the country. Everything in construction was labor intensive.

---

[36] Unfortunately, the once rich vast farmland is no where to see today, and it has been replaced by concrete roads and rows after rows of buildings during the mass construction era entering the 21st century.

First the *Hongxing* reservoir was built below Yao'sville. Although it was solely to benefit those down stream, every village in *Hongxing* commune was required to contribute to the construction of the dam, which relied on manual labors. Dai-shan remembered his parents went there too but not sure what they did exactly. He also remembered that one family who lived in the reservoir region migrated to Yao'sville, becoming the newest family in the village.

It was not sure when the gravel road down the hill was built. But Dai-shan remembered it was the main road from many counties and cities to Zhongdu-fu. Because it had only gravel surface, it required continuous maintenance year-round. There was a road maintenance team with a dozen of permanent workers under the provincial transportation department. They had a simple residential building on the top of the mountain, called *daoban fang* 道班房. Their duties were to keep the road functional in the section from the other side of the mountain near *Jingdian-zhen to this side of the mountain down to* Yao'sville at the county border.

The major maintenance would require resurfacing by adding gravel to the surface. Well, gravels were not shipped from a quarry pit but made on site: That area had mostly sandstone which was not hard enough for road surface and granite rocks, in 1' to 2' size, were shipped from somewhere to be piled up along the roadside. Then gravels had to be made manually with a hand-held hammer on site, one beat at a time, a process called *za-sui-shi* 砸碎石 (crushing rocks). That was time consuming and not an easy task. It was usually done in the wintertime when there was less farming work. Yes, you have guessed, the task was assigned to local peasants in every village. Dai-shan remembered his parents had to do that with other villagers for a few days in a row. They had to take their own lunches and have cold food on the roadside. By the time they completed the job, their hands often had cracks on the back and finger joints because of the cold weather and the vibration of hammer.

Every time after raining, there would be potholes and washouts on the road surface. The maintenance workers needed to follow up by spreading gravels to the uneven surface and fill potholes. If there were large damages which required major reconstruction, local peasants would be required to help with some compensation.

Cousin Dong-wu somehow got to know those maintenance workers when he grew a little older and then got temporary jobs doing heavy work from them from time to time, earning a good pay, up to ¥1.0 a day.

Chapter 3

Little Dai-Shan Experienced the Rural Cultural Revolution
小代山经历了乡村文革
(*xiao dai-shan jingli le xiang-cun wen-ge*)

13 Cultural Revolution Begins 文革开始了 (*wenge kaishile*)

In 1966, Dai-shan was in Grade 5. He had attended that school for five years. Like other pupils, he was expecting to graduate from elementary school in just one more year but did not know what will happen next.

According to his father, Dai-shan had been in school so long and learned more than he needed for his life as a peasant. He could count, read, and write a letter now. What else did he need to learn? He received more education than anyone in the Yao family history since his ancestor settled on this land twelve generations ago. For many ordinary families, Dai-shan's education was among the highest for their generations too. Besides, his family urgently needed more laborers to work in the Farming Group to earn a few more Gong-fen to support the family.

By that time, Dai-shan already had three younger siblings. The first one was a brother who had started elementary school in the village below Yao'sville. Then two sisters. However, the first sister only survived for about one month and died unexpectedly. He remembered the healthy lovely baby sister and wanted to take care of her whenever he could. Since there was no heating in the house, it had been a custom to keep an infant with parents on the bed at night to keep the baby warm. One morning when he woke up, he heard his mother crying with heartbreak. He asked what happened. His father said the baby died. A neighbor was asked to take the baby's body out to bury. Later he heard that the baby's body was purple, a sign of suffocation. His second sister was born the next year. The younger sibling was also a brother who was still an infant and required lots of attention.

With four children in the family, his father would need

more help to feed the family. However, Dai-shan was still too small to be much help on the farm. All he could do was some light chores and help looking after the two younger siblings. He remembered his sister as a very good helper since she was very young. She was helping taking care of the youngest brother who was that year and gave lot more help to their mother as she grew older.

School suspension for students to join the Cultural Revolution 停课闹革命 *(ting-ke nao ge-ming)*

Well, Dai-shan didn't need to think about school anymore, and his father didn't need to worry about it either. 1966 was the year when something unprecedented in Chinese history, or across any country's history, occurred. The *Great Proletarian Cultural Revolution* 无产阶级文化大革命 *(wu-chan jieji wen-hua da ge-ming*, or for short, Cultural Revolution 文革 *wen-ge*), a sociopolitical movement started in the People's Republic of China. People were talking about the "May 16 notification" released by the CP central committee. There was a rumor that the CP government had been infiltrated by *counter-revolutionary revisionists*.

In August, Chairman Mao released a short document, titled "Bombard the Headquarters 炮打司令部 (*paoda siling bu*) – my big-character poster 我的一张大字报 (wode yizhang *Dazi-bao)*". Shortly after, the CP official propaganda newspaper urged masses of people across the nation to "clear away the evil habits of the old society" by launching an all-out assault on "monsters and demons[37]" 横扫一切牛鬼蛇神 (*hengsao yiqie niu-gui-she-shen*).

---

[37] They referred to all of "people's enemies" including those classified in the five categories.

They also heard that schools and universities in the cities were already closed. Students had walked out of their classrooms to join the cultural revolution. It was hard to say if these youngsters knew what they were doing.

The news soon spread across the entire nation, including Dai-shan's school. They first heard about the school closure but did not know what it would mean to them. All policies came from the upper levels of the government. The grassroots would only follow. Soon, his school was supposed to close indefinitely as well. The regular end-of-school ceremony was cancelled. All pupils were sent home to join the revolution in their local communities.

Dai-shan, at the age of eleven, had his opportunity to study interrupted. He went back home to Yao'sville, which was the 4th farming group of the Alliance *Dadui* in the *Hongxing Gongshe* 红星公社. He was unaware of what happened in his school afterwards.

He, too small to be a peasant yet, couldn't do much farm work and had no idea what he was supposed to do, but simply wait and see, while helping with some chores to his parents.

The students from universities and middle schools were the major force during the cultural revolution. They became *Red Guards* 红卫兵 (*hong wei-bing*) of Chairman Mao. They all wore red sleeve bands 红袖套 (*hong xiu-tao*) as a symbol. In nearly every level of government, schools, factories, there was a *Red Guard* organization. They often belonged to larger organizations called *Red Guard Corps* 红卫兵团 (*hong wei-bing tuan*). In rural areas, there were also red guard organizations at the *Dadui* and Commune levels. They would belong to the organization at the county level.

Dai-shan was too young to be a red guard and could only be a little red guard 红小兵 (*hong xiao-bing*), like other kids in elementary school. He didn't get to wear a red sleeve band and was not part of the red guards' activities, except as helpers in some occassions. Most of the time, like the other kids, he could only follow the crowd and watch the red guards in action, which often puzzled him.

During that period, there was a cultural revolution leading committee 文革领导委员会 (*wen-ge ling-dao wei-yuan-hui*), for short, revolutionary committee 革委会 (*ge-wei-hui*), at every level from the central government to local communes. These committees were made up of one to two delegates deployed from upper-level revolutionary committees plus a couple of people at the local level. At the highest level of the central government, it was the small central revolutionary leading team 中央文革领导小组 (*zhong-yang wen-ge ling-dao xiao-zu*) calling the shots. The red guards basically followed whatever the revolutionary committees planned to do. This chain of committees for a period basically replaced all the governments and factory administrations in performing their functions. That meant many of the existing administrative officials were sidelined or became targets.

Liu Shao-qi 刘少奇, the then President of the People's Republic of China was the first to be publicly criticized as the commander of China's "bourgeoisie headquarters 资产阶级司令部 (*zichan jieji siling bu*)". He was put in prison the following year, purged from the CP government, prisoned in different locations and eventually died later in confinement[38]. To Dai-shan and many ordinary people, they didn't really understand what was going in the central government and all governments at the lower levels. How could the President of the country suddenly become the public enemy and confined to death outside of the court system? Was there a court system?

Open field movie showing 露天电影 (lu-tian dian-ying)

In the cities, it was an ordinary thing for people to go to the cinema to watch movies with a purchased ticket. Perhaps, everyone in the city took it for granted. Well, that was not the case in rural areas. There was no cinema around. The cities were far away. Besides, as a peasant, who has the spare time and money to go far away just to watch a made-up story? It might be entertaining, but it was not edible and couldn't help you survive.

The government intended to enrich culture in rural areas by taking movie shows to the countryside. *Jingdian* 京甸 county had a Cultural Bureau, which administered a few cinemas in the cities and major towns, plus a few mobile film projection teams. Every few months or half a year, these mobile movie teams packed up the gear required for the movie show, such as a generator, a film projector, a large white fabric screen, etc. and went on tours to the rural areas. Each team would be a on separate route. So, Dai-shan and his little friends got to watch movies once in a while when a mobile movie team came to their commune at a location half a kilometer away in the

---

[38] He was rehabilitated by Deng's government in 1980 and there was a national memorial service for him.

neighboring village down the hill.

Usually, the movie show was in an open field where a large white fabric screen was hung at its four corners onto two posts. A projector was put in the center of the open space. Everyone could just go in and find a spot  on the ground to sit. No ticket was required to watch. It became routine to show documentary films about political events at the beginning and then a movie.

It was through venues like the mobile movie shows, plus local mass meetings, that the government educated citizens on its policies and political movements. It was also by such venues that Dai-shan and the other villagers got to hear what was happening outside their village. Therefore, they only knew what they were told or were allowed to hear.

Hill-top propaganda 山头广播 (shan-tou guang-bo)

To strengthen the education of ordinary people on government policies and current politics, hill-top propaganda was set up in almost every village. It was

Hill top propaganda

Yao-Jia LiangZi hilltop propaganda 姚家梁子山头广播

91

carried out by a team of two youngsters (or little red guards) from the village. Under the upper level's instructions, every evening, around dusk, Dai-shan and his partner took a kerosene lamp, a hand-held speaker, and a red book of Chairman Mao's quotations to the hilltop beside his home. The two youngsters, one holding the lamp and another holding the speaker and the red book, would read a few paragraphs. They were little and naive. The speaker was not amplified: it was just a metal funnel. They tried to read as loud as they could, to make sure every villager could hear what Chairman Mao had to say. Perhaps they believed that was what they could do to be a part of the culture revolution. To be fair, it was not sure how much the peasants understood what he read from the red book.

In only a couple of days, little Dai-shan lost his voice from reading so loud and could hardly speak for two weeks afterwards. That made him take the supportive role in holding the lamp, instead of reading.

Sometime later, the county government established a wired-broadcasting network 有线广播网 (*you-xian guang-bo wang*), which was connected to the broadcasting-relay stations 广播转播站 (*guang-bo zhuan-bo zhan*) in every local commune. Wooden posts were erected with a single wire to all villages, where there was still no electricity. Loudspeakers were installed on hill tops in nearly every village. This broadcasting network replaced the hilltop propaganda.

The loudspeakers broadcast local and national news three times a day: early morning, lunch time and evening. They awakened the quiet mountainous villages, and you could hear from a kilometer away.

But later, those loudspeakers were again replaced by smaller speakers installed on residential buildings throughout the villages, so that people could hear it better when they were doing house chores and having meals. That also reduced the noise from the loudspeakers.

With the wired-broadcasting network in place, the local revolutionary committee leaders very frequently spoke via the system on policies, political events, etc. Often, they spoke for a long time: one hour or longer was not uncommon. The content in a speech could be shortened to less than 10 minutes but they still spoke for an hour. The leaders liked to do that. Perhaps they were enjoying the moment that they were in charge, and everyone must listen to them.

Red Guards nation-wide mutual touring 红卫兵大串联 (hong wei-bing da chuan-lian)

As the cultural revolution progressed, villagers could hear from the media many things that were happening outside of their villages. Soon, they started seeing red guards in groups holding a flag and wearing red sleeve bands from other places passing by the marketplace, on the road, beside the villages. The road near Yao'sville was a main road to the provincial capital *Zhongdu-fu.*

"Who are these people and where are they from?" some asked.

"They are the red guards touring from a neighboring county", someone replied.

Whenever the red guards passed a crowd or places where people gathered, they loudly shouted slogans, such as, "Down with the Capitalist[39]打倒走资派 (*da-dao zou-zi-pai*)",

---

[39] Referred to those people who held authoritative positions in an organization and embraced capitalism.

"Sweep Away All Monsters and Demons 横扫一切牛鬼蛇神 (*heng-sao yi-qie niu-gui she-shen*)",

"Long live the Great Cultural revolution 文化大革命万岁 (*wen-hua da-ge-ming wan-sui*)",

"Long live Chairman Mao 毛主席万岁 (*mao zhu-xi wan-sui*)", etc., etc.

That was the nation-wide red guards mutual touring 红卫兵大串联, called for by the upper revolutionary committees. At the beginning, the red guards walked by foot. Later, they got the privileges of riding buses, and trains to far away places, staying in hotels and eating in restaurants, all for free. All they needed to show the host was an introduction letter with a red stamp from their local revolutionary committee.

Red Guards touring on foot
红卫兵步行大串联

As shown in the photos above, the red guards were very excited and so determined. In their

Red Guards touring by train
红卫兵免费坐火车大串联

minds, they seemed to be onto something huge, something secret, some historical mission and were prepared to do anything.

The reasons for the mutual touring were believed to be for the red guards to learn from each other on their progress and support each other in the cultural revolution, on how to dig out the "monsters and demons" and to criticize them. Another important reason was to travel to Beijing, the nation's capital to see Chairman Mao, who would greet them at *Tian-an-meng Square* 天安门广场（*guang-chang*）.

Red Guards greeted by Chairman Mao 毛主席接见红卫兵

Throughout the cultural revolution, there were eight times that the red guards gathered in mass at *Tian-an-meng Square*. Each time, the red guards were numbered in millions. The young generation felt it like a lifetime of happiness to see Chairman Mao in person at that time. No wonder the red guards who made it to Beijing were so excited and so proud of themselves.

Dai-shan could only watch those events on the documentary films, see the red guards on the roads and hear about them from the broadcast. Like many other kids, he really envied those big brothers and sisters who were there just at the right time for such historical events. He thought he could be just like them if he were born a few years earlier.

Yes, you may have noticed, in addition to the red sleeve band every red guard also wore a badge of Chairman Mao 毛主席像章（*mao zhu-xi xiang-zhang*）

Chairman Mao's badges 毛主席像章

95

on their front left chest (where the heart is). It was a symbol of loyalty to Chairman Mao from the heart and it also made them proud of being red guards. Almost everyone was eager to have one and many had a large collection. Dai-shan also managed to get a few.

14. Cultural Revolution Events in Small Mountain Villages
小山村的文革之事 (*xiao shan-cun de wen-ge zhi-shi*)

Abolish "4 olds" – Foster "4 news" 破四旧-立四新 (*po-sijiu li-sixin*)

The very first thing that touched ordinary people's lives in rural areas during the cultural revolution was to abolish the old ideas, old culture, old customs, and old habits (for short, abolishing the "4 olds") and to foster new ideas, new culture, new customs, and new habits (fostering the "4 news"). To be specific, it primarily focused on the following four areas:

1) Change old names. Old names of historical places, streets, communes, etc. were changed to new and revolutionary names. In Dai-shan's hometown, the name of the commune was changed to Hongxing, which meant "red star" . Nearly all names at the *Dadui* 大队 level, below the commune, originally named after the landmarks in their locations, were changed to reflect the new ideas. Here are some examples of the new names, *Happy* Dadui, *Star* Dadui, *Bright* Dadui, *Advance* Dadui, *Big-step* Dadui, etc. The Dadui for Dai-shan's home village was changed to *Alliance* Dadui. Generally anything representing old ideas or things would be changed to something new and revolutionary.

2) Change old clothing and eliminate superstitious activities. Old style of dresses was not to be used, hair

styles had to be new and short. On the market  at that time, there seemed to be only one style of outfit for men – the 4-pocket cloth 中山装（*zhong shan zhuang*）, which was also called Mao's jacket.

For women, mono-color and less colorful seemed more appropriate and acceptable to society.

Inspection stations were set up on major roads, road intersections, entrances to markets, etc. to check for any unwelcome clothing and superstitious items, which would be confiscated once discovered.

A few times, Dai-shan went to the market and saw people carrying farm products on their shoulders in a pair of 箩筐(luo kuang) or on their back in a 背筐(bei kuang), walking on the smaller trails rather than on the main road, or running away from some people who were after them. These poor peasants were trying to avoid being caught by the inspectors, a bunch of red guards.

At the market, often people were inspected and products confiscated, creating hardship and desperate conditions, especially for some of the older women. It was their only possesions, their livelihood. Just because it was considered "not new", "not appropriate", it was taken away.

3) Demolish and reform historical structures. In many places, churches, public shrines, and private homes were

ransacked or destroyed as the assault on "Feudal" traditions began. In Dai-shan's village, there was no church or historical buildings like that so there was not much to damage. However, every family was told to get rid of all their belongings in the "old" category. Worshiping their ancestors was not allowed.

If someone wanted to worship, they had to do it in secret behind closed doors at night and get rid of the ashes from burning paper money immediately.

4) Search and ransack homes. For ordinary citizens, this category probably had the biggest impact on their lives. As the campaign progressed, it reached every corner even in the rural areas. Every family was told to get rid of all of their old belongs and submit their valuables (like jewelry, antique furniture, antique paintings, even precious metal utensils). If the red guards suspected any family still held onto anything in the classified "4 olds", they could just enter their homes to "search" and ransack the home when they wanted. If anything classified as the "4 olds" was found, it would be confiscated. This action destroyed many people's personal properties, including collections and buildings. When they did this, there was no need for a court order. All they needed was verbal consent from the local revolutionary committee, which was often one- or two-people's decision at their discretion.

Family shrine and the Yao's family roots 神龛与姚家的根
(shen-kan yi yao-jia de gen)

For many generations, it has been tradition for the descendants to worship their ancestors during festivals and their ancestor's birthdays, to wish them happiness in the "other world" and to pray for them to protect their descendants in good health and prosperities. Since there was no church in Yao'sville, villagers usually worshiped in their own home at a dedicated spot.

Repaired shrine
修复后的神龛

In Dai-shan's family, they had a shrine 神龛(*shen-kan*) situated in the middle of the main room 堂屋 (*tang-wu*) against the rear wall, just next to the simple stretcher where Dai-shan slept. The shrine was simply a wooden structure with some carved symbols.

At that time, his grandfather Wang-da's family and his grand uncle Wang-er's had split into four families, but they all went to worship their ancestors at the same shrine.

Since he was little, Dai-shan would see the other uncles' families separately on the Spring festival's eve. They would bring cooked meat (often a large piece of pork, a whole chicken, etc.), light some incense and burn paper money to worship their ancestors in front of that shrine. The father of each family would say a few words to wish the ancestors happiness and hope for them to protect his family. The children would follow their father *kowtow* 磕头 (get on their knees and bow to their ancestors). The ceremony would take 10 to 15 minutes and then they would take all the food back home and just leave some ashes there. Dai-shan's parents would often clean up after them. Dai-shan followed his father to do the same thing. Although in his early years he was too small to understand what they were doing, he knew it must be important and just followed.

Now, during the campaign of abolishing the "4 olds", no one could escape. Dai-shan heard of what happened in other villages and asked his father what they should do with the shrine in their home. Ancestor worship was considered feudalism and not allowed. If they didn't do something about it or remove it themselves, the red guards would come and do it for them. His father said he didn't believe much in worship anyway and it didn't matter what to do with it. However, his mother insisted on keeping it. They finally came up with a compromise: cutting the four legs of the shrine shorter and using the top as a table and storage inside. That way, it didn't prevent them from continuing doing worship as long as they didn't leave any ashes or evidence. Dai-shan helped his father cut the four legs shorter with a hand saw. They also saved the cut-off parts[40]. That seemed to work because no one asked about it afterwards.

For as long as Dai-shan could remember, the shrine was a sacred place. Children were not allowed to play in front of it or to put anything on top. Now they had to remove everything from it. What was interesting was that Dai-shan found a sacred thin wooden box on top of the shrine.

Out of curiosity, he opened it by sliding down the rear cover and found some characters written inside the box, including a name *Yin* "印" and a location of "车子园 (*che-zi yuan*), a wagon garden". He asked his father what that was. His father shook his head, unsure. He went to ask his Uncle Shi-qing who explained that it was most likely the record of their ancestor, Yao Yin-Dru, who settled here a few hundred years ago and the location was probably where their ancestors came from, but that can no longer be found or verified today.

---

[40] Many years later when worship was allowed again, his father found the cutoff parts and put them back again, as shown in the photo.

Then Uncle Shi-qing continued: It could be reckoned that their ancestor *Yin-Dru* 印祖, the 6th generation of the Yao family, settled in *Yao-Jia liangzhi* and Dai-shan would be the 12th generation descendant of him.

The home of the "Rich Peasant" ransacked 一个富农的家被抄了 (*yige fu-nong de jia bei chao le*)

One evening, Dai-shan with another young man holding a kerosene lamp went to attend a meeting called for by the local red guard branch in Alliance *Dadui*. There were a few young fellows, some of them looked familiar to Dai-shan. It was a small group, about 7 all together. When all arrived, they started discussing something which seemed to be a secret. Dai-shan was invited as a representative of the little red guards. All he understood was they were to search someone's home next day.

One person said, red guards in other places had lots of activities and had made quite the achievements. They also needed to do something here. Based on the information they gathered, the "Rich Peasant 富农 (*fu-nong*)" in the #12 farming group was reported to have had a gun at the liberation time in 1949 and he didn't seem to have surrendered it as requested by the government at that time. He had been informed to hand it over, but he denied he possessed it. They needed to search his home and everyone in the meeting was told to keep it confidential. To Dai-shan, he was simply curious what kind of gun it was. He had seen a muzzle loader in his village, which was loaded with gun powder and shots for shooting small wild animals. He would just have to wait and see the next day.

The next morning, they all gathered at the same place they had the meeting the night before. When Dai-shan got there, there were already quite a few young men wearing red sleeve bands, some had tools for picking and digging. Many of them were not in the meeting the night before. He wondered why they brought those tools. When everyone arrived, they set off towards that village through a trail on the hill, where Dai-shan had not been before. One person in the front held a large red flag, which had a label: "Red guards of Alliance Dadui". The rest just followed. This definitely caught the attention of other villagers.

It was not very far, less than 2 kilometers away and they got there in about 30 minutes. Dai-shan was at the end of the line and almost the last one to arrive. When he got there, he saw a single bungalow house in a lower flat spot in the middle of the hill, made of clay walls and a straw roof, with a small flat yard in the front. A middle-aged woman stood at the edge of the yard with her arms hugging a young child. An older boy and a girl stood beside her. They seemed scared. An older man in his 50's, who didn't look strong, stood nearby separately with his head down staring at his own feet. He was accompanied by a red guard. He was most likely the "Rich Peasant" the red guards were looking for.

"How many guns do you have? Hand them over right now", one red guard told the older man rudely.

"I don't have any gun", he replied softly.

"You are still not being honest; We will search your house". By that point, some red guards had already entered the house. They first searched by visual inspection and did not find anything. Two red guards whispered something to each other and then told the other red guards,

"Dig! we will find it even if we have to dig 3 feet in the ground".

Then they started digging into the walls, the floor and

then outside in the yard, ransacking the whole property. Dai-shan was watching first from outside and then entered the house to see what was going on. Someone found a bundle of old currency wrapped in old newspaper hidden in a crack in the clay-wall. That may tell you the condition of that house. The bundle of currency, not a big amount even at the standard at that time, was issued by the old government 国民党政府 (*guo-min dang zhengfu*) and was no longer useful. Some others smashed the furniture and whatever in the kitchen, in the name of "searching for a gun, or something valuable".

Dai-shan couldn't watch anymore and went back outside. In a short while, the whole house was completely turned upside down, dust covering everything. He couldn't understand what was going on and why they did that. No matter how shabby the house was, it was a home for that family. Now, it was gone, in the matter of one hour. The only thing left was broken clay walls with a broken roof, broken furniture, no longer a home.

There were some by-standers from neighbors. They watched. Some were in disbelieve but some seemed happy to see it. Dai-shan glanced around the yard and saw the young child crying, the mother had tears on her cheeks, the other older children were frightened and seemed lost. When he looked at them more carefully, that boy of similar age to himself looked familiar. He couldn't help but walk towards that boy. After a few steps, he saw him more clearly. Yes, that boy was his classmate, and the older girl was the boy's sister. They both were in the same class as Dai-shan a few months ago before schools were canceled. "Is this their home?" Dai-shan wondered. He stopped and couldn't move his feet anymore.

In those days, people in the Five-Categories were considered enemies of people, and their children were labeled as "educatable children". Often, parents would teach their own children not to associate with them. In a situation like this, Dai-shan wanted to say something to that boy but didn't know what to say in front of the red guards. Eventually they looked at each other and exchanged glances, without saying anything.

By the end, the red guards did not find a gun, or any firearm, or other valuables, but the house was completely ruined, no longer habitable. This was not searching. It was ransacking! Dai-shan had never seen anything like that and didn't know where the whole family would live after that.

That "Rich Peasant" did not seem rich at all. He was targeted simply because he had that title in his 成分 (*cheng-fen*) at liberation when everyone was classified into categories.

Then the red guards decided to take the Rich Peasant to the Dai-dui administration compound, which was just a few buildings housing some machinery and offices, to keep him in confinement in a storage room until he would confess.

After that day, Dai-shan couldn't stop thinking about his two classmates. "Where are they going to live now"?

Public humiliation on the market 游街示众 *(youjie shi-zhong)*

Two days later, it was an open market day. The market was a very crowded place. Farmers and villagers in neighboring areas all went there to buy what they needed and to sell what they had, such as vegetables, seedlings, seeds, etc. Dai-shan went there with his father to help sell and buy necessities for the family. When that was done, he told his father he wanted to go to the main street (just one road with a variety of things for farming and the household) to look for something. As usual, the street was very crowded, and he had to squeeze through the crowd in some areas. On the way, he saw a crowd where someone was standing on a bench, a large plate sign with a thin string hung around his neck, wearing a tall paper hat, with red guards beside him. That was a typical way to publicly humiliate someone at the market 游街示众 (*you-jie shi-zhong*). Dai-shan was too short and couldn't see much inside the circle.

He moved on and again saw another crowd not far away. This time he heard the man in the center of the crowd saying something which sounded familiar. He managed to get into the crowd. There, on a bench stood the "rich peasant" he saw two days ago during the home search. In addition to a tall paper hat and a large cardboard sign hung on his neck, he held a large metal plate 锣 (*luo,* a kind of instrument used in a parade) in his lefthand and a stick in his righthand. He looked in much worse shape than two days ago, exhausted, and weak. There were two red guards standing beside him. They pointed fingers at him and shouted:

"You must be honest and confess 老实交代 (*lao-shi jiao-dai*)",

"What do I confess for?", he replied in a weak voice.

"Tell everyone where the gun is hidden".

The "rich peasant" raised his stick and struck on the metal plate, generating a loud sound "bang…" and said:

"He is Gong xian-kui", he struck on the plate again,

"He had a gun", he struck on the plate again,

"He didn't surrender it", he continued striking the plate after each sentence.

The crowd seemed confused. Someone whispered, "who had a gun?" One red guard seemed to have realized something and quickly shouted back:

"Who is *he*?" "Say *I* had a gun", "Go on, you must confess honestly".

"He is Gong xian-kui", the "rich peasant" continued.

"He had a gun",

"He didn't surrender it".

"Why did you say *he*?" Another red guard shouted.

The "rich peasant" turned his head slightly towards the first red guard, implying he meant that red guard.

That made the red guards enraged. They kicked the man on the bench and beat him with sticks. That man repeated his "confession" again and again like that, but he never admitted "*I* had a gun".

Dai-shan learned later that the "rich peasant" was confined for more than two weeks. When he was let go home due to deterioration of his health, there was still no confession or evidence of the alleged gun.

Oh, did he still have his home to go to? Perhaps, the clay building might be still standing, but the inside might not be a home anymore. Dai-shan never knew what happened with that family after.

Public criticizing in mass meetings 批斗会 (pi-dou hui)

The public humiliation was just the beginning. The actions against the "five categories 五类分子 (wu-lei fen-zi)" escalated further shortly. There would often be public criticizing mass meetings 批斗会 in the Dai-dui and the commune levels. Meetings were called for by the local revolutionary committees. Usually, each family was required to send at least one representative. The number of attendees would be in the hundreds at the Dai-dui

106

meetings and up to a thousand or more in the commune meetings.

During those meetings, a few people in the "five categories" would be put on the stage, with their hands tied to their backs, each wearing a tall paper hat. They were often made to stand on a small bench, where it was very difficult to keep their balance. As  further punishment, a large plate made of heavy material was hung around their necks with a thin string.

Then some pre-arranged people would go up to the stage, one by one, to make a speech against them and criticize them for whatever they were being blamed for. Sometimes, when the person accusing them got excited and emotional, he/she would hit the person. This kind of meeting would normally last for two hours or longer. Apparently, older people could not endure that long on a small bench and would fall off and suffer from various types of injuries.

That "rich peasant" could not escape from such meetings. Whenever these meetings were scheduled at the *Dadui* level and sometimes at the commune level, he would be required to show up, either to be on the stage as a target or to accompany those on the stage. Otherwise, severe punishment would happen to him.

There was a *Di-dru* 地主 named *Yi* 易 in a neighboring village. He was obviously a target in those days because of his family class. Dai-shan did not know this person. During one meeting in the Alliance Dadui, *Di-dru* Yi was put on the stage and made to stand on a small bench. The red guards tried a few times, but he seemed too old to keep his balance on the bench. Then they forced him to stand on his knees on the ground instead. However, he was very resistant and refused to get on his knees. His refusal was followed by kicking and beating by the red guards until he was no longer able to resist. Then two red guards, one on each side, held him to the ground while criticism progressed.

Dai-shan learned later that *Di-dru* Yi owned some farmland prior to the liberation, but he seemed to have behaved as he was told to. He was picked to be criticized in the meetings just because of his family's status 成份 (*cheng-fen*) as a Di-dru 地主.

Public trial convention 公审大会 *(Gongshen dahui)*

Another big event in those days was the public trial convention 公审大会 (*Gongshen dahui*). It was usually held on the level of *Qu* 区, which administered a few communes. The attendees numbered in the thousands from various neighboring communes. In the conventions, there would be at least one person or a few people from the area to be publicly executed. The most common crimes included active anti-revolution 现行反革命 (*xian-xing fan-ge-ming*), murder 杀人(*sha-ren*), breaking up a military personnel's marriage or engagement 破坏军婚 (*po-huai jun-hun*, referring to having an affair with the spouse/fiancée of, falling in love with or marrying a woman who was engaged to a military personnel), rapist 强奸犯 (*qiang-jian fan*).

This type of convention was not long. At a scheduled time and date, one hour after attendees arrived, an open truck carrying hand-cuffed criminals, accompanied by armed police officers, would come to the site, which was normally in an open field with a temporary stage. An officer would make a short speech on government policy and list the crimes of each of the criminals. There was actually no trial on site but just the final sentences. If they were sentenced to jail, or to delayed death, they would be put back on the open truck and taken to their confinement place. If they were sentenced to immediate death, they would be put on the truck and be driven out of the meeting site to an open field, to be executed on the spot by gunshot. Dai-shan attended a couple of such public trial conventions. He followed the huge crowd to watch the execution but not in time. When he got there, there was already a big crowd surrounding the dead body, waiting for the family to collect the body. Perhaps he was afraid of seeing a dead body and never tried to get close to look at one but only heard what others described.

15. Armed Fighting Starts 武斗开始了 (wu-dou kai-shi le)

The idea that rebellion is justified 造反有理 (Zao-fan you-li) was promoted by the small central revolutionary leading team 中央文革领导小组 (zhongyang wenge lingdao xiaozu) during the cultural revolution. During the nation-wide mutual tours, red guards from different places were actively engaged in various activities that were considered rebelling, such as openly criticizing authorities at any level, not respecting elders, pointing fingers at anyone they wanted to, doing the opposite of what their parents wanted them to do, doing anything that was against tradition and common sense, or simply doing anything against anyone they didn't like.

These red guards were so free to speak and act. Inevitably they would have different opinions on something, some idea, or someone. Gradually this led to the division of the red guards into different factions. The two major factions of red guards were the Rebels 造反派 (*zhao-fan-pai*) those who wanted to overthrow someone or abolish/change something old, and the Royalists 保皇派 (*bao-huang-pai*) those who wanted to protect someone or values they believed were good. No matter what the arguments were, they were against each other, shouting at each other. That was all they did in those days. They had free accommodations and no worries in life.

The red guard factions grew larger and larger in organization and recruited more and more members across large regions, forming Corps with commanders, etc., just like the military organization.

At the beginning, they were just shouting at each other impolitely, then behaved rudely, eventually becoming violent. In December 1966, an event occurred on *Kang-pin lu* 康平路 in *Shanghai* 上海 and the 12.4 (December 4th) event occurred in *Chongqing* 重庆, signaled the beginning of the nation-wide armed fighting.

A few months later, *Jiang-qing* 江青, the wife of Chairman Mao, was quoted on national news suggesting the red guards to *wen-gong wu-wei* 文攻武卫, which might have been interpreted as an instruction to criticize and harass targeted individuals and opponents verbally, but to defend themselves with force. Well, that was just like dropping a burning match in the dynamite. The two major red guard factions were already heated up and this turned on the green light for open conflict by force between the factions, sometimes within the rebel faction itself too. Harassment evolved into abuse. They started fighting first using sticks, then metal bars and knives, eventually real firearms: rifles, machine guns, grenades and even cannons, resulting in a huge number of casualties. Most of the wounded and dead were young people, in their late teens or early twenties. The nation-wide armed fighting lasted over one year. Interested readers can read more details from other sources.

You may ask where the red guards got the firearms from. That was hard to say, and it was anyone's guess. In China, weapons were strictly controlled and for use only by police and military in those days. The red guards were not able to manufacture weapons themselves that fast. The weapons must have been from somewhere. Some rumors said the red guards forcefully "robbed" military units and others said they were provided with weapons by some organizations.

The military was the only organization that was not supposed to openly get involved in red guard activities. It was said they must not interfere with those activities and stay neutral. That was what ordinary people heard.

Battlefield beside Yao'sville 战场摆到了姚家村口 (zhan-chang bai-dao-le yaojia-cun kou)

One morning, in the early summer in 1967, while some villagers were up early, and some still at asleep. Suddenly, there was sound of gunshots. It was a surprise to them since no one had ever heard of a continuous real gun shot in the areas, even during the civil war before 1949.

"The red guards have started using guns to fight each other now", one villager said. In the middle of the village, many started gathering and chatting.

"Where are they from?", some asked.

"Don't know, they seem to be from elsewhere", some responded.

"Who are they fighting with? What are fighting about?" some kept asking.

While they were chatting, they saw a few red guards from the village below walking up to the top of the hill in Yao'sville, where Dai-shan often went there to cut grass and shepherd. Some red guards carried guns and two of them even carried a machine gun on their shoulders.

These red guards were said to be from the neighboring *zhongxin* county. They were the rebels, and they were there to fight the royalists. Their slogan was "*wen-gong wu-wei*", "to kill and take back *Zhongxin* 杀回中新 (*sha-hui zhongxin*)", which was the capital and a major city of Zhongxin County.

As explained earlier, the top ridge of Yao'sville was at the boundary of the neighboring Zhongxin County. The royalist faction formed a Hero Corps 英雄兵团 (*ying-xiong bing-tuan*), named after a war hero who was reported to have silenced an enemy's machine gun without use of any weapon, as they wanted to protect what they believed in. The rebel faction also formed a Rebel Corps, 造反兵团 (*zao-fan bing-tuang*) and they had very different opinions. The rebel faction seemed to have lost their territory during their struggle with the royalists and wanted to take it back by force with the help of the rebel faction in Jingdian County. That was why they had set up a battlefield along the boundary of Yao'sville and a few other villages. Their first step was to take over the *Longsheng market* 隆盛场, the major town of Longsheng commune (where Dai-shan had walked through every weekday to get to and from school) and then advance towards the capital of Zhongxin County.

Those red guards were stationed in the village below Yao'sville, which was beside the main road, convenient for transportation of heavy equipment. Villagers were told not to go up the hill during those days to avoid being shot by blind bullets. The neighboring marketplace was closed, became quiet, and no one went to buy or sell.

After daybreak that day, the fighting intensified, and many gunshots were heard. For a short while, the machine gun seemed to have been used, generating a "Tu, Tu, Tu, …" sound, a scene Dai-shan had only seen in movies.

Things like that have never happened in this village before. It seemed to be a venture worth exploring. Dai-shan had never seen a real bullet or machine gun before. Out of curiosity, Dai-shan and a couple of his buddies went out to explore. They told their parents that they were just going out to cut grass to feed goats. They carried *bei-dou* 背篼 on their backs and set off for the venture. They tried to get around and then go up the hill. They changed their direction after a while and turned towards where the fighting was taking place, hoping to pick up some empty cartridges.

Before they approached halfway to the fighting place, they saw at a far distance two red guards carrying someone on a stretcher down the hill towards the village below.

"Someone may have been wounded", they thought. They stopped and tried to find out.

A villager came from that direction and told them, "Don't go over there. It's dangerous!"

"What happened?" they asked.

"It was a young boy, only 15 years old", he replied. "He was killed right on site and his intestine has leaked out. His comrades said he even didn't eat enough rice-sweet potato porridge at breakfast". He shook his head and went on his way. What Dai-shan and the other kids heard sent a chill down their spines. They reluctantly retreated.

Some informed person said later that the young red guard was a junior high school student in his first year; he was not supposed to fight, but to patrol the border as a sentry; he got up early that morning and ate some porridge before he went on duty. A very short while after fighting started, that young boy lost his life. Maybe he was in the wrong spot at the wrong time, didn't follow instructions, or simply didn't have experience in a real battlefield.

The villagers learned later that the major battlefield was in the marketplace of *Longsheng market* 隆盛场. Yao'sville at 2.5 kilometers away was only a peripheral battlefield 外围战场 (*wai-wei zhan-chang*) to cut off the enemy's possible reinforcements.

The next day, the gun shots died down. A few days later, no more gun shots were heard, and the red guards left that fighting ground. It was said the rebel corps had taken control of the *Longsheng market* 隆盛场 and was on its way towards their destination, the headquarters of the royalists. Villagers felt relieved. After a week, the marketplace also resumed its activities. As you may have guessed, the most popular topic people talked about was still the fighting over the past few days.

Uncle get tangled in the armed fight and wounded 舅舅卷入了武斗受伤了 (jiu-jiu juan-ru le wu-dou, shou-shang le)

It had been about one year since school was suspended. Dai-shan used to pass the marketplace twice a day on his way to and from school. He had not been there very often in the past year, except for when he occasionally went there to help his father sell vegetable seedlings and other things. When the marketplace reopened after one week closure due to the red guards fighting, Dai-shan went to the marketplace, hoping to hear some news about the fights.

The *Longsheng Market* was a one-street market with two large open fields behind it for livestock and poultry. After years of walking by, Dai-shan had become very familiar with the place. That day, after he sold what his father wanted him to sell, he walked through the main street and around the livestock market, hoping to find someone or hear something. He did overhear some people talking about the intense fighting, the winners and the losers.

The marketplace was very crowded. Cellphones had not been invented yet. If you wanted to find someone, you would go to the place where you would normally expect them to be or simply ask someone else whether that person had come to the market that day. If needed, you just leave a verbal message via someone you know.

After walking around for a while, he bumped into one of his cousins, the second son of his uncle – *Jiu-jiu* 舅舅 (mother's brother). The two had not seen each other much since school was suspended. They greeted each other and talked a little about their own lives these days. Then their conversation turned to his *Jiu-jiu*,

"How has *Wai-po* 外婆 been?" Dai-shan asked.

"She is fine", his cousin answered, "just worried about my father".

"What happened to Jiu-jiu?"

His cousin pulled him aside to a quiet place. After making sure no one else was around to overhear, he continued:

"He left home the night before the fighting started to
help and has not come back home for over a week now.

"We also heard from a friend that he retreated with others, but we don't know where he is".

"At least you heard about him, he should be OK", Dai-shan said, not sure how to comfort his cousin or himself.

His Jiu-jiu was a middle-aged man, a little over 40. People knew him as a quiet, honest and responsible person. He would not become a red guard because that was mostly for younger people and students. He, as a peasant with four children and an older mother (Dai-shan's *wai-po*), carried a big responsibility and would normally focus on farming to support his family.

However, he was also a man with principle. Like many ordinary people, he didn't like what some rebel red guards were doing, sometimes they seemingly destroyed things for no reason. The royalist faction – the Hero Corps, was said to be protecting existing values and were against the rebel faction's radical actions.

Dai-shan did not know exactly how his Jiu-jiu got involved in the fighting. But he learned later that some younger friends of his Jiu-jiu were in the Hero Corps. They were posted to fight the rebels with force when needed.

However, their headquarters was 30 kilometers away and they did not have sufficient people to fight in the first battle front at *Longsheng Market*. They started recruiting helpers. Somehow his Jiu-jiu was persuaded to help on the eve of the fight. He didn't realize until he got there that they were supposed to use firearms. He probably had never fired a gun before and would have learn how to shoot on the spot.

It was said that they were outnumbered by the rebels who had superior weapons. As they were retreating, his Jiu-jiu was stabbed in the waist by a red guard. Luckily, it was not fatal. He managed to escape with the others and retreated to Zhongxin city, and a few days later retreated again to an undisclosed place when that city was taken over by the rebels. Jiu-jiu was said to be on rehabilitation for a few months thereafter. He eventually returned home after the fighting settled down later. What exactly happened to him during those months was not known. His Jiu-jiu would not tell anyone.

16. The Uncertain Times 迷茫的岁月 (*mimang de sui yue*)

During those years, many young people were lost and did not know what to do. They did not know what would happen ahead either. In rural areas, when classes were suspended at the beginning of the cultural revolution, students were dismissed and sent home, perhaps because there were no resources or means to keep them around. In the cities, it might have been different. After classes were suspended, students might not have been completely dismissed, or they were still able to do various things on campus or in the names of their schools.

In rural areas, students were not easily able to gather

or do much together because of the vast geographic distance between homes and lack of communication devices and transportation. What they could do was to help on the farm to keep themselves busy. That was probably one of the reasons why so many young people from the cities were later sent by the government to the countryside in the name of "re-education by peasants".

On the other hand, the population was very dense in cities and students at home would not have much to do to keep themselves occupied, sitting idle and easily getting bored. They were young and restless. They must do something. It was reasonable to say the situation was like an "opened can of worms". That could be one of the reasons why so many red guards did things together in large groups and actively engaged in many activities.

Students who were in school were not required to attend classes when classes were suspended. Some would devote their time completely to the cultural revolution activities, criticizing what they thought was wrong, whom they considered to be a target or just fighting with each other. No wonder armed fighting fumed so fast and spread across the whole country so quickly.

Perhaps and just perhaps, when the problem was noticed, a joint notification to students later in 1967 was issued by the then governing authorities: the CP Central council, the Central military council, the State council, and the small central revolutionary leading team. They collectively wanted students to go back to classrooms and called to 复课闹革命 (*fuke nao geming*) - resume classes while engaging in the cultural revolution at the same time.

You may be confused here. You are not alone, and many ordinary people were confused as well. If it was an educational matter, why was the Central Ministry of

Education not part of it? Oh, that agency might not be functioning any more at that time. And for the students to resume classes while engaging in the cultural revolution? That would be a nice wish, but was it possible and practical?

Many schools did resume, and students in the cities went back to school. However, for Dai-shan, there was no school to go to. Grade 6 had not resumed in his school and there was no junior high nearby yet. The closest middle school was at least 20 kilometers away. The distance does not sound very far today but at that time, the only transportation available was one's own feet on small trails among the hills and that was quite some distance. Not to mention questioning what students could learn in those days at school, the cost involved in sending a child to school was a big hurdle for many ordinary peasant families. Under these circumstances, Dai-shan had no hope to continue his schooling and he stayed in Yao'sville.

Educated youth sent to the countryside 知识青年上山下乡
(zhi-shi qing-nian shang-shan xia-xiang)

It was around the end of the year 1968 when the *People's Daily*, the major propaganda newspaper of the CP published an article quoting Chairman Mao's newest instruction, calling for "the educated youth to go to the countryside to receive re-education from the Poor Peasants and the Lower Middle Peasants 贫下中农[41] (*pin xia zhong nong*). It is very necessary". That is right, to learn from the peasants, the vast majority of whom never had any formal education but hardship in their daily lives. Really? Perhaps, they could learn from them on how to farm and

---

[41] See class composition given earlier.

119

how to get by with their daily lives. We will not discuss pedagogics here. There were many rumors about why those young people were really sent to the countryside and we will not explore them further. For Dai-shan, he was too young to understand any of these anyway.

After the new year started, many young people in the cities, some volunteered and some picked by local authorities, were deployed in groups to various rural areas across the country. They were mostly students who entered middle school in 1966, 67 and 68 and many had not graduated yet. They were collectively referred to as "the old three classes", 老三届 (lao san-jie). Many of them were sent to remote areas, far from the cities, often in large groups. There were also some being sent to southern China in rural areas surrounding the cities. In the latter case, they were often in small groups, a few people together to settle in a village. They would usually be provided with their living shelters, either built specifically or renovated for them. A quota came from the province to the counties and then to the communes, and eventually to the Dadui, the grass root level.

Initially every village was required to prepare for a few newcomers. Village leaders were instructed to prepare for those youth. The news of 知青 (zhiqing, the educated youth) coming spread very quickly. People were chatting about it, old and young.

The villagers in Yao'sville were surely talking about it too. It was on a fine day when they were seeding peanuts, all working in the same field but in small groups. In each group, one person dug a small hole in the loosened soil with a hoe, another person threw one peanut seed in the hole, followed by someone to put dry compost in the hole, and the last person would cover the whole thing with soil using a hoe. Dai-shan was among them. He couldn't do much heavy and skilled work but covering the planted peanuts was something he could. Simple, he just needed to push some loose soil to cover it.

Wait a minute. Was Dai-shan still a child and how could he be doing work on the farm? Yes, he was a child. He was not alone and there were many more children like him in the village, in other villages and all over the country. No one would say anything was wrong with children helping their parents do chores around the home. There was nothing wrong with kids, like Dai-shan, helping their parents earn something to support the family either. Did I mention before that his father working a whole day would earn 10 points of 工分 (*gong-fen*)? His mother only earned 8 points, and Dai-shan could earn 3 points. That was a huge help to his parents.

Now back to the peanut seeding field. Dai-shan was in the same group as his mother who put peanut seeds in the hole, and he would cover it as the last step in the process. The first person who dug the hole was a young adult, his aunt 姑姑 (*gugu*) of a neighboring family.

Needless to say, the most popular conversation among the villagers was about the *zhiqing* 知青 coming to the countryside.

"Did you hear that *zhiqing* from the cities are coming to our rural areas?"

"Yah, all over the broadcast speakers. I wonder what they can do here".

"Growing up with a comfortable life in the city, they may not be used to our lives here".

"I heard that many of them are very young and may have never been away from their parents".

"Yah, making food for themselves and walking on the trails will be the first challenge, let aside farm work".

You can imagine the conversations, more out of curiosity than anything else. Dai-shan was listening. He thought that it took his mother a long time to make a pair of shoes for him. He watched her, using old clothes to make the bottoms of shoes and then sewing it one needle one thread at a time, thousands of times to complete the work, not to mention the skill required. He thought his mother was the greatest. Then he jumped into the conversation: "I bet they don't know how to make shoes".

"Haha, Dai-shan expects to find a *zhiqing* 知青 to make shoes for him", the *gugu* in the front teased him.

"They are not here yet. You have to wait", another person in the neighboring row followed.

"You, you, you, Dai-shan ⋯", others teased him and made a face at him.

Poor boy, he didn't have a clue what had just happened. He was completely lost, looking back at those adults. His mother knew exactly why they were teasing Dai-shan and quickly tried to rescue him from the awkward situation he got into, saying "tell *gugu*, I'm still young. Don't tease me".

What was that about? This was what happened. In the rural areas, the tradition was that if a girl had a sweetheart in mind, either having fallen in love by herself or being arranged to marry, she would usually spend her time making a pair of shoes for him to show her love quietly. So, unless one was in that kind of relationship, a boy would never expect shoes or any clothes from a girl.

With his mother's hint, Dai-shan seemed to have realized what trouble he got into with his words. But he couldn't repeat what his mother just said, and his face turned flush, feeling embarrassed.

However, no *zhiqing* came to his village in the end, most likely due to the hardship in that half-hill village where water was in short supply during the drought season in the spring. The other villages at lower terrain had a few youths from *Zhongdu-fu* and nearby cities.

Those young people, who mostly didn't have a clue what they were getting into, came by buses with their simple belongings, one to two pieces of luggage of clothing and essentials. Once they arrived, usually by truck or bus, at the Commune complex, they were greeted by a village leader, then made their way to their destinations on foot. There were no roads accessible by any automobiles yet. Their belongings would be carried by villagers who came to help.

They would then be taken to a place which had been prepared for them. A simple bungalow with one or more rooms. If there was a girl, she would be in a separate room in the same building. They would have a simple bunk bed and a place to cook which normally burned hay or wood sticks. Their new lives had begun, with no electricity, no telephone, no library, just like other peasants.

Once those youth settled down, they became new members of the village and were supposed to do the same thing as the other peasants. Their personal files and *Hukou* 户口 (registered residence) would be transferred to the local county office. In those days, no one would be able to find any work, do anything or even buy something without a *Hukou* in a place. That meant they were no longer residents of a city and would no longer have the privileges they enjoyed before. However, they still had some special treatment for *zhiqing* from the government.

How well did those *zhiqing* merge into the lives of peasants? This won't be explored here simply because no one came to Dai-shan's village and there are plenty of stories about the lives of *zhiqing* elsewhere.

These youngsters were supposed to be there for re-education. Logically, they would graduate one day and move on with their lives elsewhere. That was, however, unknown indefinitely for them and for any ordinary person in those days. Nevertheless, some *zhiqing* who had connections with authorities through their parents or parents' friends, returned to the city or found a job somewhere after one to two years. That process is what was called *dujin* 镀金, which literally meant "coated with gold" and here meant "did it for the show".

At a later time, the government gave a quota to each county for "the well-behaved 表现好的 (*biao-xian hao de*) zhiqing" to return to city or to take a job somewhere. But it was to be recommended by and at the discretion of the local authorities. The majority of those *zhiqing* stayed in the rural areas for a long time and returned to the cities in large numbers between the late 70's to early 80's when policies changed.

Knowledge was useless and the stinky NO.9 知识无用和臭老九 (*zhishi wuyong he chou laojiu*)

During that special period of time, the students who were sent to the countryside were stuck out there. Their new daily lives had nothing or little to do with what they learned in school in many cases. The students who remained in schools were wondering what they were learning for. For a period, knowledge became useless 知识无用 (*zhishi wuyong*) and "The more one had learned, the more they would be reactionary[42]". Intellectuals who had profound knowledge would be generally classified as the "stinky No. 9 臭老九 (*chou Lao-jiu*)".

What was that about? As stated earlier, after the People's Republic of China was established in 1949, the CP government outlined five categories of enemy: *Di-dru* 地主, Rich-Peasant 富农 (*fu-nong*), Counter-Revolutionaries 反革命 (*fan ge-ming*), Criminals 坏分子 (*huai fen-zi*) and the Rightist 右派 (*you-pai*). During the Cultural Revolution, another three categories of enemy were added to the list: Traitor 叛徒 (*pantu*), Enemy Spy 特务 (*tewu*) and Capitalist-Authorities 走资派 (*zou zi-pai*). The first two categories were related to the last Chinese civil war. The third category was created specifically for those "people who were in power and embraced capitalism 走资本主义道路的当权派 (*zou ziben zhuyi daolu de dang quang pai*)", literally, the authorities who followed a capitalist route, for short 走资派 (*zou zi-pai*).

This brought the total number of enemies to eight categories on the list. The intellectuals were then added on the list as the No. 9 category. Perhaps, it was not reasonable to make someone an enemy just because they had knowledge. Then the word "stinky" was added as a prefix. Now it was Stinky No. 9. That sounded more acceptable, didn't it?

The term "Stinky No. 9" was commonly used as a derogatory label for intellectuals during the Cultural Revolution, particularly those who were perceived as not being supportive of the CP ideology or policies. Now that some intellectuals were on the enemy list, you can imagine

---

[42] It meant that if someone had more knowledge, he would be more critical to government policies and would be the target for punishment.

125

what their lives were like during that time. There are many stories on this subject. We will not get into any in detail. Besides, Dai-shan was still a young boy who merely heard about this.

It is worth mentioning however that during that period, many intellectuals (new university graduates and teachers) were deployed to rural areas to teach. A few went to Dai-shan's hometown – *Hongxing middle school* 红星中学. It was those teachers whom Dai-shan benefited from and they played a big role in changing his life. This happened a couple of years later so we will talk about it in a later chapter.

It is also worth mentioning that the title of "stinky No. 9" for intellectuals was removed about 10 years later. It was said that during a high-ranking central government meeting in 1975, Chairman Mao quoted a line in his speech: "老九不能走啊 (*lao-jiu buneng zou*) – (we) can't let *Lao-jiu* go!", a line from a model opera 《智取威虎山 (*zhiqu weihu shan*)》 – The taking of Tiger Mountain by Outsmarting[43]. This implied that the contributions of intellectuals could not be completely negated, and they were still needed. Three years later, most of those intellectuals who were sidelined got their reputation back and resumed their positions.

---

[43] This was one of the eight model operas established during the cultural revolution by the then authority which was headed by Jiang-qing – Mao's wife. The other seven model operas are 《海港(*haigang*) The Habor》, 《红灯记(*hongdeng ji*) The Red Lantern》, 《沙家浜(*shajia bang*) The Shajia Beach》, 《奇袭白虎团(*qixi baihu tuan*) Raid the White-Tiger Regiment》, 《红色娘子军(*hongse niangzi jun*) The Red Detachment of Women》, 《白毛女(*baimao nu*) The White-Haired Girl》, and 《沙家浜》交响乐(*shajiabang jiaoxiang yue*) The Shajia Beach Symphony.

17. Dai-shan's Life in the Wondering Years 代山度过了迷茫的年代 *(dai shan du guo le mimang de nian dai)*

How did young Dai-shan spend his life during those uncertain times? Here are a few examples below.

Earning work points 挣公分 *(zheng gongfen)*, *Picking herbs* 采草药 *(cai caoyao)*

Dai-shan had no more school to go to or anything meaningful to do but stayed at the village like other kids. Doing something interesting or having fun at his age was just wishful thinking. He probably never knew what life should be like for a child. He was trying to understand everything that had happened and what would be ahead.

Although he was too young to be a peasant to do real labor work, he helped do whatever he could. Oh, it must be noted that farming in that village was labor intensive and really hard. There was no machinery, and everything relied on human hands and strength. Plus, the terrain was hilly without much flat area. Every step carrying something required muscle strength. At that time, all peasant families had to work collectively in the field to earn their living.

During busy seasons, Dai-shan would help do work that a child could do. Other times, he would go out with his buddies, most times his two older cousins *Dai-er* (the 2nd son of his uncle, the older brother of his father) and *Dong-wu* (the 2nd son of his aunt, the 2nd older sister of his mother). They were not out there to have fun like kids in the cities but to explore and see how they could help outside of the farm.

As mentioned before, on a market day, people buy and sell livestock. If the buyers were butchers for meat or farmers from out of town, they would usually walk the live cattle all the way to their destinations, which might take a few days depending on the distance. They had to keep the cattle in a temporary stable and had to feed the cattle before their journey. The cows were fed mostly grass, occasionally grains which was more expensive. Dai-shan had seen people selling grass to the cattle buyers when he was going to school. He knew the place to sell grass.

After talking to his buddies, they decided to give it a try. One day he went out to the field to search for and cut fresh young grass. Like other kids, they carried the grass with a *Bei-dou* 背篼 on their backs to the cattle stable and sold it. Usually, the bigger kids could make ¥0.25 for a *Bei-dou*-full of grass. Dai-shan could only make ¥0.10 at the most because of the smaller size of *Bei-dou* and the quality of grass.

The difficult part was to find a place where the right type of grass grew and was young. Often one had to get up early in the morning and get to the market at the right time. Getting the grass to the market required strength too, which was certainly another challenge for Dai-shan.

Dai-shan used to help his *waipo* 外婆 pick wild herbs in the field of his village whenever she came. He recognized some of the herbs. They were just different types of weeds to him. He saw people paying money for the herbs on the market. He thought that might be an opportunity to earn some money. He knew where to find these herbs and talked to his two cousins. They then went to the field to pick the herbs, such as dandelion 灯笼花 (*deng-long hua*). They tied it in small handful of bundles and took them to the market to sell.

To their surprise, there were so many people at the market, but no one seemed to be interested in buying the herbs. Once in a while, an older woman might drop by and ask some questions but then left. Dai-shan realized that they didn't seem to know what the herbs were, but they were the same thing his *waipo* 外婆 provided to her patients who appreciated it. Then he had an idea, "tell them". But how? He started calling out "买草药来喽 (*mai caoyao lou*) – Buy herbs". It did attract the attention of some people, but they were just looking, not buying.

An elder man walked by and told him "Young man, people may not know much about herbs. You need to tell them what it is for". Then he started yelling like other vendors and added more words:

"清凉解暑 (*qingliang jieshu*) – Cool off",

"祛火 (*qu-huo*) – Expel internal heat",

"助消化 (*zhu xiaohua*) – Help digestion",

"治头疼 (*zhi tou-teng*) – Relieve headache", etc.

That really helped. More people came over and started asking questions "does it really work"? "You won't fool us, will you?".

Dai-shan remembered somewhat his *wai-po* used to say about the herbs and started explaining it to these customers. He eventually sold one bundle for 5 *fens* (¥0.05, a nickel)! That was great. Remember his father could only earn a maximum of 10 *fens* working a whole day.

What happened next may sound kind of strange. As soon as there was one person that started buying, another and then another person would come over to examine it. Dai-shan continued his selling call and added:

"相因[44]卖喽 (*xiang ying mai lou*), Sell cheap now",

"五分钱一把 (wu fen qian yi ba), Only 5 *fens* a bundle",

"快来 (*kuai lai*) – Hurry, 要卖完喽了 (*yao mai wan lou*)

---

[44] "xiang yin", local dialect for cheap, 便宜 (*piang yi*).

129

- Almost sold out".

Believe it or not, they didn't ask questions anymore and Dai-shan sold 8 bundles in a few minutes. That was all he had. When he turned around to his buddies, they still had all their bundles and were waiting for people to come. He told them "You have to yell and tell them what it is for". They followed and you know what, they sold theirs very quickly too. This is known as advertising today to let customers know what the product is for.

This seemed to be something worth continuing. However, it was not always possible to find what they were looking for in the field. Herbs were just like other wild weeds and took time to grow. You could not go to the same place to see the herbs all the time. You need to find them. Therefore, this type of venture was only possible once in a while.

Young laborer for hire – pulling a loaded monowheel cart 小力工拉鸡公车 *(xiao li-gong la ji-gong che)*

In those days, transportation was a big problem. You could see buses and trucks on the road, but they normally belonged to factories, the government, or the army. None for peasants in the rural areas. In the mountainous areas, the primary transportation would be a human's shoulders and back. In flat terrain and on the main roads, two-wheeled or four-wheeled carts may be used, and they were normally pulled by horses or cows/ox.

The most popular transportation was the monowheel cart, called *Ji-gong che* 鸡公车 (literally rooster cart), perhaps because of its shape.  It was almost completely made of wood except for a metal ring surrounding the wheel and a metal shaft through the wheel. The cart was usually pushed forward by one person with both hands on the two handles. Often a strap would cross the driver's shoulder and be tied to the two handles to transfer the load from his hands to his shoulder.

When the cart was fully loaded, or when the load obstructed the view of the driver, or when it was going up a hill, a second person would be required to help by pulling from the front.

Dai-shan often noticed on market days that people from other places, 10 to 30 kilometers away bought stuff and transported it away using a *Ji-gong che*. The road from the bottom of *Yao'sville* to the top of the hill was up the hill all the way for over 5 kilometers before descending to the other side of the hill. That was the main road with gravel surface and almost every one of the loaded carts required a helper to pull to the hilltop. Sometimes the very heavily loaded cart needed two helpers. It would take one to two hours to get to the hilltop and the helpers would be paid for his labor.

Dai-shan and his cousins chatted about it, and they decided to try it as well. Those far-away buyers usually came very early in the morning and would try to get back home on the same day. Therefore, they would buy what they need first thing in the morning and start going back as soon as they could. When they got close to *Yao'sville*, it would be near noon or early afternoon. Dai-shan and his cousins would each bring a rope, sometimes a little dry food (*momo*) and go to wait on the roadside at the spot where the road started ascending.

When they saw someone pushing a cart with a load coming up, they would go to ask, "do you need help up to the hilltop?"

When the driver had a heavy load or was in a hurry, he would just say yes if the helper looked strong.

Sometimes, some would say "no, I can handle it myself" until he went up a little further and realized it was not possible.

His two cousins both were bigger and stronger. They had no problem at all getting hired right away. They sometimes could make two trips a day. They normally earn 25 to 35 fens in each trip.

However, it was a little different for Dai-shan. The driver would look at him and say, "no I can do it myself", or "do you have the strength to pull this up the hill?" He would try to convince them by saying, "yes, I have strength, and I can help you get up there".

You can guess, he would not be selected if there were other stronger boys around. Even when he was hired, they would pay him less "I am not sure if you have enough strength. We can try but I can only pay you 20 fens". Eventually he got hired. Often the man behind the cart would keep saying "pull harder", "use more strength".

It was hard for him. Once they got to the hilltop, he would feel very tired and then had to walk back home. He would eat some dry food if he had it and drink cool boiled water from a tin bottle.

Oh, it would be a big joke if anyone drank bottled water in those days. It was just not a normal thing to do. Plastic bottles were probably not invented yet.

He tried a couple of times as a young laborer and realized that was not for him. Maybe it would be better by the time he grew bigger?

Helping his father on night duty to guard the crops 帮父亲守夜 (*bang fuqing shou ye*)

When it came to working on the farm, there was no fixed age or schedule and time in the day. You just had to do what needed to be done when it needed to be done. During those days, food was scarce and was the most important supply item for everyone to think about. Perhaps it was historically always like that. Maybe, that was the reason why in China people usually greet each other by saying "have you eaten yet 吃饭了没有 (*chifan le meiyou*)?" instead of saying "how are you 你好吗 (*nihao ma*)?" or "it's a fine day", like one would say in North America.

Well, people can't resist hunger. When they were hungry, they would try to find a way to search for food or when desperate, they take from others' land in secret. At a young age, Dai-shan understood that when the crops were almost ready for harvesting, they needed guarding from thieves. That was particularly so for peanuts, corn, watermelon, cotton, and anything that is worth money.

In the collective farming team, usually there would be two people on night duty to watch the crops. Each family was required to have a major laborer (usually a man) available, in turns. Often the duty was overnight, from dusk to dawn.

Usually, a simple hut made of straw or corn stalks was built in the field with two ends open as monitoring windows. Inside, there is a simple bed with a wooden frame, bamboo-made lattice panel, bamboo sheet and sometimes straw too. Whoever was on duty would just need to bring their own quilt with cover. There was no sleeping bag. The hut could be moved to different places when needed.

When the turn came, his father would go home to do some chores after the day's work and have supper before going on night duty. In the meantime, Dai-shan and another kid would go to fill in on behalf of their fathers and watch out the crops in the hut until the adults came to take over for the night.

Watermelon was the first crop to be watched in the summer. The watermelon field was very open. No one would be able to pick one without being noticed. A thief would 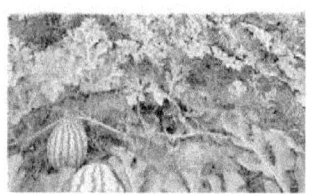 normally come at night, especially on a dark night. The night watchers would be there before sunset.

During a hot summer, it was tempting for the kids themselves to try some. Dai-shan and his watch partner faced the temptation themselves too one evening. A watermelon normally weighed a few pounds or more. It would take two kids to eat it together. However, they had to do it in secret without anyone noticing it.

One said, "I would really like to try some melon".

Another replied, "Me too, but what are we going to do with the melon rind (西瓜皮 *xigua pi*)?"

"Bury it in the ground?"

"No, someone will notice the fresh soil tomorrow".

"Take it home to feed the pigs then?"

"Are you not afraid of someone seeing you? Maybe we shouldn't do it".

They faced a dilemma and were not sure what to do.

In the Fall, peanuts, corn, and cotton would be ready for harvesting. Corn can't be eaten raw, and cotton is not

peanut   corn   cotton

edible. But raw peanuts are very tasty: crunchy, juicy, sweet, and fresh.

The temptation of fresh peanuts was hard to resist for kids and adults alike. However, pulling out a whole plant was not good practice because others could easily recognize that one plant was missing. On the other hand, pulling out one or two pods from one plant was not easy to notice. Some people just did that and buried the peanut shells in the soil after they ate the nuts. That would however be noticed later when the whole plant was dug out during harvest time.

Swimming in dug-water pits 沙凼里游泳 *(shadang li youyong)*

In the hilly mountain terrain, there was no river or pond for swimming. There was a large reservoir down the hill more than one kilometer away, but they would not go that far just for a swim.

Water shortage was an issue for the village. There was small spring water seeping out of the hill, but it was barely sufficient for drinking, cooking and feeding animals. Irrigation would rely on the storm water collected in the Summer. Villagers used their wisdom to build many water storage pits by digging out the earth and/or blasting stone at the lower areas. Those water pits were in irregular shape, some were small, less than 100 square feet and some were large, up to 2000 square feet in surface area. The depth varied up to 10 feet. Often the pit bottom followed the outcropped bedrock sloping downwards.

When a storm came, villagers would be busy in the rain diverting water to the pits. The storm water normally carried plenty of sand from the silty soil. The water would be used for irrigation. Sand was deposited at the bottom and

沙凼 (*shadang*)
A dug water pit

could fill up the whole pit during the summer. So, these pits were called 沙凼 (*shadang*), meaning "sand pit". They needed to be cleaned up before the next storm season.

The village kids, including Dai-shan, enjoyed the large *shadang*. After a storm, they would go there to swim, often in groups. Sometimes adults too. Parents would usually not allow children to swim by themselves, out of concern for their safety. One kid had drowned in a large water storage pit which was over 20' deep.

However, once these kids were determined to do something, they got creative in getting to the *shadang* without catching their parents' attention. They had developed a secret code: for example, scratching one's face meant "let's go swimming". The other kids would respond by giving the same gesture if they agreed. When parents asked where they were going, they would say "going out to collect fresh grass for the goats", or just "to collect some grass" as cooking fuel. Of course, the grass needed to be dried before it could be used for cooking. It was the dug-pit that gave Dai-shan and many other kids an opportunity to learn how to swim, not with proper techniques, more often in a dog style, simply to stay afloat.

Thirsty for knowledge 渴望知识 *(ke wang zhi shi)*

Yao'sville was really poor. As a mountain, it didn't have many natural resources, and large trees were cut down during the great leap years. As a farmland, it didn't have much rich soil nor much flat terrain. Water was in short supply every spring. Villagers were simply struggling to survive year after year, with no hope of a better life. Many just considered it to be their fate, it wasn't possible to change it. When policies were relaxed at a later time, all they could do to subsidize their living was to feed a few rabbits by picking grass after work hours, to raise a couple of goats by taking them to the field every day, or to feed a couple of pigs. Most families had at least one pig. There weren't many other options.

Young Dai-shan and his buddies often asked themselves "Why is our village so poor? How can we improve our lives?" They heard of people in richer places, like those vegetable farmers near *Zhongdu-fu,* who could earn up to ¥1.00 or more a day and workers who had a job in the factories could earn ¥30 to ¥50 a month and at the end of the month, they would just collect their pay. But why was there such a big difference between those places and Yao'sville? Are some people born to be poor and others born to have a better life? That was probably what people said fate (命运 *mingyun*) was about, a predetermined course in life. Is it possible to change your fate?

They couldn't find any answers. No one could explain it to them either.

In those days, Hukou (the registered residence) locked people in a place forever. You couldn't find a job, go to school or do anything outside your own place. The only exceptions were if someone being recruited to a factory or some organization, which was usually reserved for people who had connections with somebody who had some authority. Being recruited to the military was on the top of the list and a dream for many rural youths. However, there were certain physical requirements in addition to various rules. Dai-shan thought of it but knew it was not possible to meet the requirement of 1.5 meters height and 45 kilograms weight at his age. Marrying someone in a better place was usually an option for girls, because by tradition, a girl after marriage would normally live with her husband's family.

For Dai-shan, none of those options were available. The only way to change his life was to learn something and make himself capable of doing something. It was on himself. He wanted to learn something. He was thirsty for knowledge. But how and where to learn from?

At the time when knowledge was considered useless, little Dai-shan was still determined to learn, because he knew that was the only hope for him. His mother often said he should learn some skills which might become useful someday. She used her own language to emphasize the importance of learning: "if you have walnuts, you don't need to worry about having a stick to crack them". When people asked him why he was still learning, that was what in his mind.

There was a medicine clinic in the village down the hill. There were two medicine doctors, one in Chinese medicine and the other in Western medicine, for all the surrounding villages. Dai-shan passed by there often and one day went there to observe them at work. Knowing there was no other hope, he thought why not try to learn to be a doctor. One day, he went to see the Chinese medicine doctor all by himself to ask if he could be an apprentice. The doctor looked at the young boy, hesitated for a while and said, "when we have an opening, you can apply through your Dai-dui".

He was too young and naive, not knowing medicine was a profession, a highly respected and privileged occupation in society. It was not something you could do just because you wanted to. Besides, in many cases, Chinese medicine was passed on from generation to generation in the same family. There was no hope for Dai-shan to be a doctor at all!

Attempting to help his mother weaving fabrics 想帮妈妈织布 *(xiang bang mama zhibu)*

As time passed by, the economy was not as good as expected, and the supplies did not meet the demand. The governments gradually allowed people to make something for their own use and sell the surplus, in the name of revitalizing the economy. In a short time, many old trades which had disappeared in previous years resurfaced, carpenters, lock smiths, bamboo craftsmen, etc. Various types of goods, all manually made by individuals, were being sold on the market.

You may remember that in those days, nearly everything from government shops / stores required government issued tickets to purchase. For example, *Bu-piao* 布票 was required to buy fabric for making clothes. A ticket of 5 meters of fabric per person per year was not enough for a tall person and many people needed more. At the same time, there were not much fabric available in fabric shops.

Therefore, people would buy 土布 (*tubu*) - homemade fabrics, at the market.

One day, Dai-shan's mother came home from the market and said to his father, "I saw people selling tubu on the market today".

"Yes, old things are coming back, because there is not enough supply", father responded.

"Well, I'm thinking, maybe we can make it too".

"What did you say? Making tubu"? His father was very surprised and never dreamed of doing something like that. "I don't know anything about it and haven't heard of anyone who can make it".

"I know how. I helped my brother make tubu when I was home". His mother got excited. She was talking about nearly 20 years ago before she got married.

"You?" He stared at her for a while and said, "Even if you can remember how to make it, where do you find the equipment?" His father looked at his mother, half excited and half doubtful.

"The equipment we used before is still stored in my brother's home and has not been used since. His wound is not completely cured, and he is not in the physical condition to do it at present. His wife does not know how, and their kids are still small. The equipment would just sit there idle". His mother continued, "Maybe we can borrow the equipment from my brother for a couple of years and return it to him when his health improves".

"But I can't help you with anything on that". His father felt helpless. Actually, he probably couldn't learn either.

"I remember everything. I can do it myself. You just need to do more house chores and give me a hand when needed". His mother was very confident.

His father did not say anything further and went into deep thought: That would be a big help to the family if it was possible. It would also mean more chores at home with all the kids and animals to take care of. Most importantly, how could we even "open mouth[45]" to ask to borrow the equipment?

The next week, Dai-shan's mother went back to see her mother and brother and discussed the idea with them. As you have guessed, they both agreed to let her use the equipment. His mother came home with a smile on her face. A few days later, his father went to pick up the equipment and carried it all by himself for over 4 kilometers on his shoulders with a shoulder pole 一根扁担 (*yi gen bian dan*), made from a half-split tree. It took him two trips to bring all the required gear.

In the clay bungalow of Dai-shan's home, there were three rooms: one bedroom for his parents, another bedroom for his siblings (a total of four by that time). Dai-shan slept on a simple stretcher type of bed in the main room 堂屋 (*tang wu*) where there was a table for eating and guests to sit. The kitchen was moved to the outside on the front porch, which was over 8' wide.

They moved things around and away from the *tang-wu* except for Dai-shan's sleeping place in the corner and made space to put the weaving equipment, loom – 织布机 (*zhi bu ji*) which occupied one quarter of the room.

Now the loom was in place. His mother got to work on it. Upon hearing the news by word of mouth that his mother was making tubu, neighbors started bringing cotton and yarn and asking her to make fabric for them.

---

[45] It implies to find a rationale without being considered as inappropriate.

It was a very complex process to make fabric from cotton. The first step was to remove the seeds from the cotton picked in the field and make it loose to a condition like cotton candy. This was done by specialty equipment in commercial services.

Loom 织布机 (zhi bu ji)

The second step was to make the cotton in small rolls and twist it into yarn. In small operations, this was done by a hand-spinning machine 纺线机 (*fang xian ji*).

To save time, his mother would tell customers to have yarn made from cotton so that she could focusing on weaving. But there was still lots to do before weaving could begin.

The yarn was sorted in bundles, soaked in light fluid (Dai-shan saw his mother use light rice soup) and then hung out to dry. This process was to make the yarn strong to endure the tension on the waving machine later. Up to this point, there was not much Dai-shan could do to help.

Once the yarn was ready to use, it would be wound onto spindles and then properly arranged to fit on the loom. Normally, one bundle of tubu was approximately 2′ wide and 30′ to 50′ long. The yarns were to be cut to the same length and aligned one by one and rolled onto a beam (like a drum) in sequence. Dai-shan saw his mother count but didn't know exactly how many. Well, you probably can calculate the number of yarns to line up for 2′ width.

The part of work was completed on a large open space. Dai-shan helped his mother clean the flat ground in the larger yard near his home and drive sticks (as many as the number of yarns required) into the ground. On each stick, a spindle of treated yarn was placed.

The next step was a delicate process. Every strand of yarn would be brought through the reed 筘(*kou*), which had many vertical slits, like a comb. The width of the reed determined the width of the fabric to be made. Then every second strand of yarn had to be sorted and loosely hooked on a harness. Once they were all sorted out, the yarns were simultaneously wound onto a beam in a big bundle.

The beam which stored the yarns would sit at the rear of the loom. All necessary parts were to be connected to the loom frame. The two harnesses, which were hung on the top and bottom, would separate the yarns in two rows up and down during weaving. When the weaver pushes one foot down, one harness pulls one row of yarns down. When the weaver pushes the other foot down, another harness pulls another roll of yarns down while the first roll of yarns going up. When the two rows of yarns were separated wide open, a shuttle 梭子 (*suo zi*) with yarns in it would travel through the open space swiftly. The shuttle was activated by the weaver pulling a string and it traveled back and forth when the string was pulled continuously. Each time after the shuttle passed through, the weaver had to pull the reed back to compress the traverse yarn in place and push the reed forward quickly before the shuttle came back again. During weaving, the four limbs of the weaver had four separate sequential tasks, and they must coordinate very well to allow the process to go smoothly and swiftly.

Needless to say, this was highly skilled work and Dai-shan had no place to help. He often just stood by and watched his mother weaving. The shuttle just traveled so fast and made a trip every second. Every once in a while, for 30 to 40 seconds, his mother would stop, wind the weaved fabric, and advance the yarns to the proper position before continuing.

Occasionally, some yarn broke. She had to stop and reconnect them. She also told Dai-shan how to properly make connections to allow the nut to pass the reed smoothly.

His mother worked so hard, often very late at night once the yarns were put on the loom. Dai-shan would stand by or sit on his bed just to watch his mother. The different sounds made by the harness strings, foot pedals, the reed, the shuttle string, and the traveling shuttle gradually become his lullaby. Even today, when Dai-shan closed his eyes, he can still hear the symphonic sound his mother made on the loom.

Sometimes, his mother would work overnight, just to catch the market day the next day to hand the completed fabric to a client, probably for ¥2 to ¥3 for the work.

To his memory, his mother did this for a couple of years before returning the weaving machine to his jiu-jiu. However, he didn't remember if his jiu-jiu ever got started again.

Chapter 4

Classes Resume - Middle School
学校复课 - 中学时代 *(xuexiao fuke -*
zhongxue shidai）

18. A New Junior High School Opens without Classrooms 一所无教室新中学 (*yi-suo wu jiaoshi de xin zhongxue*)

Although the central government called for classes to resume, that didn't happen in rural areas right away. In Dai-shan's hometown, there was no grade six class nearby and the original school he attended did not resume that class either. Therefore, there was no way for him to continue school. This continued for nearly three years.

Time passed by day after day. Dai-shan did whatever he could in his village to help. Deep in his mind, he was still expecting to go back to school someday or to learn some skills somewhere. In the Spring of 1970, the population in *Yao'sville* peaked to 120[46]. There were many children of his age who barely had any education.

One day as they were tilling soil for planting sweet potato, Dai-shan heard people chatting about something, news that a new junior high school would be built in their commune, to be located right in the village just down the hill from Yao'sville. That was huge news because there had never been a junior high there or in the surrounding areas.

"Is this true?" "How can it be possible?" You can imagine how excited Dai-shan was. He just couldn't believe what he had heard. It was not just a chance to return to school. It was historical, a new school was opening. He had to confirm whether the news was true.

After they finished work that morning, he went down to the Commune complex, which had a few buildings forming a courtyard with the front facing the main road. There were also a few shops on the main road: a butcher store where

---

[46] It dropped to below 40 in 2000' s due to massive migration of famers to cities.

146

pigs were slaughtered and pork sold, a clinic, a store selling fertilizer and a corner store primarily selling salt, oil, soy sauce and other very basic items. They were all government-run businesses.

There were two entrances to the courtyard, which was covered under a roof with a stage at one end, a setting for mass meetings. The buildings surrounding the yard were partitioned into small rooms, as offices or residence for the Commune officials.

Dai-shan walked into the courtyard through the side entrance off the trail from his village. Nothing was going on, and it was very quiet inside the complex. A moment later, someone came out of a room.

"Who are you looking for, young man?" the person asked.

"Ah… I'm … not sure". Dai-shan stuttered. "I heard a new junior high will open here. I wonder where to … find some information."

That person happened to be associated with education. "Yes, that is true. But it is still too early. There will be more detail coming once the teachers have arrived".

"Where will the school be?"

"It will be around here, but everything is still being planned, nothing has been decided yet. Come back to check again at a later time."

Wow, that was exciting news. Although nothing was clear, it was not just a rumor. He started thinking about what he should do and how to convince his parents to allow him to continue school.

Let's pause for a second here. Establishing a new school from nothing was not a simple matter in a rural area or anywhere. It had never happened in the history of this place. How could that become possible suddenly? Maybe, just maybe, this had something to do with the overall national and international situation at that time. Let's take a look at what was happening across the country.

Zhenbao Dao event 珍宝岛事件 (zhen bao dao shijian)

There was a tiny island in the northeast of China, named 珍宝岛 (zhen bao dao), approximately 1700 meters long and 500 meters wide, located in the middle of *wusu li* 乌苏里 river, which bordered *hei long jiang* 黑龙江 province of China and the former Soviet Union. It did not sound like an impressive place but there was a boundary dispute.

It was reported that there had been small conflicts between the border guards on both sides since 1967. The dispute was territorial over who owned the tiny island. The conflicts escalated in 1968 but both sides restrained themselves to non-armed fighting. However, open armed fighting broke out eventually in March 1969. Large casualties were reported. That led to the official breakdown of the China-Soviet Union relationship[47].

As a result, combined with other events occurred within and outside the nation around the same time, the relationship between China and foreign neighboring countries became tense. There were discussions to deploy citizens from large cities to rural and mountain areas to reduce and avoid casualties in case of foreign attacks. The whole nation was in a mode of "preparing for war" 备战 (bei-zhan). Duotong province is located in the southwest interior of China and is far from the border in all directions. It also has many large mountains and was

---

[47] The dispute was reportedly settled in 1991. At the end of that year, the former Soviet Union was officially dissolved.

therefore considered a grand retreat area 大后方（*da houfang*）in case of any events.

Migration of higher education institutions 高等学院搬迁 (gaodeng xueyuan banqian)

In the early 1950s, just after the establishment of the new China, the central government made a huge effort to establish major higher education institutions in order to train urgently needed personnel for the reconstruction of the country. Through reorganization and restructuring of some existing universities (including 清华大学 *qinghua daxue*), eight specialty higher education institutions were established along *Xue Yuan Lu* 学院路 in *Haidian* 海淀 district 区（*qu*）, Beijing. They included:

Beijing Medicine Institute 北京 医学院（*yi xueyuan*）, later become Faculty of Medicine, Beijing University 北京 大学(daxue) 医学部（*yi xuebu*）.

Beijing Steel & Iron Institute 北京 钢铁学院（*gangtie xueyuan*）, later known as Beijing University of Science and Technology 北京 科技大学 (keji daxue).

Beijing Petroleum Institute 北京 石油学院（*shiyou xueyuan*）, later evolved into China University of Petroleum (Beijing) 中国石油大学 (zhongguo *shiyou daxue*)（北京)and China University of Petroleum (East China) 中国石油大学（华东 huadong）.

Beijing Agriculture Machinery Institute 北京 农业机械化学院（*nongyei jixiehua xueyua*）, later known as China Agricultural University 中国农业大学 (zhongguo *nongyei daxue*).

Beijing Aviation Institute 北京 航空学院（*hangkong xueyuan*）, later known as Beijing University of Aeronautics and Astronautics 北京 航空航天（*hangkong hangtian*）大学(daxue).

Beijing Geology Institute 北京 地质学院 (*dizhi xueyuan*) , later evolved into China University of Geosciences (Beijing)中国地质大学（zhongguo *dizhi daxue*, 北京）and China University of Geosciences（Wuhan）中国地质大学(武汉 *Wuhan*) .

Beijing Coal Mining Institute 北京 矿业学院（*kuangye xueyuan*）, later evolved into China University of Mining and Technology 中国矿业大学 （zhongguo *kuangye daxue*) and China University of Mining and Technology (Beijing)中国矿业大学（北京）.

Beijing Forestry Institute 北京 林学院（*lin xueyuan*）, later known as Beijing Forestry University 北京 林业大学 (*linye daxue*).

You may have noticed that all the institutions have changed their original course of specializing in a specific field and evolved into universities to include more fields of study. Most noticeably, some of them became two separate universities with nearly identical names plus a suffix to distinguish their locations. That was due to what happened during those few years in preparing for war.

Under the escalating situation of "preparing for war" and retreating to a safe place, many large cities were also trying to evacuate people to rural areas. Out of the eight institutions five were ordered by the central government to relocate to different and safer places around the nation. In a short period of time, four institutions moved away from their Beijing campuses and migrated to other places. They packed up essential teaching and some research equipment and other necessities in containers, hopped on the trains and moved away from their home campuses in Beijing. Only a few people were left behind to take care of whatever remained and the buildings.

Beijing Geology Institute migrated to Wuhan in Hubei province and stayed there. Some years later when the overall situation changed, the Beijing campus was reused as part of the institute, and it eventually evolved into two independent universities.

Beijing Coal Mining Institute first migrated in 1969 to a place near Chongqing in Sichuan Province and later relocated to Xuzhou in Jiangsu province. Its fate was very similar to the Geology Institute and eventually evolved into two universities, one in Beijing and one in Xuzhou.

Beijing Petroleum Institute migrated to Shandong Province, with a similar ending, splitting into two universities, one of which eventually settled in Qingdao in Jiangsu province.

Beijing Agriculture Machinery Institute first moved to Chongqing then to Hebei province, eventually back to its Beijing campus.

Beijing Steel & Iron Institute was initially on the relocating list but for some undisclosed reason on the eve of moving, got an order to halt the move and avoided the chaotic journey.

Now back to Yao'sville. Although the village was merely 50 kilometers away from *Zhongdu-fu*, the capital of Duotong Province, its education system and many other things were not much different from those in remote rural areas. Given the overall situation at that time, it probably made sense to provide more resources and increase support to the areas like Yao'sville because they were not very far away from the capital city. Maybe, that was part of the reason a new junior high[48] was to be established there. Whatever the reason was, is not for us to explore. Dai-shan and many other young kids in that area benefited from this historical and new development.

At the same time, every other commune in Jingdian county probably opened a new junior high school if none existed before. The education affairs were directly administered by the Education Bureau of the county, which was responsible for curriculum, teachers' salaries, school supplies, etc. The local government would play a supportive role, providing support such as temporary accommodations for teachers, land for the school and assisting in the school's construction.

Now Dai-shan knew a new junior high would open, but when and where? He kept his ears open to the commune's broadcast and went to the Commune complex from time to time. Eventually, one day in late August of that year, a voice from the broadcasting speaker announced that elementary school graduates were encouraged to register in the commune complex for the soon-to open middle school.

Hongxing Junior High opens 红星中学开学了 (Hongxing zhongxue kaixue le)

In September of 1970, the day finally came. Four years had passed since Dai-shan left elementary school. This was an opportunity to make up for the lost time. In comparison to those who never had this opportunity, he still considered himself among the lucky ones.

On the day of registration, he went down the hill trail to look for the registration place. It was in the commune

---

[48] Unfortunately, the junior high as closed about 30 years later, most likely due to population decrease from mass migration to the cities.

complex. About a dozen kids from neighboring villages were already gathered in the courtyard. A little later, a middle-aged man came out of one of the rooms. He wore a pair of glasses and looked like a teacher from out of town, from a major school. He greeted the youth and said, "My name is Lin. You can call me Teacher Lin". "I am the principal of the new junior high school. Today, you need to fill a form with the required information". He continued "We will start class next Monday morning".

"Where will we have class?" someone asked.

"We will meet here. Other teachers will join us, and more information will be provided at that time".

Dai-shan was excited. The day had finally arrived. But where would the classrooms be? He was still puzzled.

That was nearly four years after schools were suspended during the cultural revolution. Many students like Dai-shan had never officially graduated from elementary school, not to mention receiving the elementary school graduation certificate. There was no mention of entrance exam in that year, perhaps the education system was still in a rehabilitation process after the drastic damages. To the teachers, they would probably feel lucky to have enough students to make up a full class under the circumstances.

Now Dai-shan had to solve a dilemma. At that time, his youngest sibling, the 5th child of his parents, was born, increasing the total number to 7 in the family. His other two younger siblings were also in school. He understood that the family was in need of support. How could he convince his parents to let him continue school? He understood his family responsibility as the oldest child, but he also knew going to school was the only hope, even only a tiny hope, for him to get out of poverty of this village and to have a better future and to help his family.

At that time, elementary school and middle school were free education, no tuition fees, except buying textbooks and exercise books. Dai-shan was determined to grab the once in a lifetime opportunity. In the short term, he planned to earn money by selling grass, herbs and raising rabbits to pay for his school supplies. In the longer term, he would have a better opportunity and potential to help support the family after finishing middle school, which was just three more years. There were not many middle school graduates around there at that time.

He explained to his mother that he would help with chores and farming work in the evenings and on the weekends. Fortunately, the school was only 15 minutes walk away and there was plenty of time to help at home in the summertime. This was no problem with his mother at all. She always wanted the best for her children and the family. No matter how hard it was for her, she would always support him. She never complained about the chores at home and the hard work she had to do. She, a kind woman with no education, spent her entire life supporting her children. Dai-shan thought he had the greatest mother in the world.

However, his father was a little different. In his mind, some education enabling one to read, write and count would be sufficient for a peasant to live in a rural area. Even in the surrounding larger areas, no one had heard of any case where a person had achieved great success or became someone important. That was only in stories and reserved for privileged and rich people. For an ordinary peasant, don't even think about it, except in our dreams. Besides, the family needed a laborer to help earn *gongfen* to support the family.

After convincing his mother, Dai-sha asked her to talk to his father. Fortunately, he never agreed nor openly opposed it this time, with an attitude of "let's see how it goes".

The first day of school after 4 years of interruption arrived. Dai-shan went to the meeting place and saw a large group of youth, over two dozen, gathered already. This was the very first middle school in the Hongxing Commune and there were students from the surrounding areas up to 15 kilometers away. There were also a few more teachers.

Teacher Lin greeted the group and introduced other teachers: Teacher Jia, who wore a pair of glasses and seemed to be from the city, would teach Chinese language. Teacher Sun would teach Physics. Teacher Wang would teach English. Teacher Ye, who was from the neighboring Ye'sville, 5 minutes away and graduated three years ago from high school, would teach Mathematics. There was another teacher for Chemistry and Teacher Lin would teach Politics and Physical Education.

Among the five teachers, aside from Teacher Ye, they were all from different cities and with formal education from universities or normal institutes 师范学院[49] (*shifan xueyuan*). They all stayed in the commune complex and Teacher Ye went home to stay with his family at the beginning.

"Attention students 同学们 (*tongxue men*), welcome to *Hongxing* middle school 红星中学 (*Hongxing zhongxue*)", Teacher Lin announced. "Thanks to our government, our junior high school officially starts today. Although we currently do not have a school campus and classrooms, we have our students and teachers. We are going to make history. We will start classes in temporary classrooms

---

[49] A higher institution for teacher-training.

while waiting for the new school to be built". Everyone looked around but couldn't see a room large enough to have class. "Please follow Teacher Ye to our temporary classrooms", he continued.

"Please follow me everyone", Teacher Ye, the local young man, announced.

"Where are we going?" Someone asked.

"We are going to walk to Ng'sville, the #7 group of the *Alliance Dadui*, just 10 minutes away, across the creek". As a local, Teacher Ye walked in the front and the students and other teachers followed behind.

The creek was the main water course towards the reservoir at the bottom of the hill. It normally had little water in the dry seasons and people could walk on the stones to cross. However, during the rainy season, the volume of water running down from the upper stream was huge, making it impossible and dangerous to cross. The only place to cross then would be on the dam but much further away down stream.

Ng'sville was not far from the commune complex. People often communicated with each other on both sides by shouting out something along the creek, like:

"Mr. Ng, we will have a meeting at 10 o'clock this morning in the *Dadui* office".

Someone on another side could hear it and would relay the message. That was the way to communicate in those days.

However, the path was not flat. It winded down for over 20 meters to the creek and then up again. For the youngsters who grew up there, it was probably a 10-minute walk. For the teachers from urban cities, 20 minutes might not be enough.

The group followed Teacher Ye through the trail path and crossed the creek 20 minutes later. They ended up at a storage building 仓库（cangku），a bungalow made of clay wall and straw roof. It had an open space in the middle with no desk and no table. On the wall there was somehow a black patch. Not sure how they made it. Teachers could write on it with chalk.

All the students gathered around and sat on the benches provided by villagers in Ng'sville. Teacher Jia gave them the first class on literature for 45 minutes. As he spoke, the students took notes. The next class was math by Teacher Ye. Similarly, students took notes while he taught some math exercises.

Before the Cultural Revolution, the education system had six grades for middle school, equally split between junior high and high school. However, with the new school, the school system was reformed to finish middle school in 5 years, 3 years in junior high and 2 years in high school. As a result, some subject materials had to be omitted, the rest reorganized and new textbooks printed. All classes were supposed to have universal textbooks designed by the provincial education ministry for rural areas. But the books were not ready yet and were supposed to arrive in two more weeks.

That was the temporary classroom for the new junior high. That was how classes were held at the beginning.

19. Class in Progress while School under Construction 边上课边修建学校 (bian shangke bian xiujian xuexiao)

The practice of crossing a creek to teach students in a storage house without any facilities may sound necessary, but not practical in real life. It was particularly hard for the teachers who had lived their lives in cities. After about two weeks, they stopped walking to the storage house. Instead, they had classes in the Commune complex courtyard or on the stage at the end. It was not ideal schooling conditions, but nobody seemed to complain. Perhaps, they still thought it was the best thing that could happen to them in their lives.

At the same time, construction had started on a piece of land just next to the Commune complex.

红星水库（Hongxing shuiku）

Site of New Junior High

View from Yao'sville

The construction had a higher standard than a straw residential house. Red bricks instead of clay blocks were used to build the walls with mortar between bricks. A crew from a neighboring town was hired. Apparently, construction of the school was the priority for the Commune and the higher-level government. The construction was pretty fast. In about two months, two classrooms were built with a roof. Soon, a black board was built on the wall in each room and wooden desks and benches were placed on the leveled clay dirt floor. The walls were just bare brick and mortar, not painted. There was no electricity, no water supply, and no sewer system. They were just like shelters. Classes were held in the new classrooms as soon as they were completed.

The teachers however remained in their rooms in the

Commune complex until a few months later when their residence was built. At night, teachers, like everyone else in the rural area, used kerosene lamps for lighting.

Fortunately, they did not have to cook for themselves at that time. They ate together with the Commune officials in a *shi-tang* 食堂, which had one cook to make three meals a day for all, except on Sundays, which had only two meals supplied. The cook was also responsible for purchasing supplies, carrying water on his shoulders from the village about 300 meters away, cooking and serving food at mealtimes. Everyone would hand him pre-purchased *fan-piao* 饭票 to buy the main food: rice, *mantow*, etc. and cai-piao 菜票 to buy vegetables and/or meat when it was available. The price was calculated based on cost-recovery. The salary of the cook was paid by the government.

For students, many brought their own cooked food if they were from far away. The cook helped them by warming up their food by steaming it in a large wok, which was extra workload for him, of course. Students who lived nearby, like Dai-shan, would just go home for lunch. There was about two hours break during lunch time.

It was mentioned earlier that no sewer system existed. Actually, there was none at all anywhere in rural areas. Then how about the washroom? A washroom in the rural area was called *Ce-suo* 厕所, which is not the same as what you use today. At that time, a *Ce-suo* was simply a dug pit, sealed around by stone and concrete, partially covered on the top. The covered part would have two rooms, one for girls and one for boys and each room had a few rows of ditches, for doing one's business. Yes, it smelled bad inside. The open part of the pit on one side would allow farmers to take away the human waste for use in the farm.

There was no water fountain for washing hands, no toilet paper, and no light. People would just use a kerosene lamp or a flashlight at night to go to the *Cesuo*.

Approximately half a year later after school had started, all the teachers moved into their own residence rooms, which were as simple as the classrooms. Many started cooking their own meals in the evenings and on the weekends using portable kerosene stoves, which was a way to improve their lives and enjoy something they like to eat on their own.

20. Teachers' Dedication and High Quality of Education 教师的奉献，高质量的教育(*jiaoshi de fengxian, gao zhiliang de jiaoyu*)

At this point, it is worth talking a little more about the teachers. Except for Teacher Ye, all other teachers were graduates from Normal Education Institutions, and some had taught for many years in well established middle schools.

Teacher Jia, who taught Chinese literature, wore a pair of glasses, and had the appearance of an educated gentleman 斯文(*siwen*). He was from *Zhongdu-fu* and had years of teaching experience. He was also the designated head teacher 班主任 (*ban zhu-ren*) for the first-year class in the new junior high. In addition to teaching his own subject, his extra duties included monitoring and supervising all students in the class. Whenever a student had any issues, he would be the one to go to for solutions. Teacher Jia was passionate about teaching and his students. He also often volunteered to provide free hair cutting services to students.

Teacher Ye, a local, graduated from the high school in the county capital just before the start of the Cultural Revolution. However, he had no chance to go to university because higher education institutions were suspended. Most likely, it was because of his excellent achievement in school that he was selected to teach mathematics in this new junior high. He was good at math. Dai-shan loved this subject and often asked him challenging questions. Teacher Ye was passionate and patient. A number of times, when he could not answer Dai-shan's question right away, he would say, "I have to look into it and will get back to you later". He always did with satisfactory answers.

A little sidetrack story. Shortly before that time, there were two high school graduates including Teacher Ye in the same class and they both were in the neighboring areas. The other graduate was Mr. Zhang, who was said to have always been on the top of his class. However, his birth family class 家庭成分 (*jiating chengfen*) was said to be Middle-Peasant. His 2nd older brother was one of the officials in the Commune. In a normal situation, he should have benefited from his brother's position. However, it was said his brother somehow was not on the right side during those years of politically correct environment. As a result, he was ignored and stayed at home farming until 1977 when entrance exams for Higher Education Institutions resumed. He proved himself and passed the entrance exams in 1978, 10 years after high school.

Now back to the teachers. Teacher Sun, who taught physics, was from a middle school from a neighboring county. He was good in his field and loved students who asked him difficult questions. Since the education material from that year was compressed from the previous 6 years to the then 5 years, some materials might have

161

been cut out. He often found some challenging questions from the old textbooks and let Dai-shan solve them in his spare time.

Teacher Wang, who taught English, was the second younger teacher, from a neighboring middle school. It might sound a little odd. In a poor rural area like Hongxing Commune, even a junior high was a historically new thing, how much would ordinary people understand and need English? Presumably, Teacher Wang would have had some challenges in delivering his class in that situation. In the first class, Dai-shan remembered they learned the alphabet. The were the same letters as those they had used to spell Chinese 拼音 (*pinyin*) but pronounced differently.

"That is the language of English and English speaking people use". "If you want to communicate with foreigners, you must learn their languages". Teacher Wang told the class.

Communicating with foreign people? Maybe that was taking it too far, Dai-shan thought. Since it was one of the subjects all middle school students were required to learn at that time, they would have to learn it, whether it was useful or not in their lives. After a few classes, Dai-shan found it fun and liked it. He became one of Teacher Wang's favorite students.

Another one was Teacher Lin, the school administrator (not titled Principal yet). He was teaching real time politics 实时政治 (*shishi zhengzhi*) and physical education 体育 (*tiyu*). The first subject was all about the then politics and the CP policies. After all, the government wanted all students to be 又红又专 (*youhong youzhuan*), which basically meant to excel in all subjects and at the same time to follow and support CP ideology and the government's policies. Complaining about or being against the policies was not welcome. Not actively supporting the policies was also not favoured and that would be labeled as 白专（*baizhuan*）, meaning only good at the other subjects but not actively supportive to the CP policies.

The subject of physical education was not much about learning health but just about doing exercises to keep fit, twice a week, 45 minutes each time, and included running, playing basketball, gymnastics following the radio 广播体操（*guanbo ticao*）, etc. To the peasants, that didn't seem necessary because they all had to do physical work anyway.

There was one more subject in the curriculum, chemistry. Somehow there was no teacher to teach it at the beginning and no facilities for laboratory experiments. It was only in the second year when one teacher took on the challenge to teach chemistry following the book, but no lab work was involved.

Despite the primitive conditions in the rural area, all teachers did an excellent job. Dai-shan benefited from their hard work and dedication.

21. Cherishing very much the Rare Opportunity 机会难得，十分珍惜 （*jihui nande, shifen zhenxi*）

To Dai-shan, going to junior high was a rare, once in a lifetime opportunity. He cherished it very much and eagerly 如饥似渴地（*ruji sike de* - literally like being hungry and thirsty） learned everything he could in the classroom and beyond. After school, he helped his parents by doing house chores and field work, as much as he could. At night, he used his little kerosene lamp to finish his homework before going to bed. He never left it overnight. Somehow, he didn't seem need to spend too much time on it.

Dai-shan was keen on self learning all the school subjects. He usually finished the homework quickly and spent time previewing new material before the next class and was always prepared for new lessons. While some students were struggling to follow the teachers in class, he was using the opportunity to review and confirm what he already understood. In his mind, there was nothing that was beyond what he could learn. As long as he put his mind to it, no matter how difficult, he would eventually solve the problem.

Dai-shan's industrious learning attitude and ability to learn certainly rewarded him. In those days, no marks were allocated for assignments. The grade of a course was solely based on the result of the final exam. He excelled and his grades in math 数学 (*shuxue*), physics 物理 (*wuli*) and chemistry 化学 (*huaxue*) were always over 90%. 100% was very common and even often 120% in math.

Wait, 120%? Teacher Ye noticed Dai-shan and another student *Shi-hui* in the same class achieving way above the class average. Teacher Ye intentionally introduced extra questions in the exam with 20% bonus marks, in an attempt to see how wide the range was in the class. Often, after completing all the necessary questions, Dai-shan still had time to tackle the bonus question before the exam ended. Teacher Ye would normally mark Dai-shan's answering sheet first and use it as his marking template.

All his teachers loved students who understood the material quickly and were eager to learn more. They often found challenging questions from old textbooks before the reformed system and gave him more opportunities to learn and challenge himself.

In English class, he was always at the top. However, he was not doing as well in Chinese literature. He could calculate, think and reason logically, but was just not as good at describing things or putting together statements. His mark in that course was usually between 65% and 75%. He just didn't like to write. Teacher Jia noticed that and asked him why he did not do as well in this class. "I just don't have much to write or to say".

Believe it or not? He didn't understand Chinese grammar until he learned it in English class. Unlike native English speakers who typically picked up the language from daily conversations, he learned English starting from the alphabet and grammar. Only after that, he understood there was usually a subject, a verb, and an object in a complete sentence.

Dai-shan appreciated his teachers and the unexpected, rare opportunity to be their students. He remembered them well even after he grew up.

Fascinated by radio 无线电的吸引 *(wuxiang dian de xiyin)*

Dai-shan loved mathematics. However, he was even more attracted by the subject of radio waves in Physics. It was fascinating to be able to talk and communicate with someone at a far distance without any direct contact in between. Radio was still a rare thing in the rural areas in the early 1970s. In his simplified Physics textbook, there was not much detail on radio waves, and the learning environment in his school was further restricted by a lack of access to laboratory experiments. But Dai-shan wanted to learn more about them.

There was a young man who usually sat at the *Longsheng* market during market days, to set up a service to repair radios. His gear would consist of a small set, a few small items he used. A kerosene lamp was his heat source for soldering. Dai-shan was there a few times, standing by and watching him repairing. When a radio box was opened there were a few resistors, capacitors with wires connecting one to another. He was fascinated by what that guy was doing. A dead radio, after he soldered some elements and wires together, became alive again.

Dai-shan decided to give it a try. He asked his teacher for more information, and he was recommended to get a book on introductory radio waves. Money to buy the book was the challenge. He managed to earn and save some money and eventually bought a book for ¥2.50, from which he learned the basics of radio waves and the required

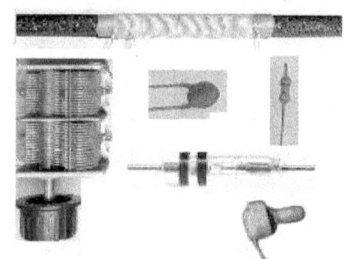

diode radio components

electronic elements. He managed to buy a diode, a magnetic rod, an earbud, some resistors and capacitors in a store in the county. He then started his experiment.

He used the half inch flame on his kerosene lamp as his soldering source to heat up a peanut size piece of metal. After connecting the elements together, tuning and repeatedly trying, he eventually managed to capture some radio signals. However, the signal was too weak and there was too much high pitch and background noises. He needed to have a better design and add transistors and other components to complete a radio. Due to lack of money and other necessities, he couldn't finish the project at that time. More will follow up this later.

The 9.13 Event 9.13 事件 (shijian)

It was the Fall of 1971, shortly after school started. Suddenly the People's Central Broadcasting Station (PCBS) 中央人民广播电台 (zhongyang remin guangbo ditai) made an important announcement that shocked the whole country about *Lin-biao* 林彪, who was the then second most powerful person in China. It was very unusual to refer to a high-ranking person without his title or "comrade". This must be something huge. Everyone was eager to hear more.

The PCBS continued: "… he was on the way escaping to an enemy country when his aircraft crashed in Mongolia, in a place called Öndörkhan, killing everyone on board. On the plane with him were his wife and his son."

"Why?" you would ask, "would a person of that high rank do such a thing? The official propaganda made a long list of his crimes. To Dai-shan, other young students in his class and ordinary people, it was hard to understand. The previous day he was the second most powerful person, Chairman Mao's closest comrade and the designated successor of Chairman Mao, which was even written in the Constitution of China (something you may have not heard of before). The next day he became a traitor, a counter revolutionary. It was just like driving on the highway at 150 km/hour and suddenly making a 180° turn, making you feel dizzy and lose consciousness.

This news was followed by a series of political movements across the nation, criticizing *Lin-biao* and Confucius 批林批孔 (*pilin pikong*) together. Now, that was another hard-to-understand thing for young people, and adults too. How could *Lin-biao* be connected to Confucius who lived more than two thousand years ago? The students were told that they both had followed the same principle: *keji fuli* 克己复礼 (restrain himself and return to the rites or observe for the opportunity to make a return). Instructions were given to criticize the two people together, who lived over 2000 years apart!

22. A Juvenile's Mind 少年的初心 (shaonian de chuxin)

A girl in the class 班上有个女同学 (ban-shang you-ge nu tong-xue)

Dai-shan had turned sixteen, but he was a shy boy due to lack of opportunity to socialize and encounter peers and opposite sex. He could hardly speak or make conversation with girls; except the ones he knew well. He often tried to walk away when a female student was on his path.

There were a few girls in his class. He did not have any time to pay attention to them as he was focusing on his studies. All he wanted to do was to learn and gain as much knowledges as possible. But there was one girl in the class who was an exception to him. She was about the same age, or might have been slightly older, named 玉芳 (Yu-fang). She was an average student academically, but she could sing, perform, and even dance. She was considered a school beauty 一朵校花 (yiduo xiaohua). Because of her talent, she was appointed by teachers as the *Wenyi Weiyuan* 文艺委员, the class leader in charge of arts and musical activities.

Yu-fang was pretty in Dai-shan's mind. More importantly, she appeared to be nice to him, at least that was what Dai-shan thought. The way she talked to him was gentle, sweet, and caring. Even just some general conversation made him feel good, a kind of feeling he had never had before. Somehow, he often felt like being around her, or having her around. However, whenever there was an opportunity for them to face each other, he couldn't say a thing and just blushed.

Once in a while, not often, when there was a really difficult question on their assignments, she might ask him for some help. Only in that situation, was he able to talk to her normally.

Dai-shan always had his poor family and poor village at the top of his mind and tried to remind himself: "You're in school to learn, nothing else". Besides, she never said she liked him. Maybe she was nice to everyone, and this was just his one-sided imagination. He tried to restrain himself and keep a distance from her, but that was not easy to do.

A person's political identity and future 一个人的政治身份与前途 (*yi ge ren de zhengzhi shenfeng yu qiantu*)

To those readers who are not familiar with Chinese society in those days, here is some useful information to know. For anyone who wanted to be able to do something or to be successful in his/her life, it was very important to join the CP (communist party) and become a CP member when they grew up. It was however not an easy thing to join CP. It required one to have "red roots" (being born to the poor and lower middle peasant families) and to be actively supportive of the CP government and socialism. If one's birth family class was not in those categories, it would be very difficult to become a CP member.

There was also a political organization for youth, called Communist Youth League (CYL) 共青团 (*gong-qing-tuan*). A young person would normally first join the CYL before joining the CP later.

Like the CP organization, the CYL organization was rooted in every level of government and in society. There was a CYL branch in the junior high as well. To join the organisation, you must first submit a formal application, but only when you were invited to do so. If an existing member discovered you had political potential, this person

169

would approach you to have a formal conversation on behalf of the organization and encourage you to submit an application.

The application was not a form to be filled out but a personal letter to show your determination and loyalty to the organization, to the CP and its policies. Once an application was recorded, there would be an indefinite period of test, not a written test on a piece of paper, but a test via real life which could take months or years.

You could voluntarily approach the organization and submit an application, but the test period could be much longer, and you might face additional challenges.

During the test period, the applicant needed to do everything as instructed, be on the same side with (or supportive to) the CP, the government policies and be politically correct. Whenever you were put in a difficult situation, whether it be some hard work or to sacrifice something, you would be told that was part of the test.

It was not uncommon for some people, in an attempt to show off, to do superficial things to flatter superiors 拍马屁 (*pai mapi* - meaning literally to pat the horse's butt). Only when you were considered to have passed the test and the local branch had approved your performance, would you become an official member. At that time, you would swear under the organization's flag in a secret meeting.

She seemed to care about him afterall 她好像关心他 (*ta hoaxiang guanxin ta*)

Now back to Hongxing Junior High. One day, at the end of a class meeting, *Yu-fang* approached Dai-shan and told him she had something to talk to him about.

"What ··· about?" he asked, with his head down looking at his feet.

"You know, you have been excellent in your studies".

"Em···", he didn't know how to respond.

"Have you thought about setting a goal for yourself?"

"What goal?" He was puzzled.

"To try to make some progress for yourself on the political side 在政治上要求进步 (*zai zhengzhi shang yaoqiu jinbu*)."

"What do you mean?"

"Strive to join the CYL 努力争取入团 (*nuli zhengqu rutuan*) and write an application".

Dai-shan understood that if he wanted to be successful in his life, he must join the CP eventually, but first the CYL. That was the only route to success in that country and it was what every young person was hoping for at that time. He thought he should think it over. He was excited but also reluctant. He asked back, "are you a CYL member?"

She smiled and just said, "you should try".

"But ··· how?"

"First, write an application to show your interest and to voluntarily join the CYL, be supportive to the CP and socialism, and behave well." She continued.

"Then you need to put those words in action, to behave politically correct and to do good things, etc."

Wah, that was a baggage full of stuff to do. He thought it over. Maybe he should try but what would be the chances he would get approved? So, he replied "I will think about it".

He would always try new things when he had full confidence to do so. Anyone with knowledge of the political environment in China in those days would know that simply writing a letter without showing something in action would lead him nowhere. Dai-shan realized, he could not make a promise which was not possible. He disliked saying things that were not true and doing superficial things just to show off. Most importantly he hated flattering people. He couldn't come up with a politically promising application and decided to wait until he could do some good things first to improve his chances.

One day, at the end of classes, all students gathered in the playground, lined up by classes and groups for a day-end speech by a teacher or the principal, Teacher Lin said a few words as usual and then praised a group of students for cleaning up the dirt on the playground voluntarily. "I hope we have more students doing good things like that", he ended the speech with that comment.

Two days later, Dai-shan saw a few students sweeping part of the playground where they normally did their exercises. *Yu-fang* was among them.

Dai-shan thought to himself that kind of good action was achievable for him. One day soon after school, he saw the classroom floor was dirty and decided to sweep the floor after classes finished. As a reminder, the floor consisted of dried clay surface and was not very even, collecting plenty of dust. He followed the normal procedure. First, he put all the benches on the top of the desks, spread some water with a basin and his hands on the dusty floor, and then picked up a broom to sweep the dirt on the floor. Even with water on the floor, there was dust floating in the air and out the door.

Someone saw him and came over. Dai-shan noticed it was Yu-fang. She didn't say anything and picked up another broom in the corner, started helping him. It was quite some work, taking them 20 minutes to finish. Then she said to him in a soft tone: "It was good you did something like this. But it was a lot of work. You didn't really need to do it all by yourself".

Apparently, she knew why he had done it. She didn't exaggerate nor blame his action but lent him a hand to avoid making him uncomfortable. She was obviously more mature than Dai-shan. Her words seemed to hint that he had over done it. He seemed to have got the message and felt a little embarrassed when he thought it over. You could imagine that some political climbers would score more political points with less effort. But he didn't like playing that kind of game anyway. Nevertheless, her actions and words gave him comfort and made him feel good.

School musical and performance event 学校文艺汇演
(xuexiao wenyi huiyan)

One day, during the school gathering, Teacher Lin announced that the school would organize a musical and performance event 文艺汇演（*wenyi huiyan*）. Several students had been approached to start preparing the program. Yu-fang was going to have a group performance plus a solo song.

Teacher Lin asked Dai-shan and another student *Xiao Lin* (not related to the teacher), who was the same age and similar in height, to go to his office and said, "I'd like you two to prepare a two-person crosstalk show 相声 (*xiang sheng*)" and handed over a few pages of notes to them to speak to. Another teacher in the room asked: "Do you think you can do it?" showing a little concern.

"I don't know, I have never done it before", *Xiao Lin* replied.

"I have never been on stage before", Dai-shan added.

Teacher Lin encouraged them by saying, "with practice, you should be able to do it". He then added, "the first thing to do is to memorise these notes and get back to me next week".

Dai-shan had never been afraid of challenging questions in class. But on stage to perform with many people watching? He had no confidence, really. *Xiao Lin* and he talked about it and decided to give it a try. Dai-shan was keen in analyzing, following logic and reasoning, but was not good in memorizing things which did not seem to have much of a pattern or relationship. A few days passed; he still couldn't memorize the speeches.

When Teacher Lin checked on their progress, Dai-shan still needed to read the notes rather than be able to speak from memory. Apparently, they both didn't make as much progress as was expected. Teacher Lin said, "it's OK to look at the notes during practice. Now you two need to work together. While you talk to each other, you need to look at the audience and add actions: facial expressions, hand gestures and postures, etc. to get their attention".

It sounded so simple. But that was what the Performing Arts was about. Not everyone had that talent. Apparently Dai-shan didn't have it either. When Teacher Lin checked on their progress again, they could only read with the notes and with some clumsy and mechanical movements. He and the other teachers didn't say anything. You might have guessed, on the day of the performance, their crosstalk show was not on the list.

On the other hand, Yu-fang did so well. In addition to practicing her group performance, she learned a new song by herself. During the show, when it was the time for her solo, everybody was silent waiting to hear what she was going to sing. She was dressed up and walked to the front of the stage.

Suddenly, a beautiful soprano 女高音 （*nu gaoyin*）voice appeared: "the loquat turned yellow in the full garden ….满园的枇杷黄橙橙（*manyuan de pipa huang cheng cheng*）…".

Dai-shan couldn't believe the voice was from her. She surprised everyone with her new voice.

There was no music teacher in the school. Sometimes, she taught the class how to sing new songs.

Dai-shan realized that she would deserve a lot more than what he had to offer. If he was to think of her as anything in

Loquat 枇杷

his life, the only possibility was for him to be successful in his future. That certainly stopped him from thinking about her too much in the short term and pulled him right back on track to focus on school.

23. Middle School Ends 初中结束了 （*chuzhong jieshu le*）

During his three years of junior high school, Dai-shan got along well with *Zhan-hui* (another top student in the class) and Ye-zhong (one of Teacher Ye's brothers). They three became good friends and often spent time in Ye-zhong's home, discussing schoolwork, the future, or sometimes just hanging around. Apparently, another reason was for them to discuss things with Teacher Ye, who loved to be with them and had lots to talk to them about.

Their teachers often told them that: they were at the best time in their lives to learn. The time was extremely specious, as the famous saying goes: 一寸光阴一寸金（*yicun guangyin yicun jin*），寸金难买寸光阴 （*cunjin nanmai cun guangyin*）. That is to say: If we could measure time by length as one inch per minute, "A minute of time is worth

175

one inch of a gold bar. However, you can never buy back one inch of the time in the past with one inch of gold".

Time passed by quickly. Before they noticed, they had finished junior high. They had completed final exams in every subject by early June 1973. They were also told that there would not be an entrance exam to high school that year and the marks from their third year of junior high would be evaluated to assess their qualification for high school.

There was no high school in Hongxing Commune. The new high school that had opened two years ago was Yangjia High school, located in a neighboring commune, most likely because of its central geographical location for the five communes in the area. Graduates from the surrounding five junior highs would all go to that high school to make up two classes (approximately 30 students each). There would only be 20% graduates from junior high going to high school on average that year. The majority of students would not be able to continue schooling.

During the school gathering on the last day of school, everyone was told to go home and wait for official notification of high school entrance. There were mixed feelings in everyone's mind. Those students with good academic results and without a bad political record would feel confident of continuing onto high school. Those students with poor academic results would not expect to continue. Most students who fell in between did not know their outcome and had to wait. In Dai-shan's mind, there was no doubt what his result would be, and he had full confidence.

Nevertheless, everyone tried to put a smile on their face. After all, they had just completed three years of junior high and eventually would have their graduation certificates. Some students exchanged presents to memorialize their friendship. Everyone did it in their own way. Dai-shan received a notebook from *Yu-fang* as her wish for him to continue to excel in his future. He also realized that she was nice to many other students, not only to him. Dai-shan didn't prepare anything for her or anyone, because he didn't have a clue what to give a girl anyway! But he thanked her for the notebook. For his buddies, they just shook hands and wished to see each other again in high school.

That was it. Everyone then left for their homes, and some never saw each other again. Although his home was only 15 minutes away, Dai-shan was one of the last few to leave the campus, which was a very basic and primitive place with nothing comparable to today's school campuses, but it was a place full of memories. Somehow, he felt like he had lost something, but was not sure what it was. He went home via the same trail but felt different that day.

Believe it or not, after three years in that school, there was not a single photo taken, individually or in groups. There was a photo shop in a nearby town, but it was over 3 kilometers away and it would be too expensive to get them just to take some photos. For poor peasants in those days, taking a photo was really something unnecessary and luxurious.

At this moment, it is necessary to mention two of Dai-shan's siblings: His brother, the 2nd eldest sibling, did well in school too but unfortunately did not have the chance to go to middle school after elementary school. His sister, the 4th sibling, was also a good student, though she started school very late for her age and stopped going to school before finishing elementary school as she felt embarrassed about being the oldest student in the class.

Dai-shan felt very sorry for them both but there was nothing he could do at that time to change anything. In his mind, all he could do was to give them a hand in the future when he has the means to.

Curios of family roots 好奇寻根 (haoqi xungen)

Up until that time, Dai-shan had learned a lot of new things but he was still unclear how his middle name was determined and why his village lived in such a poor place. He decided to find out.

He first asked his mother, and she told him that his middle name, like everyone else, was predetermined by their ancestors, though she did not know the details. As for why their family ended up there, she told him to ask his father or his uncle.

His father simply replied that all the children in his generation was called Dai and didn't know much the rest.

Dai-shan was not satisfied with that answer and he decided to ask Uncle Shi-qing, who was the older brother of his father, grew up earlier and knew more about family things than his father. When Dai-shan asked him those questions, he was happy to explain to him everything he knew.

Uncle Shi-qing started telling Dai-shan what he had heard from his grandfather who had heard it from the previous generations. That was a rare day when Uncle Shi-qing seemed to be not busy and just sat there recalling from his memory everything he could, telling Dai-shan the legendary story. Soon, many other kids had gathered around to listen. What happened was described in the Prologue at the beginning of this book.

"That was how we ended up living here." Uncle Shi-qing ended the story.

"Then what happened?" Dai-shan wanted to know more.

"Not sure exactly. There was no record. Now you are in the 12ᵗʰ generation. All should remember our ancestors. "

"What about our middle names?" Dai-shan asked further.

Uncle Shi-qing then told him the family ranks and the generation sequence.

"This was what I heard from the elders", he said.

"The generation ranking was predetermined, after consulting a wiseman, by our original ancestor who lived in the previous Guangdong province, long before ancestor Yin-Dru came to this land. "

Uncle Shi-qing spelled out the 30 characters representing the generations of the Yao family with a local dialect. it sounded like a poem but Dai-shan couldn't understand their meanings.

"Those characters were supposed to be good for the Yao family. " Uncle Shi-qing continued. He told Dai-shan to write them down in sequence and to be used by future generations of their families.

Each character was designated for a generation. The first generation was *Qi* "旗" and the 6ᵗʰ generation was Yin "印" . Every descendant in a generation would use the same letter as their middle name as identification of their generational sequence and all they needed to name a newborn child was to add another letter at the end. For example, Dai-shan was in the 17ᵗʰ generation Dai "代" and needed to add shan to have his full name, Yao, Dai-shan.

Dai-shan did some analysis. In spoken Chinese, one sound could mean several different characters and the local dialect would deviate more. After trial and error a few times, Dai-shan finally came up with the 30 characters which had the closest sound and had some meaning. He listed them in the Yao ancestry table on the next page.

Yao ancestry

Yao family generation ranking 姚氏輩份 (Bei-Fen) [50]				
Qi 旗 1st	Jui 举 2nd	Qing 擎 3rd	Kong 空 4th	Ying 英 5th
Yin 印 * 6th	Zhan 蒼 7th	Cheng 成 8th	Yu 御 9th	Wen 文 10th
Wei 卫 11th	Yuan 苑 12th	Ming 铭 13th	Fa 发 14th	Wang 旺 15th
Shi 世 16th	Dai 代 † 17th	Yong 永 18th	Yuan 远 19th	Cun 存 20th
Ren 仁 21st	Liang 良 22nd	Ben 本 23rd	Shang 尚 24th	Da 達 25th
Da 大 26th	Dao 道 27th	Xian 献 28th	Chao 朝 29th	Ting 廷 30th
Repeat the above thereafter.				

* The first generation that settled in Yao'sville.

† The latest generation of the Yao family at that time.

In an attempt to understand the minds of the Yao ancestors, they could be interpreted as follows:

Line 1: to hold the flag up high in the sky like a General (an imperial general),

Line 2: to stamp a paper making it an imperial order (an imperial court officer with power),

Line 3: to guard the imperial palace and the family becomes well known and prosperous,

Line 4: the success continues from generation to generation,

Line 5: kind, honest, do well on own duties,

Line 6: all to be contributed to the imperial court.

It indicated their loyalty to the empire and the hope to be associated with and be a part of the imperial system.

---

[50] The Yao generation ranking is adopted from a family in *Yao'sville*.

Chapter 5

High School 高中时代 (gaozhong shidai)

24. Going to High School 上高中（*shang gaozhong*）

Not long before high school was about to start, Dai-shan received his official admission letter from Yangjia High school. Through word of mouth, he learned his other buddies all received their letters as well. In the first week of September 1973, the high school opened for the second group of new students since its establishment.

For Dai-shan, this time it was quite different from junior high. First, it was located over 10 kilometers away and daily commuting was not possible with no transportation options at the time. In fact, all students were required to stay on campus during the weekdays. He met up with his buddies, and they all decided to go the day before classes started. There were plenty of things they needed to do: find the residence, the location to have food, their classrooms, etc., etc. This was the first time Dai-shan was going to live by himself and away from his mother. There were concerns and uncertainty ahead but there was also excitement.

The first day of high school was the biggest family event for many students. They needed to bring all the necessary things required for day-to-day living, such as a mosquito net 蚊帐（*wenzhang*）to cover the bed, a quilt 被子（*beizi*）, a straw mat 草席（*caoxi*）, a suitcase 箱子（*xiangzi*）, a wash basin 脸盆（*lianpen*）, clothes 衣服（*yifu*）, shoes 鞋子（*xiezi*）, a large rice cup 饭盅（*fanzhong*）, etc. Those were their supplies for the whole semester. In addition, many students brought some raw food (mostly yam and rice) for a whole week, while some could just buy them from the local market. All those things together would be a full load for even a full-grown adult to carry. For many students, their parents helped bring their supplies to school. It was a big thing for the family too.

For Dai-shan, this was also a family event, as he was the first person to go to high school in his family's history. His mother made a quilt with a colored cover which had flowers and said, "this is a new quilt I made for your school".

"Mama, I couldn't take that. It's too colorful. It's for girls. I will just take my old one, the faded black quilt".

The whole family had only one very old suitcase made of leather (though probably not real leather). It was big and heavy. "No, I won't need the suitcase. I will just use a *beidou* 背篼 (a back carrying bamboo basket)", he decided.

His mother bought a new washing basin for him. After packing everything together in the beidou with the quilt on top, he said bye to his mother and headed down the hill to fetch his buddies Ye-zhong and Zhan-hui. Instead of the main road, they decided to take a small trail over the mountain, which was supposedly a shorter distance, as an adventure. That was the first time they went that way; it zig-zagged, up and down the hills, but it was not difficult to follow. On the way, there were peasants and herd boys here and there. They asked for directions and came to the top of the last hill probably two hours later and saw a small town in the distance.

"That looks like the Yangjia Commune", one pointed out.

"The school should be just there", another added.

They descended to the bottom of the hill and came to a creek, which had running water, similar to the creek near

Hongxing junior high. But the water in this creek seemed to run all the time, even during the dry season.

There were a few young people washing their clothes in the creek, and someone was taking water from the river with a pair of pails. They were told that the creek was called 杨家河 (*Yangjia he* – river). Storm water was huge during the rainy seasons and there was a large spring, 3" to 4" in diameter gushing out of the riverbed. The water quality was very good, and it tasted fresh[51], none of the tap water in cities was comparable. Probably that was why the creek got its name of river.

They crossed the river on the stones and arrived at the school campus a few minutes later.

25 Yangjia High School 杨家中学 (*Yangjia zhongxue*)

Yangjia high school had its own campus, located a few hundred meters away from the local market / town of Yangjia commune, to avoid the noise and crowd during the market days. The junior high was also on a separate campus.

The high school sat on the bank of Yangjia river, one side facing the river and another side facing a small hill. The site and its surrounding areas were flat. There were a few local residential houses nearby. Down the main road a few hundred meters away was the town and marketplace.

The water source in the river was very good. However, there was no running tap water on campus. All domestic water supply had to be carried by pails on one's shoulders.

The area was relatively quiet, a good location for school. On the campus, all residence buildings and facilities were fenced off by a peripheral brick wall.

---

[51] No one would believe then, 20 years later the spring site was covered with a commercial building to make bottled water for sell.

184

The classrooms were outside next to the open playground. There was one main entrance door and a rear door.

The *Ce-suo* 厕所 (washroom) was very similar to the one at Hongxing junior high. One side of it was outside the peripheral wall for waste removal by local peasants.

Most people would normally walk through the town/market to the main entrance. Dai-shan and his buddies came from the river side to the rear door, which led to the *shi-tang* 食堂, where a few people were busy preparing food.

Dai-shan and his buddies explained they were new students, looking for registration and asked for direction.

"Oh, you are in the wrong place. You need to leave this room, make a left turn and a right turn, then exit the main entrance, and go to one of the classrooms. Registration is over there".

It was a small campus with four rows of buildings. All were one-level bungalows with no basement or attic. It didn't take them long to get to the main entrance. The building next to the entrance was the student residence. Some students were in and out of those rooms, busy getting settled. One came over and asked:

"Which class are you in?"

"Don't know, we haven't registered yet".

"You can leave your stuff here first and come back to get it after registration".

Dai-shan and his buddies looked at each other. That student seemed to know what they were thinking and said,

"Oh, don't worry, we are all new students here".

They left the heavy stuff beside the door of a room, walked out the main entrance, and found the classroom for registration. There were a few teachers and some early-arrived students there. They greeted the new arrivals and took them to the first desk where the students' names were listed.

One teacher said, "Dai-shan, you are in class one. Ye-zhong and Zhan-hui, you two are in class two". All the students had already been separated into two classes.

"Go to the next desk to fill out the forms and then get the school material. Classrooms, class schedules, your residence rooms, everything will be there.

"After you have finished everything, get your key to your residence rooms 寝室（*qinshi*）, then take all your belongings to your room".

"Oh, don't forget to buy tickets at the food services desk".

They followed instructions and completed registration shortly after. Then they found themselves in three separate bedrooms. Dai-shan was in room one, at the end of the student residence building. The other two were in the other rooms.

Then they went to the last desk for food services to buy some tickets for their meals. Dai-shan purchased some *cai-piao* 菜票 for immediate use. We will get back to this with more detail a little later.

Students from five different junior high schools 学生来自五所不同的中学 *(xuesheng laizi wusuo butong de zhongxue)*

Let us pause for a second. Yangjia high school was built for the whole *Xingxing qu* 兴兴区 (district), in which there were five communes:

- *Hongxing* 红星 (red star) commune,
- *Xingxing* 兴兴 (prosperous) commune,
- *Jinji* 金鸡 (Golden rooster) commune,
- *Yangjia* 杨家 (Yang'sville) commune,

186

- Yingxiong 英雄（Heros）commune, in memory of the martyrs during the liberation war.

Each commune had a junior high school and so there were five junior highs that fed into Yangjia high school.

Yangjia high school was a rural school. In comparison with city schools, it had much less school resources available. Nevertheless, it was much better than Hongxing junior high. Students were normally from the local areas. As mentioned before, it would be very difficult for someone to attend schools outside their registered residence community. There were exceptions for those kids whose parents were moving due to a job or other situations. If someone was going to change to another school, it would normally be a school with better education and better conditions.

There were two students, one boy and one girl, that year who came from outside the Xingxing *qu*, from two small cities in Jingdian county. It had nothing to do with their parents' jobs. They simply came to that school to have their high school education, and they came two weeks after school had started. That was apparently not a normal situation, a situation with complex connections. Perhaps, their parents asked their friends who had connections and eventually let them join the school. Why didn't they attend school in their own cities? There could be many possibilities on their individual situations. We will not explore this matter any further.

Student residence and roommates 学生宿舍和室友（*xuesheng sushe he shiyou*）

After registration, Dai-shan gathered his belongings and headed to the residence building. There were about eight rooms, side-by-side, in that building, all for boys.

The girls' residence was in a separate building near the teacher's residence. In the boy's rooms, each had four bunkbeds, two on each side of the room, with a total of eight beds. Six students were assigned to each room. The two extra beds were used as storage space.

Dai-shan came to the first room at the end of the building. The door was open. Four of his roommates had already arrived and the four beds at the bottom were taken. He chose one on the top at the end of the room. It was not convenient to climb up and down but more private. He preferred to be in a space alone.

They introduced themselves to each other. Some were from Jinji junior high and some from Yangjia junior high plus Dai-shan from Hongxing junior high. "We have one more roommate who lives not far from here and will move in tomorrow", someone pointed out. The six roommates had a variety of backgrounds:

Yue-gong, handsome and well behaved, was a small city boy. He grew up in Jingdian county and came to Yangjia High school with his father when he took a position on the school administrative services but did not engage in teaching. His mother was teaching in a nearby elementary school. The rumor was that his grandparents were among the richer family classes. That may have affected his father's family class and was sidelined during the cultural revolution. Both of his parents seemed to be respected by teachers and staff.

Gong-hua, handsome, grew up in a peasant family in Yangjia commune. He was the youngest among his siblings, a "richer kid" with more resources than others in the rural area but behaved like he was an urban kid. He was very close to Yue-gong and hung around him all the time.

Liu *banzhang* was a mature and honest student, who grew up in a peasant family in Jinji commune. He was patient and often tricked by naughty classmates. He was chosen as the class leader 班长（*banzhang*）by teachers, well suited to his personality.

The other two boys had similar background to Dai-shan, one from Jinji commune and another from a nearby village.

School meals 学校用餐 （*xuexiao yongcan*）

Once they were settled down in the bedrooms, the next immediate thing to do was to figure out their meals and water.

There was a *shitang* 食堂 in the school, for preparing meals for staff and students. Water supply for the whole school was from the spring down the river, taken by labor and stored in a large stone-made water tank 水缸 （*shui-gang*）. That water was basically for cooking, dishwashing, and drinking, but not for washing clothes, which would be done at the river by individuals themselves.

Meals could be purchased in the *shi-tang*, as teachers usually did. However, no cash was accepted but only tickets, to be purchased in advance at the facility service office. Alternatively, you could bring your own raw food and put it in a cup to have it cooked through the steaming cooking service, called 蒸饭（*zhengfan*）.

To buy food at mealtime, one must use a *cai-piao* 菜票 for cooked vegetables and a meal ticket 饭票（*fanpiao*）for the main food, such as cooked rice 干饭 （*ganfan*）, *mantou* 馒头, *baozi* 包子, noodles 面条 （*miantiao*）, etc. Meal tickets had different face values: 1 两 （*yi liang* = 50 grams）, 2 两（*er liang*）, 5 两 （*wu liang* = *0.5 jin* 斤）. The nomination referred to the raw food amount before cooking and the amount of the cooked food would be more.

189

Normally, a girl would need 2 *liang* for a meal but a boy would eat 3 liang or more.

To purchase meal tickets, cash and *liang piao* 粮票 were required. As mentioned before, liang piao was not distributed to peasants but only to urban citizens. However, to help students from the rural areas, the government would allow each student to use their own food (such as corn, wheat, beans, etc., but not yams which was perishable) to exchange up to 20 *jin* 斤 *liang piao* per month in a government food store. The exchange was not necessarily on a one-to-one basis.

Like many other kids, Dai-shan would exchange for some *liang piao* and use it to supplement his own food. That ability to exchange did not exist at first and came about some time later. Therefore, most students would usually rely on their own food and buy meal tickets for use when really needed.

To buy cooked vegetables at mealtime, *cai-piao* 菜票 was used, which would be purchased in advance with cash. *Cai-piao* also came in different face values: 1 fen 分 (¥1.00 = 100 fens) for steaming one cup of food, 2 fens to fill one large thermal bottle with boiling water or one small plate of pickles, 5 fens for stir-fried vegetables 素菜 (*sucai*), and 20 fens for other use. A dish of stir-fried vegetables with meat 荤菜 (*huncai*) would cost 25 fens.

Dai-shan purchased some *cai piao* at the registration desk and brought his own raw food (yam and rice purchased on the market). He learned to prepare his first meal in the school by washing and cutting the yam into small pieces, adding a little rice, washing in a cup, and adding proper amount of water. He then left his cup, covered with a lid, on a large counter together with the other students' cups. A chef later put all cups on multiple layers of steaming rackets on top of a large wok (over 4' diameter). That cooking service would cost 1.0 fen.

In the rural mountainous areas, people usually cooked yam and cornmeal to make corn porridge 玉米粥 (*yumi zhou*), also known as 包谷犒犒 (*baogu kaokao*). The cornmeal would normally be added later when the yam was almost cooked. Apparently, in Dai-shan's case, that was not possible with the steaming process in the school. So, only rice was used instead. If cornmeal was added before cooking, it wouldn't taste good.

Once cooking was finished, all cups would be put back on the counter just before the mealtime. Students would all go there to fetch their own cups. Then some might line up to buy some cooked vegetables and those who had brought their own pickles would just go back straight to their bedroom to eat. There was no designated eating place.

Dai-shan went to his bedroom, opened the jar of pickle his mother had made with dried vegetables. Some other students did the same. When the "richer kid" and the "city boy" came back to the room with purchased dishes, Dai-shan had almost finished eating.

"How come you are so fast", they asked.

"Oh, I had my own pickles and didn't need to line up", he replied.

The first day of school was nothing much. After supper, a teacher dropped by to check out every room and told students to go to bed earlier and to be ready for the next morning. Most students had traveled from quite far away and felt tired anyway.

Dai-shan put his straw mat on his bed, set up his mosquito net around his bed, made his bed and then went to sleep. Well, you can guess if he was able to sleep at all that night.

191

School timetable 作息时间表（*zuoxi Shijian biao*）

The next morning, around 6:30 am, there was a sudden loud bell sound. A teacher shook a hand bell while walking along the residence buildings and loudly announced "Time to get up and go to the playground 操场（*caochang*) for the morning exercise 早操（*zaocao*）". He would knock on bedroom doors if no light was on.

20 minutes later, all the students had gathered in the playground. A tall teacher dressed in sportswear with a whistle hung around his neck, blew his whistle and said,

"Attention everyone. Today it took 20 minutes for you to get here. You must get here in 15 minutes tomorrow".

"Class one stand on the left and class two on the right, each class make 3 rows, with sufficient distance between each other. Now let us do exercise".

He then played a loud radio with an exercise recording 广播体操（*guangbo ticao*）. He led the exercise and everyone followed. As you can imagine, some students were well dressed for the exercise, while others were not, like Dai-shan who wore his normal clothing.

After the exercise, the teacher announced:

"From now on, we will get up at 6:30 am every weekday morning to do exercise and I will knock on your door at that time. 7 o'clock is breakfast time. 8 o'clock is self-study 自习（*zixi*) time. All classes will begin at 8:30".

He then continued, "10:30 to 10:50 is for between-class exercise 课间操（*kejian cao*) and you are all required to come back here to do exercise. Lunch break and nap is between 12 and 2. Please read the timetable you are provided with for more detail".

Dai-shan followed the crowd and went to have breakfast.

The food was usually *mantou* 馒头 and porridge 稀饭(*xifan*) with pickle, to be purchased.

After breakfast, they immediately prepared their lunch cups and left them on the shi-tang counter for cooking before going to classes. Dai-shan stood there in front of the shi-tang for a few seconds and looked around. "Looking for someone?" his friend asked. "Not really" Dai-shan responded. "Hurry, we will be late for class".

Eventually saw her 终于看到了她 (*zhongyu kandao le ta*)

Dai-shan, together with other students, headed to their classroom as quickly as they could and arrived just in time. One student came in and announced, "Hello everyone, please bring your bench to the open playground outside for the opening ceremony".

Soon, the students were assembled outside, with class one on one side and class two on the other side. They were all new students in the school that year. "Where are the senior year students?" Someone whispered.

In the crowd, Dai-shan suddenly spotted someone at the back, someone with a familiar figure. "Is that her?" he wondered. Then she turned around. Yes, it was *Yu-fang*. He waived at her. She saw him and smiled at him. Then she turned around, busy instructing other students.

There were a couple of desks in the front, set up as a temporary stage. Soon teachers arrived too. The tall teacher who led the morning exercises went to the front and announced,

"Good morning, everyone". He paused and the audience quieted down quickly.

"My name is Jia-xin. I am your sports teacher, and we met already early this morning".

"Today we gathered here for our school opening ceremony. Now please join me to welcome the Principal of Yangjia High School to address the ceremony". There was applause.

Behind the desk, sat an old man, probably over 60. He put on his glasses and cleared his throat.

"Goo⋯d morning, every⋯one", he started speaking in a slow tone and a deep voice.

"Today, is the first day of the class 1973. Welcome to Yangjia High School!" Applause. Then he continued.

"You may be wondering where the previous year's students are. They graduated two months ago. We are a new school, established two years ago. We did not have new students last year. Therefore, you are the second group in this school."

He continued with quite a long speech, from the current politics and the changes in the nation-wide education system, to the school rules, courses, etc. Eventually, he introduced two teachers as the head teachers 班主任 (*ban zhu-ren*), Teacher Sun for class one and another teacher for class two.

26. Classes and Dedicated Teachers 课程和尽职的老师 (*kecheng he* jinzhi de *laoshi*)

After the ceremony, Teacher Sun led the whole class into the classroom which was also dedicated to class one for self study when no class was in session in the room. They brought the benches back too. On the way when Yu-fang was close, Dai-shan wanted to ask her something but didn't know what to say and only said "Hi".

"Hi, Dai-shan. When did you get to school?" she asked.

"Yesterday afternoon, through the mountain trail with

two friends. How ⋯ how about you?"

"I arrived quite late yesterday afternoon".

"Oh, that's why I didn't see you around yesterday".

Yu-fang lived in the same Dadui but in a different village, at least 3 kilometers further into the gully from Hongxing Junior high and it would take her longer to walk to the high school, unless she got a ride on a tractor.

"Let's get in the classroom now", she followed up.

Inside the classroom, there were a few rows of desks, a bench behind each desk, with a corridor in the middle of the room. The seats in the center and front were already taken.

Although seats were not preassigned, students normally wanted to seat close to the front to better hear what the teacher was saying. To Dai-shan, any seat would be the same and he had no interest in striving to find a better seat. Dai-shan just chose one at the back of the room.

When they all entered the classroom, Teacher Sun went to the front desk and announced:

"Please sit down everyone. I'm Teacher Sun, your English teacher and also the head teacher of your class. We will be together for the next two years. When you have any questions or concerns from now on, you can come to see me".

"First, there is a CYL branch 共青团支部 (*gongqing tuan zhibu*) in Yangjia high school. *Hu-chou*, a student in our class, is the CYL branch secretary 团支部书纪 (*tuan zhibu shuji*)".

A tall skinny student stood up with a big smile on his pumpkin seed-shaped face and nodded to the class. Teacher Sun continued:

"After discussions with other teachers, we have selected a class committee for class one based on their individual political status and past school experience. The class committee is comprised of:

"Liu *Banzhang*, class leader 班长 (*Banzhang*), and the following members:

"Zhong-lin, in charge of CYL affairs 团支部委员 (*tuan zhibu weiyuan*),

"Ben-xue, in charge of study issues 学习委员 (*xuexi weiyuan*),

"*Yue-ben*, in charge of physical exercises 体育委员 (tiyu *weiyuan*),

"Yu-fang, in charge of arts and musical activities 文艺委员 (*wenyi weiyuan*).

"If there is any issue in class, please bring it to the class committee". Teacher Sun continued with an introduction to the curriculum, the courses, and teachers.

The condensed two-year high school curriculum included the following courses:

Chinese literature, 语文 (*yuwen*), by Teacher Liu.

Mathematics, 数学 (*shuxue*), by Teacher Cheng.

Physics, 物理 (*wuli*), by Teacher Chen-ju.

Chemistry, 化学 (*huaxue*), by Teacher Huang.

English, 英语 (*yingyu*), by Teacher Sun.

Current Politics, 政治 (*zhengzhi*) and History, 历史 (*lishi*), by the principal.

Sports, 体育 (*tiyu*), by Teacher Jian-xin.

The sports class was for learning basic skills and doing exercises. Most courses lasted for the whole two years, while some continued only for one year.

At the end, Teacher Sun announced:

"We will have a course representative 课代表 (*ke daibiao*) in each of the core courses. … and Dai-shan will be for the English course". At that moment, Dai-shan was a little surprised as he was not prepared to play any role as a course representative, nor had he expected to be selected.

"What am I supposed to do?" he asked the teacher afterwards.

"As a course representative, you just need to collect assignments, distribute them after I have marked, collect feedback from students, and help with things related to the course".

"I probably can do that", he thought.

After the class, a junior high schoolmate walked over and teased at him: "Hi, Dai-shan, 朝中有人好做官，呃？(*chaozhong youren hao zuo guan, eh*). It meant literally; it would be easier for someone to become an officer if he/she knows someone in the upper level".

"What is that supposed to mean?" Dai-shan protested. Like everyone else, he didn't know anyone in the school or in the class committee. That student just gave him a smile and made a face before walking away.

"Oh, dear", he probably meant Yu-fang, the only person from Hongxing Junior high in the class committee. "Could they possibly know what is in my mind?" Dai-shan wondered. "But that is not possible", he thought.

Dedicated teachers 尽职的老师（*jinzhi de laoshi*）

Math, Physics and English were Dai-shan's favorite subjects. The math teacher was Teacher Cheng, a tall and handsome middle-aged man. It was said he had been teaching math in another high school before coming here. He knew the subject very well and his teaching was good. Dai-shan had no difficulty in the class and just like before in Junior high, he was always at the top of the class, even did much better in many exams than the *xuexi weiyuan* 学习

197

委员, who often became jealous. Dai-shan quickly became known to the teacher.

Physics was taught by Teacher Chen-Ju, a middle-aged man, who spoke and walked in a proud and elegant way. Students often called him Teacher Ju. He had also taught in another high school before coming here and was certainly knowledgeable about physics. However, students often had difficulty grasping the concept. Some people commented that he should be teaching in a university with his complex explanations. To teach high school students, he needed to make the complex subject easier to understand. However, Dai-shan had no difficulty in his class. Teacher Ju probably knew the physics teacher Sun in Hongxing junior high as he seemed to know Dai-shan well from the start.

One day Teacher Ju was teaching the concept of the three-phase alternating electric power. There was 120° delay in each phase current. Unfortunately, there was no physics laboratory for any hands-on experiments. There was no basic tool to demonstrate the power phases alternating and it was not easy for everyone to understand. Teacher Ju asked Dai-shan if he could help put together some demonstrative device to show each phase current following a sine wave with a phase delay. They discussed how to do it and used wires and light bulbs to build a demonstration device.

The English teacher Sun was surely happy to have a student like Dai-shan in his class. At that time, the education system was gradually getting back to normal after the disruption of the cultural revolution. However, the "door" of China was still tightly closed to the outside world. Learning a foreign language was promoted but it was hard to see its direct use in real life, particularly in rural areas. Many students were learning it just because it was a required course. However, Dai-shan, as mentioned before, wanted to learn whatever he could, to maximize the opportunity and not to waste any time. He spent time on memorizing new English vocabulary every morning and he liked the new language. The only thing which was lacking was the opportunity to speak and listen to native English speakers.

The Chinese literature teacher was Mr. Liu, a very quiet person, who was not tall but looked strong, and always had a slight smile on his face. He never seemed to socialize with anyone more than he needed to, or to greet anyone on the way. He went straight from his bedroom to the classroom and vice versa everyday. His behaviour certainly got the attention of students. It turned out that he was from a Di-zhu family somewhere out of the county, part of the enemy class in those days. Apparently, he was trying to protect himself by not saying anything. However, he was very talkative in class, but it was limited to the textbook's content.

At a later time, when he noticed that Dai-shan was on the top of the class in other courses, but not in his course, he asked to meet Dai-shan in his room after reviewing his assignment, which was to write an essay.

"Your essay was very short. You need to expand more. I heard you did well in other courses, why not in this course?" he asked softly.

"Sorry, Teacher Liu. I tried, but I really didn't know what to write and how to write".

"Writing an essay is just like making a speech. Write more when you have more words to say. Write less when you don't have much to say. Not too much, not too little, but enough to make your point clear". He tried to inspire

Dai-shan. It sounded easy but it was not as simple to do. Dai-shan attempted to follow his advice.

The school principal taught the Current Politics 政治 (*zhengzhi*) and History 历史 (*lishi*) over the two years. This old man was probably used to making long speeches in mass meetings, a typical phenomenon during the cultural revolution period. He did the same in the classroom, in a slow tone, word-by-word. During the course of Politics, he would read a bit in the newspaper or a document and explain for a whole hour until the class was over. Or let the class discuss what it meant or implied, and how to follow it. Dai-shan disliked that course but had no choice but to attend and participate.

What gave Dai-shan the biggest impression by this teacher was the History course. They had a textbook, a thick book over 300 pages. In the first class, the teacher started reading the Preface and within the first paragraph these two characters appeared: 悠久 (*youjiu*), meaning "long long time".

"Ah-ha! This is so right", The principal said as he got excited. "We have a very long history. I can spend the whole semester just explaining these two characters".

That was what he did exactly! He started explaining and expanding on the two characters, from the invention of writing paper 纸 (*zhi*) to the printing technology using a movable typing system – assembling individual characters 活字印刷 (*huozi yinshua*), and to the steam engine 蒸汽机 (*zhengqiji*). When the semester was over, they had not turned the book to chapter one!

"As I said at the beginning, our history was very long. More detail is given in the textbook. You are encouraged to read more". He then ended the class.

Continuing to excel 成绩继续领先 *(chengji jixu lingxian)*

In high school with dedicated teachers and better teaching facilities, Dai-shan did not waste time and continued studying hard. As before, he never missed a class unless he was very ill. He would normally preview the new contents before class, and he always completed assignments on time, with a full understanding of the subject. During exams, he usually achieved over 95%, sometimes 100%, ranking at the top of the two classes, except in Chinese literature where he was generally in the middle of the class.

Very soon, students knew him, and teachers noticed him. Most fellow students congratulated him for his achievement and admired him. He got along well with most students and all of his roommates. However, not all students were like that. The *xuexi weiyuan* - a class committee member in charge of study issues, was one. He probably had done very well in his junior high and was the center among his peers. When he did not rank at the top in an exam, he could not accept that he was no longer the "best". He would try harder and after a few times ranking behind, he became upset. He was jealous of others who did better and often make sarcastic comments. Dai-shan just ignored his behavior and was not bothered by him at all.

One day, Dai-shan's roommate, Gong-hua, the "richer kid" who was average in the class, returned to the bedroom with excitement. "You know what, guys?" He couldn't wait to share what was in his mind.

"What?" someone asked.

"I happened to hear our teachers commenting on our roommate, Dai-shan and another student, *Zhan-hui*. They both came from Hongxing Junior high".

"What about?" Another one asked.

"Our teachers were in a meeting. The math teacher, physics teacher and chemistry teacher all agreed that Dai-shan was the best in our grade of the two classes. They also said Zhan-hui sometimes was faster but could make mistakes. Dai-shan on the other hand was fast and seldom made mistakes. Overall, he is considered the top student, with the best chance to go to university. "

"Well done, Dai-shan" his friends congratulated.

You may think that if a student had a good academic achievement, he would be able to go to university easily.

Well, not necessarily. It may be true in normal situations these days, but not at that time in China. It was still the middle of the Cultural Revolution. Abnormal things were normal in those days. Universities were suspended shortly after 1966, and many had gradually just started recruiting new students. The entrance criteria were however not based on the academic merits, but on the "public opinions" and the perceived behavior. To be eligible, one must support the CP and socialism, be born in a good family (not in the enemy categories), be able to pass political assessment and to be recommended by the local authorities. The academic achievement was not that important. All those criteria were actually within the control of the local authority, mostly the person in charge directly! Therefore, it was one person's decision in many cases.

Dai-shan remembered very well: One day when they were chatting in their dormitory about their futures after graduation, finding a good job, doing something interesting, or going to university which was basically a remote hope. Just at that moment, *Hu-chou*, the CYL branch secretary walked in, with a big smile on his face as usual.

He was around average academically in the class, but was a big "red" star politically, meeting all the above criteria. He joined the conversation immediately,

"Hi you guys. If there is anyone that will go to university in our class, that will be me first. If I can't, none of you will even have a chance." Although the way he said it was arrogant and self flattering, the tone he used was not annoying. It was honest and what he said was probably true in the environment of that time. Despite the fact that nobody liked it, he was right based on the above criteria and the university recruiting policy at that time. But Dai-shan was never discouraged by such a thing. He always thought that as long as you had real knowledge, it would be useful someday, somewhere.

27. The Memorable Times 那些可回忆的日子 (naxi ke huiyi de rizi)

It's seemingly an ordinary thing for someone to go to high school. For Dai-shan, it meant a huge difference. In the short two years, he learned a lot and became much more knowledgeable. He had more confidence for life in the future. During that period, there were lots of memorable times.

It was routine for him to go to school on Sunday afternoon, carrying a load of raw food on his back, plus dried pickles his mother had prepared for him. Sometimes, he walked through the main road, passing by the Longsheng market and his elementary school, for a distance of approximately 10 km. Sometimes, he walked via the mountain trail with his friends. The latter was slightly shorter but not as easy to walk. The food he brought with him was expected to last until Friday. On Friday afternoons after the last class, he and his buddies would walk back home, sometimes arriving home quite late, especially in the winter.

On one Sunday afternoon, Dai-shan and his buddy Ye-zhong were on the way to school, passing by the Longsheng market. It was just about the time for people to go back home after selling and buying for the day. They saw an older man striving to push a *banche* 板车 with a full load of logs[52] on it, while another young man pulled it hard up a small hill. They immediately went up to give them a hand and pushed it up the small hill.

"Thank you so much, young men", the old man said. "No problem", they replied.

The voice sounded familiar. They looked at him, "Lin *shifu* (the Chef in the high school) ? It is you. Are you going to build a new house with the logs?"

"Oh, you two look familiar. You are in Yangjia High school, right? What are your names?"

"Yes, I'm Dai-shan", "I'm Ye-zhong".

"Right, we are going to build a new house. Oh, this is my son." Chef Lin introduced the young man in the front. "See you in school." He continued.

They didn't expect to see the chef there, but they felt good after helping him. A few days later, at lunch time Dai-shan waited in line to buy cooked veggies. Chef Lin had sharp eyes and a good memory and immediately recognized Dai-shan when it was his turn.

"Give me your cup, young man", he said and gave him

---

[52] In those days, it was not possible to buy pre-shaped lumbers but only logs on the market.

a big scoop of veggies, almost twice as much as to others. You can imagine how happy he was as he couldn't afford to buy vegetables for every meal.

As mentioned before, there was good spring water in the *Yangjia* river 河 (*he*) just beside the school. Like many other students, Dai-shan often took his clothes down to the river to wash them with other students. He watched and learned how to wash his own clothes. He would wash clothes before going home on the weekend. You may wonder why he didn't take them back home to wash. First, his village was short of water in the spring season and the water quality was incomparable with the water in the *Yangjia* river. Besides, he thought he was old enough to take care of himself and should not pass the chore onto his mother anymore. There was no washing machine at home either.

Just a few steps away from the school's main entrance, there was a barber shop. He charged 2 *mao* 毛 (1 mao = 10 fens) and 5 fens to cut someone's hair. As rural students, many didn't have that kind of spare money. Students would usually help each other cut their hair to save money. The outcome might not be perfect, but it served the purpose.

However, no matter how capable a person is, you can't cut your own hair, right? Guess what? That barber just did that. Dai-shan saw him cutting his own hair when there was no customer around. He placed two mirrors facing each other and cut his own hair while watching both mirrors. It might not be easy, but he managed to do it, saving 2 *mao* 5 *fens*.

During his spare time, Dai-shan also learned how to

play Chinese chess 象棋 (*xiangqi*) . There was another student, named Guang-cai, from Jinji junior high. His family background was quite similar to Dai-shan's. They were about the same age and similar in height. Guang-cai was probably the master chess player in their class. Dai-shan tried to learn from him, but he often teased Dai-shan, "For you, I would only need half of my chess pieces". They got along well. They often discussed things beyond school subjects. They managed to maintain their friendship for quite some time after graduation.

As a stopgap in a music band 乐队里 "滥竽充数[53]" (*yuedui li "lanyu chongshu"*)

Dai-shan got along very well with all his roommates including Yue-gong and Gong-hua, the latter two who spent all their times together. After some time, Dai-shan also became friends with them.

This started with Yue-gong, who played the violin. Although he stayed in their bedroom, often he went back to have meals with his parents, who lived on the campus just 2 buildings away. Dai-shan gradually started visiting him in his parents' residence as his friend. Although his parents did not teach any courses to Dai-shan, they most likely heard about him and naturally would be happy to see their son socializing with this rural boy. Every time, when Dai-shan showed up at the door, his mother, Teacher Lu, who was teaching in an elementary school nearby, would greet him with a big smile, very enthusiastic, just like a kindergarten teacher meeting a kid.

Yue-gong's father appeared to be a knowledgeable and experienced scholar. However, he was not teaching but

---

[53] From a Chinese idiom, to make up numbers with unqualified.

helping in school administration and services. Dai-shan and some students wondered why. Dai-shan didn't want to ask. Later he learned that it had to do with his parents' family class (not considered as the people's friends). He was working in the Educational Bureau in *Jingdian* county and had been sidelined since the cultural revolution started. He was a talented man. He could play different musical instruments and do many things. Apparently, Yue-gong was influenced by his father.

Yue-gong often played his little violin in their bedroom after supper, which he said he spent ¥5 to purchase it in a second-hand store and repaired it himself. Nevertheless, it sounded like a violin and good music to Dai-shan.

Gong-hua played *er-hu* 二胡, a two-string instrument. There was another student in their class who also played the er-hu. From time to time, they three practiced in the room where Dai-shan was.

At first, Dai-shan was just watching and listening. One day, one of his friends said, "do you want to try it?"

"Oh no, I have never played and absolutely don't know how".

"I have a spare *er-hu*, you can borrow it and try", Yue-gong added. From then, Dai-shan started to learn playing the er-hu. With no exposure to musical instruments and no knowledge of music notes, it was not easy for him. The numbers 1, 2, 3, ⋯ were pronounced as *duo, lai, me,* ⋯ His fingers didn't cooperate properly, and he often played the wrong tune. Well, it was fine as it was just for fun.

Not sure what triggered this next idea. One day, Yue-gong said the school wanted to organize a band, which would include the cello, violin and er-hu to start. Yue-gong would play the violin, and his father would fill in to play the cello, Gong-hua and another classmate would play the *er-hu*. Now there were four of them. They wanted to have at least five members to make up the band. After some thoughts, they decided to include Dai-shan.

"But I'm not good enough to play in the band," Dai-shan worried.

"Don't worry, we are just practicing and having fun. Even on the stage, all you need to do is to move your bow by following the others. It would be hard for others to hear your playing anyway".

Dai-shan managed to learn the basics and movements of his bow and practiced a couple of pieces of music. One day, he was told that they were going to join other bands in a musical show.

"Now I am really a stopgap, just like Mr. *lan-guo* 滥郭[54]". Dai-shan thought. "But I'm not pretending, I'm learning too".

He practiced the music they were supposed to play. Eventually, he was able to manage most of the music. Whether his performance was good or not was a different story. He joined the band in the show, but he sat at the rear where the audience could hardly see him.

He tried. However, he did not become a good *er-hu* player.

Hard to read her mind 难猜透她的心 (nang caitou ta de xin)

During the two years of high school, Dai-shan was

---

[54] The king of the Qi kingdom loved listening Yu(flute) music played in ensemble with 300 musicians and treated them well. Nan-guo who had no skill on the instrument but wanted the treat. He managed to convince the King and joined the ensemble, but he could only pretend playing.

could provide him some hope for a better definitely happy because of the opportunity to learn, future. There was also another reason: the girl he knew since Hongxing junior high, was also in the same class. He felt good just being around her, but he was not sure exactly how she felt about him. It might be just in his head. He didn't want to find out because he knew he was not in a position to provide her with what she deserved. He didn't want to think what outcome it might lead to in the end. He was just happy to be able to see her. On both ways to school and back home every week, he was often hoping to bump into her and walk with her. But he didn't really have much of a chance because they lived in different villages. She sometimes might get a ride on a tractor or other vehicle. Nevertheless, he was happy to see her in school almost everyday. There were some days he didn't see her in class due to illness, which would worry him, and he would try to find out.

One evening, after supper, as usual, he took his books to the classroom for self-study. He saw at a distance Yu-fang and another girl sitting at the door of the classroom. His first instinct told him to go there to say hello to her. However, before he could get close, he hesitated because of the presence of another girl. He didn't know what to say to the two of them. But he was so close by that point, he couldn't just walk away. Then he quickly remembered that the teacher told them about an up-coming regional sports competition and the need for volunteers. That might be a potential conversation topic. He walked close to them, trying to remain calm.

"Hello. You two are here to study too", he managed to start the conversation.

"Yes, and you too", Yu-fang replied.

He was trying to say something more but didn't know how. She noticed and asked, "Dai-shan, do you want to say something else?"

"Oh, I'm just wondering if you know more about the volunteer thing the teacher mentioned to us today."

"Oh, that," she paused for a few seconds and said, "You probably should not let that distract you from your studies". She said sincerely.

"Ya, Okay". He felt he had completed the mission and turned around, about to walk away. Then he heard the other girl saying:

"Yoooh, Yu-fang. (You) have started to protect him already 开始护着他啦 (*kaishi huzhe ta la*)?"

"What are you talking about. Nothing like that", Yu-fang protested.

Dai-shan tried to understand the two girls' conversation. "I don't need anyone to protect me", he thought. "Was she, really?" "Nothing like WHAT?"

Whatever they implied in their conversation made him feel a little embarrassed, but he felt really good too in his heart, at least based on what he understood.

"Oh, I should go to study now", Dai-shan said, not sure whether to himself or to the two girls and walked into the classroom. After that day, he thought about her more often. However, whenever he was trapped in his thinking, he constantly reminded himself: learning was his paramount goal at that time.

It needs to be pointed out that in those days, dating among students was not allowed while they were in school. There would be serious consequences if caught, being expelled from the school in the worst case. Well, humans, just like other animals, grow up naturally. When they reach a certain age, they behave the way they are naturally supposed to. Therefore, if a boy and a girl were attracted to each other, they would try to make connections and date in secret. When they reached the last semester of high school, some couples would no longer hide it, and other students would not pay much attention to them anymore. Dai-shan was probably a late bloomer in that sense, or a self-conscious boy who knew what his priorities were. Hhis interest in Yu-fang was probably his wishful thinking. He didn't follow through with it and never had a real date with her, or any time being with her alone.

28. Assembling a Dual Band Radio 组装了一台 2 波段收音机
(ta zuzhuang le yitai liang boduan shouyinji)

During his two years in high school, Dai-shan also explored the radio venture further and accomplished something he never could have dreamed possible. It was all attributed to his roommate Yue-gong's father. He was a talented "handy man", and radio repairing was his hobby. When Dai-shan entered his residence with Yue-gong for the first time, he noticed various radio gadgets lying on the table. Apparently, he was fixing something.

"That is my father's hobby. He repairs radio at his free time". Yue-gong explained.

Dai-shan got excited. When he saw Yue-gong's father working on something, he would get close to watch for a while and ask him questions when he could. One day, he mentioned his attempt to build a radio with a diode and the problem of weak signal and high noises he encountered and asked for his advice.

"Radio signals are very weak in the air, especially in mountainous areas. You need a better circuit design to amplify the signal and to filter the noises." He explained.

211

Then he showed Dai-shan a typical circuit diagram, showed him how to properly lay out different electronic elements and how to solder them together. He even let Dai-shan practice soldering on his used elements.

With more knowledge of the radio and a better understanding of the circuits, Dai-shan decided to try it again. During the summer break that year, he went to the electronic store in the county and bought more components as required, including transistors, resisters, and capacitors, etc.

He also managed to find a thin wooden board, manually cut it to the proper size using an old hand saw, drilled holes with a hand drill wherever suitable for buttons and nailed them together to make a radio box. He used another piece of board as the "mother board" to install all the elements on.

With the radio book he bought before, he started assembling again, from the antenna to the speaker, step-by-step, and soldered all the components following the circuit. After a few times of trials, adjustments and tests, he got it to work - he had made a radio, a medium waveband radio! Now he could listen to the People's Central Broadcasting Station (PCPS). That was one of the very few stations which could be easily picked up in the area.

That was certainly something new in the village too. When people heard talking and singing on the radio, they dropped by to see and listen.

"My father bought us a radio a long time ago, but it stopped working. Can I bring it here for you to repair it for me please?" One kid asked. His father was working out of town somewhere and would be the only person in the village who could afford to buy a radio in those days.

"Well, I can't promise anything. But I will be happy to take a look sometime". Dai-shan replied.

The kid brought his radio to Dai-shan very shortly after. Dai-shan carefully opened the box and gently checked every element to see if anything had come loose. It turned out to be an easy fix. He found that one battery wire had fallen off. After soldering it back, the radio started working again. The mother of that kid came by with 10 eggs to thank Dai-shan for the help. "Oh, no. I can't take them. It happened to be a small problem. Otherwise, I would not have been able to do anything either".

After that, as you can guess, by word of mouth, some people from even other villages would come to ask Dai-shan for help with radios. But he could only do what he could with his resources. School was restarting soon, and he had to go back.

At a later time, Dai-shan upgraded his radio onto two wavebands by adding a short waveband magnetic rod and other elements. That increased the receiving range of the radio, and he could listen to other stations from further away.

Warning on secretly listening to enemy stations 警告偷听敌台 *(jinggao touting ditai)*

Dai-shan now had a short-wave radio and could receive signals from many more stations, even from far away. It was no longer a secret. The news soon spread to the local law enforcement officer 治安员 *(zhi-an yuan)*.

When Dai-shan was at home one weekend, his mother told him one morning, "Dai-shan, the officer is here to see you". He came out of his room and saw Officer Yi, who lived in the village down the hill, just about 10 minutes away. They knew each other.

"Hi, officer Yi. Welcome and please take a seat", he offered a bench to him and continued, "You seldom visit us. What brings you here?"

Officer Yi smiled and said, "I heard that you made a radio and can listen to stations from far away."

"Oh, yes. It's a two-waveband radio. The medium waveband can hear the People's Central Broadcasting Station and the People's Broadcasting Station of Duotong province. The short waveband sometimes can hear other stations, like the People's Broadcasting Station of the *Zhongdu-fu*". Dai-shan explained and knew why Officer Yi was here, and he continued, "But the signal is not good, often not clear at all".

"Well, I wanted to warn you that the policy is very tight these days. Anyone listening to enemy stations 敌台 (*ditai*) may face serious punishment". He made his point and said, "Just be careful".

What was that about? In those days, the governments were calling for class struggle 阶级斗争 (*jieji douzheng*), making people fight against one another internally and everyone was on high alert all the time. The whole nation was in a tightly sealed box and citizens were not allowed to know what was going on outside the country. They were told, except for few communist countries (like USSR, North Korea and Cuba), every other country was China's enemy. Communicating with enemies was a crime and would be subject to severe punishment.

It was said that during those years, a few superpowers including the United States and United Kingdom, plus Taiwan all set up powerful far reaching broadcasting stations surrounding China, such as, "The voice of America 美国之音 (*meiguo zhiyin*)", "BBC" and "The voice of Free China 自由中国之声 (*ziyou zhongguo zhisheng*, from Taiwan)". All of those stations were labeled as enemy stations. They had programs in Chinese language with many relay stations basically covering the entire country and targeting Chinese people. The Chinese government knew all about it and set up powerful anti-broadcasting stations with the exact same radio frequencies to interfere. People were forbidden from listening to those enemy stations.

As you can imagine, no one dared to openly listen to those stations. But people were curious, thirsty for news and eager to know what was happening outside of the county. There was a lack of personal earphone those days. Some would listen at night with the volume turned very low, just enough to hear at their ears when there was no one else around. It **was** a secret action, labeled "secretly listening to enemy stations 偷听敌台" (*touting ditai*).

Dai-shan tried his short waveband. Sometimes he was able to hear the Voice of America (from USA), from which he could also learn English, and the Voice of Free China (from Taiwan). The former appeared more factual, but the latter was a strong anti-communist station against the CP government. Based on the reputation of the old Chinese government, not many people would believe the Taiwan station, but the USA station was preferred. However, under that tight policy, Dai-shan didn't want to take that chance and restrained himself from listening to those stations.

29. Graduation Farewell 毕业告别 (*biye gaobie*)

Two years of high school passed quickly, and it soon was the summer of 1975. Dai-shan had finished high school. They had final exams in every course. For better or for worse, the exam results alone would be their final record of their high school grades.

That was it. On the last day, students were all packed up with their belongings and prepared to walk out of the school campus. They had a strange feeling. They had been together everyday over the past two years and didn't have that kind of feeling before. Maybe, it would be a long time before they could see each other again. For some, they might never see each other anymore. For most students, it would be like that.

Realizing what would be ahead of them or not knowing what was ahead, many of them felt reluctant to depart. It was probably an unwritten tradition that they bought some presents with their hard saved money to give to each other, as a memory. Mostly they gave each other a book, a notebook, a pen, and some other things with more personal memories. After exchanging presents, they shook hands and said goodbye.

Surprisingly, Dai-shan received a book from Yu-fang, written by 鲁迅 (luxun), a famous author and literary critic before the 1940s. "Hope you study hard and be successful in the future", she added.

"I only have a notebook for you. I also wish you luck", he responded. But no hand shaking.

Dai-shan said farewell to the other students and teachers, and walked away from the campus, with Ye-zhong and Zhan-hui, and returned to his home village. Ye-zhong lived in the village down the hill and Zhan-hui in a village further into the gully a few kilometers away.

Their school time seemed to be finished for now.

Chapter 6

The Life of an Educated Home – Return Youth 一个回乡知青的经历

(*yige huixiang zhiqing de jingli*)

30. Returning to his Hometown 回到了家乡（huidao le jiaxiang）

After spending two years in Yangjia High School, Dai-shan returned to his home village in the summer of 1975 upon graduation. That was during the later stages of the Cultural Revolution. The nation was on its way back to normal but very slowly. People were still afraid of openly expressing their opinions, definitely not to openly complain about anything or say something against the government's policies. Universities appeared to be getting back to normal as well. However, new students were not being recruited on the basis of their academic merits but on the recommendation of the local authorities. Often, one single person in charge at the local authority could decide the fate of a youth.

Dai-shan was back to a time of wondering once again. With a high school graduation certificate, he was then the most educated person in Yao'sville, together with a dozen or so graduates in the Hongxing commune. At that time, there was still not much hope on the horizon. Like many other youths, he waited, while helping do some farm work.

Building a biogas chamber 建一个沼气池 （jian yige zhaoqi chi）

During that period of time, villagers were encouraged to build a home biogas facility as a source of fuel. The major component was a large, sealed composting chamber, which could be a variety of sizes, shapes and types of construction. In his village, every option seemed too expensive, and the most common chamber would be a sealed underground pit. However, the soil was very shallow and the bedrock was sandstone. A pit would then be constructed in the sandstone.

Construction of a pit in sandstone at that time was a manual endeavor and hard work. There was no drilling or excavating equipment. It was all manual work and would require the use of a hand chisel and a hammer to break the stone

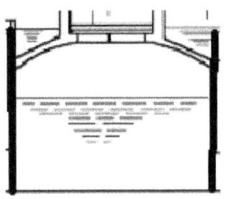

biogas chamber illustration

in the ground, one piece at a time. It would take a few weeks or months to construct an underground pit. The pit had to be sealed all around with a layer of cement paste and on the top with stone slabs to form a compost chamber.

Thereafter, the chamber must be filled with fresh weeds, grass, other organic materials and water. On top of the chamber cover, a small hole was drilled to fit a plastic tube which would run all the way to the kitchen. After a few days' composition, biogas (Methane, CH_4) was supposed to produce, which could be used for cooking, a way like that of a propane stove is used today.

Dai-shan had been thinking about building one for his family. One reason was to save on other fuel material because they normally used dried grass, hay and the remaining parts of crops for cooking. Another reason he had in mind was to help reduce his mother's chores she bore all the time. He told his parents the idea. His mother was happy to hear it but was unsure if that was possible for the family. His father liked the idea but thought it was just a dream, and said "It sounded good, but is not possible for us." His father never tried to do anything beyond his capacity and thought to it was too much trouble.

"I'm going to build one for us", Dai-shan answered.

"You?" His father seemed half surprised and half skeptical.

After returning home from high school, many of his classmates had the same unsettled feeling. His chess master friend, Guang-cai who lived in Jinji commune, wrote to Daishan by mail that he couldn't just stay home and felt like going somewhere or doing something to clear his mind. Well, where could they go? Cities were too far and too expensive. Besides, people were still not free to go anywhere they wanted to. The only possible option was to go from village to village to see the natural scenery. But that was not what they had in mind because they had grown up in that environment and didn't see it as interesting. Then, Dai-shan said to him, "Why don't you come help me build a biogas chamber?"

"What is that? It sounds interesting". He wanted to know more.

Believe it or not, a few days later, he showed up at the doorstep of Dai-shan's home.

"I can't believe it, you really came? " Dai-shan was surprised to see him. "How did you get here?"

"I took a bus and got off down the hill and asked how to get to your home. It was not difficult at all. And here I am. I thought I would give you a hand and wanted to see how it works".

Dai-shan explained the principle and the construction work his neighbors had done. These two recent high school graduates, instead of doing something related to what they had learned in school, started doing masonry work, chiseling the sandstone in the ground to build an underground biogas chamber. The selected site was about 30 meters away at a higher elevation behind his clay-built house.

There were a few inches of sandy soil on the top and the rest was reddish sandstone underneath. They removed the topsoil and drew a circle of approximately 2m diameter on the bedrock. The top part was weathered and easy to break using a chisel and a hammer. It became harder further down. The work was not easy.

They first chiseled a 4" wide channel at the boundary as deep as the chisel could reach, one hammer a time. They made two to three wedge-shaped holes along a line, put metal wedges in them and used a larger hammer to drive the wedges in sequence into the  stone little by little. When the wedges were in the stone, they started inducing a fracture along the line and eventually broke off a slice of stone.

They practiced and worked hard. After separating the stone, they had to break it into small pieces, and hoist the stone up to the surface, with one person in the pit to load using a hoe and a bucket, and another at the surface to lift it up with a string and two hands. That was not an easy task for the two new graduates. They both had a backache and sore muscles after the first day.

Cousin *Dong-wu*, the 2nd child of Dai-shan's mother's 2nd elder sister, didn't even have the chance to complete elementary school and had stayed home as a child laborer ever since he was young. When he heard Dai-shan and his classmate were building a biogas chamber, he came to help. He was almost always there to help whenever Dai-shan needed him. Cousin Dong-wu was strong and he probably did as much work as Da-shan and his classmate combined. Dai-shan's father also lent a hand after finishing work in the farming Group 生产队 (*sheng-chan dui*).

As they went deeper, they made the circle bigger each

time. The chamber would be a concaved drum shape rather than a vertical cylinder.

After a few weeks of their hard work, a pit of approximately 2.5m deep and a little over 2m diameter was constructed in the sandstone. They then sealed the top with stone slabs, left an entrance for adding materials and fitted with a plastic tube. Dai-shan appreciated the help of his friend and his cousin. Without them, he would probably never have been able to complete the chamber.

The next challenge was to fill the chamber with organic material and water. Water could only be available after a heavy rain. So, they had to wait. After the rain, he and his father collected water from various dug-water pits in the fields with wooden pails, carried them on their shoulders and poured the water into the chamber until it was almost full. They collected a variety of green grass and weeds to fill it in. Oh, home food wastes would have been an excellent material, but they were always kept for feeding pigs.

After the hard work, the biogas facility was complete. His mother was certainly happy and couldn't wait to use it. A few days later, it did produce some biogas CH_4, and his mother used it for some light cooking using a tin pot. She had a big smile on her face and was hoping to use it for more.

However, there was no extra gas for lighting. The production and sustainability of a biogas facility highly depended on the continuous supply of new organic materials. After a few days, his mother told him; she couldn't complete the cooking when the gas flame went out. Dai-shan went to the chamber site to check it out and found that the gas was depleted already in the chamber. More new materials must be added to rejuvenate gas production, or they would have to wait for more gas. That was a continuous endeavor.

Apparently, the chamber needed to be cleaned periodically to remove the old material debris and be refilled with new material. That again was not an easy task. It was probably the need for continuously feeding with new organic material and removing old material that posed the biggest challenge in biogas production. Many biogas facilities in his village and other places in the surrounding area produced less and less gas and eventually ceased to work one to two years later. In the whole village, only one or two families kept their biogas chamber working for another one to two years, primarily because they had more laborers to collect organic material to feed their chambers. But eventually, they all stopped producing gas due to the same reasons.

Orchard assistant 橘园帮手 (guoyuan bangshou)

Summer passed quickly and Autumn came. It was harvesting time, one of the busiest seasons for farmers. In Dai-shan's village, more than a hundred mandarin orange trees were planted some years ago and they all had become mature fruiting trees, producing plenty of large, sweet, juicy mandarin oranges. Each fruit was hand picked with scissors and carefully sorted by size, wrapped with white soft paper and put in wooden boxes before being shipped out to cities and sometimes even exported.

After harvesting, the primary work in the field was maintenance and preparation for the next season.

In the orchard, to keep the trees producing well every year, continuous maintenance work was needed. It included supplying fertilizer and plenty of water in the Spring and pruning after harvesting. The work in the Spring required all man-laborers in the village but pruning was technical work for a trained person only. His cousin Dong-wu was the orchard technician in the village.

"What do you plan to do now?" Dong-wu asked Dai-shan one day.

"No plan yet. Not sure really", Dai-shan replied. Although he had grown up more now, he was small in size and heavy labor work, like carrying a heavy load of water up steep hill trails, was still a challenge for him.

"It's time to prune the orange trees now. Maybe you can help me", Dong-wu suggested.

"But that's skilled work and I'm not trained for it".

"Oh, that's easy. I can show you how. As a high school graduate, you would have no difficulty learning it. I will tell *duizhang* 队长 (the production team captain) that we are going to start tomorrow".

The *duizhang* was Dong-wu's uncle. He was the one who assigned work to everyone everyday and would announce it everyday loudly to tell them what the work was and who was to do what.

"Time to go to work now 出…工…喽… (*chu-gong-low*) ", the *duizhang* shouted out in front of his home the next morning. He would do it three times a day, early in the morning, after breakfast and after lunch.

"Men 男…的… (*nan-de*), to carry compost to the field 挑干瀵 (*tiao-gan-fen*) today.

"Women 女…的… (*nu-de*), to clean sand deposits in the pits 挑沙凼 (*tiao-sha-dang*) in the field".

Since most of the farming fields in the area were not flat and had some slope, the rainwater in the summer carried soil/sand downward and deposited it at a small dug-pit at lower 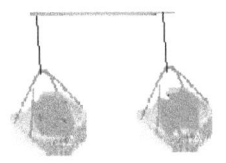 spot. These deposits needed to be removed from the pits and replaced at the higher spots in the field to make room for the next season. It was all manual work with hoes and bamboo-made soil pans 土撮箕 (*tu cuo-ji*) to be carried by shoulder. This was repetitive work, moderately labor intensive.

The *duizhang* would usually be the first one to go with a few older men and the rest followed.

Dong-wu came over to Dai-shan's home with two pairs of pruning scissors and a high bench and they went to the orchard together. He gave Dai-shan instructions on the pruning principles:

"Cut the hidden (branches), but not the exposed ones 打阴不打阳 (*da-yin bu da yang*).

"Cut the ones hanging down, but not the upturned ones 打掉不打翘 (*da-diao bu da qiao*).

"Cut the weak, keep the strong 打弱不打强 (*da-ruo bu da qiang*).

"Avoid crowding, maintain balance all around 杜绝拥挤, 保持平衡 (*dujue yongji, baochi pingheng*).

"Remove the water sprouts, nutrition last long 铲除水苔, 保障营养 (*chanchu shuitai, baozhang yingyang*)".

Dong-wu then demonstrated on a tree and coached him on each step. That was where Dai-shan learned how to take care of fruit trees and he continued to use these skills throughout his life.

An unexpected day 意外的一天 (*Yicai de yitian*)

At that time, mass meetings in the Commune, Dai-dui and farming group were still routine for the government to educate the citizens on its policies. Dai-shan as a home-returning educated youth seemed to be obligated to attend. Sometimes, if a person was required to attend a meeting but didn't, he/she could get a punishment of negative *gongfen* 公分, meaning, a one-day's worth of gongfen would be deducted from what you earned before. Dai-shan would therefore usually go to the meetings, one reason was to avoid punishment, and another reason was to get connected to the "outside world".

One day, there was a commune level mass meeting 公社大会 (*gongshe dahui*) held in the commune complex down the hill. Each family was required to have a representative present. Dai-shan went to the meeting on behalf of the family because his father never understood what they were talking about anyway. There were approximately a few hundred attendees, filling up the courtyard in the complex.

Before the meeting started, the commune's leading authorities and the cadres 干部 (*ganbu*) in charge from each Dadui, including Uncle Hua (a distant uncle of Dai-shan, who lived next to his home) – the CP Branch secretary 党支部书记 (*dang zhibu shuji*) of *Alliance Dai-dui*, were on the stage having a small meeting.

Then the meeting started, as usual first a speech by the secretary of the CP Commune Council, followed by others. Dai-shan was in the middle of the crowd, hanging around some of his junior high classmates to catch up on things.

Before the meeting was finished, he saw Uncle Hua on the stage chatting with the vice secretary of the CP

Commune Council 公社党委副书记 (*gongshe dangwei fu shuji*), whom people customarily called Mayor Tan 谭乡长 (*tan xiangzhang*). They whispered to each other for a while and Mayor Tan seemed to look in the direction where Dai-shan was. Then Mayor Tan left the stage and walked towards where Dai-shan was.

Mayor Tan walked directly to him and asked,

"You are Dai-shan, right?"

"Yes, it's me, Mayor Tan", Dai-shan nodded.

"Come with me", Mayor Tan turned around and walked away. His classmates noticed and wondered what had just happened. So did Dai-shan. It was not normal for an official to talk to an ordinary young boy unless there was something going on. However, Dai-shan soon calmed himself down because he didn't do anything wrong nor said anything politically incorrect and the mayor's tone was friendly.

Dai-shan followed Mayor Tan, through the crowd to his office/residence room. There was a single wooden-framed bed covered by a mosquito net, a small desk and a single seat bamboo chair. Mayor Tan opened his desk drawer and took out a piece of paper and handed it over to Dai-shan,

"Please fill out this form and give it back to me".

Dai-shan took it and looked it, a blank registration form for the Commune cadres 公社干部登记表 (*gongshe ganbu dengji biao*). He was puzzled, wondering "What is this for? Does he need me to help with some clerk work or do a survey?" The mayor saw the expression on his face and explained,

"You knew, we established a mobile film projection team 移动电影放映队 (*yidong dianying fangying dui*) in our commune last year". Dai-shan nodded but was still puzzled.

"One of the members in the team is a *zhiqing*. He has recently received a transfer order to return to *Zhongdu-fu*. He is leaving in a couple of days and there is now a vacancy.

"We need an educated youth, better to be from our own commune and to be close to the commune complex for convenience in case needed.

"On the recommendation of the CP Branch secretary of *Alliance Dai-dui*, the CP Commune Council had a discussion on your qualifications and considered you as the best candidate to fill this position.

"Will you accept it?" The mayor asked at the end.

"I will, of course", Dai-shan quickly nodded again but still trying to follow what the mayor just said.

"Fill out this form and give it back to me before you leave the meeting today".

Dai-shan quickly filled the form with the required information,

Name: Yao, Dai-shan,

Age: 19,

Permanent residence address: Group #4, *Alliance Dai-dui*, Hongxing Commune,

Education: Yangjia High School graduate, 1975,

Birth family class: Middle Peasant,

Personal class: Peasant / educated- returning youth,

Political status: none,

Dai-shan completed the form, came out the room and handed it over to Mayor Tan who was still beside the door.

"Here it is, Mayor Tan".

Mayor Tan glanced through the form and said, "Good. The film team will come back to show a movie here tomorrow night. You will start tomorrow. Come here a little earlier and I will introduce you to the crew".

"Yes, I will be here on time. Thank you".

The mass meeting was not finished yet. Dai-shan walked back to the crowd with great excitement in his mind. Some of his classmates were still around.

"What did Mayor Tan ask you to do?" one asked.

"He wanted me to help fill a form", he replied as if it was nothing important and tried not to show the excitement on his face.

A pie fell from the sky 天上掉馅饼了 *(Tiānshàng diào xiànbing le)*

Wow, what a great news it was to Dai-shan! When he got home, he couldn't wait to tell his mother what had just happened. It was a day that could be the beginning of a big change in his life and in the future.

"Mama, I went to the mass meeting today and Mayor Tan told me that they wanted me to show movies". He couldn't hide his excitement in front of his mother.

"Which Mayor, the one from your *da-yi* 大姨 (eldest ant – his mother's eldest sister's) place?"

"That's him, from *Yingxiong* commune and he is the vice CP secretary of our commune. "

"Where, and to show what movie?" his mother was still unsure but curious.

"You knew that our commune now has a film projection team, and they go to various villages to show movies. We watched movies down the hill too. One of the people doing the work was a zhiqing and he is leaving for the city in two days. They want me to take over his work", he explained.

"Are you sure about this?" His mother wanted to make sure.

"Yes, I have already filled the form and will start tomorrow".

"Oh, then, we should thank Mayor Tan sincerely". His mother was very happy and mumbled this, unclear whether to Dai-shan or to herself.

Dai-shan remembered that he went to see his Da-yi a few times with his mother when he was very little but never knew any connection existed with Mayor Tan's family.

"He lived in the same village and was a distant nephew of your Da-yi fu (Da-yi's husband)", his mother explained.

In Chinese history, people always thought it would be easier for someone to get a good job or to be successful if he/she had connections with someone at a higher level, most often referring to a relative, a close friend, or a political alliance. That was called 人事关系 (*renshi guanxi*, meaning "social - political connections").

His mother was trying to make the connection. Otherwise, why would good things like this happen to her son?

"Mama, I have not seen Da-yi for many years. I don't think Mayor Tan knew us at all". Dai-shan reminded his mother. In his mind, it is unlikely it had anything to do with that.

"If anyone is to be thanked, it would probably be Uncle Hua", Dai-shan continued.

"He helped you get this job?" His mother wondered.

"I heard that he suggested my name and supported me for the job".

His father had come home by then. He was sure happy to hear it too. After so many years of school, the boy could finally do something now. He asked his mother if she had saved any eggs, which was the only valuable thing they had in those days.

His mother prepared 10 chicken eggs, which she had saved to sell so as to buy oil and daily supplies. She gave the eggs[55] to Dai-shan and asked him to take them to Uncle Hua to thank him. He had never done anything like that before and didn't know how and was very reluctant to.

His mother insisted, "if you don't want to go, I will. A person should learn to be thankful if someone gave you help".

Dai-shan went with his mother to see Uncle Hua in his home, just two houses away.

"Uncle Hua. We want to thank you very much for your help. Dai-shan got this job on the film team today, it was because of your help. We don't have many valuables. Here are some eggs. Please don't mind the small present". His mother said and started to hand over the eggs.

"Thank you very much, Uncle Hua", Dai-shan added.

"Oh, you don't need to do this, *yao-sho* 幺嫂 (the youngest sister in-law)", Uncle Hua replied. "It was all because Dai-shan was the best candidate and I only provided support. It just happened at the right time when all conditions were in his favor".

What Uncle Hua was saying referred to the three necessary elements in success 成事三要素 (*chéngshì sān yàosù*): the right time and opportunity 天时 (*Tiānshí*), the right place 地利 (*dìlì*), and the right people 人和 (*rénhé*). If any of the three elements was missing, you wouldn't be successful. Only when all three elements existed at the same time, would it be possible.

In those days, a job as a film projectionist was a very sought after position, not to mention watching movies was

---

[55] Unlike in the western countries where 12 eggs are packed as a dozen, the normal whole number was 10 in his place.

still a rare thing. Many people would try their best by all means to get the opportunity. There were many local young people who were in privileged positions and had connections to people at higher levels. There were more people who were richer when it came to giving presents or bribes. There were still other Zhiqing that came from cities who had connections at various levels. These Zhiqing were referred to as "sent-down Zhiqing 下乡知青 (xiaxiang Zhiqing)", while those returning to their hometown, like Dai-shan, were called "home-returning Zhiqing 回乡知青 (huixiang Zhiqing)". The former had many government privileges, while the latter had none and they were treated the same as other peasants.

When considering the whole pool of potential candidates in Hongxing commune for this job, Dai-shan would probably not be on the short list. In a "normal situation" of that time, he would not have had the chance to get that job at all. But he did. To him, it was really "a pie fell from the sky, right in his hands 天上掉下了一个馅饼 (Tiānshàng diàoxia le yige xiànbing), an unexpected gift. He never knew how he was selected for that job exactly.

Examining carefully the above three necessary elements, it became clear that:

The time was right, and the opportunity existed: a vacancy became available and Dai-shan had graduated from high school just at the right time, not too early, not too late. A person with adequate education was needed to fill the vacancy in the film team.

The place was right: the CP Commune Council wanted to have one of their own home-grown educated youths nearby for convenience and Dai-shan was a home-returning zhiqing and lived just 15 minutes away from the commune complex.

The right people also applied to Dai-shan: he had his high school education, with knowledge no less than those sent-down zhiqing from the cities; he was born locally and grew up there and would be more reliable for long-term stability of the movie team; Most importantly, he was the best in his class.

Adding all these elements together, it appeared that no one else was more qualified than him and he would automatically get that job, wouldn't he?

Not really. There was one more thing those days which could be the deal breaker: the power 权力 (quanli) and connections 关系 (guangxi), which Dai-shan did not have, during the decision-making process. But how did he get the job?

Let us dig deeper.

At that time, the secretary of the CP Commune Council 党委书记 (dangwei shuji – the number one in power) had a son in Dai-shan's junior high class, who graduated with a grade a little below the average; Another vice secretary of the same CP Council 党委副书记 (dangwei fu shuji) had a son who was about the same age as Dai-shan and had only just managed to finish junior high; A deputy secretary of the CP Council at a higher-level government had a younger brother, an average student, who had graduated from the same high school at the same time as Dai-shan.

In terms of academic record, none of the three candidates were comparable to Dai-shan. But who said it had to be the person with the highest grade to do that job? It was very common in those days for a person with much less qualification but more power and connections to be offered a position over a person with higher qualifications but with little or no connections.

Most likely, there were serious discussions behind the scenes. Maybe, just maybe, that was a compromise solution and Dai-shan happened to benefit from it. Or, that kind of "common" practice was not as bad in Hongxing commue as in other places and big organizations. Or, Mayor Tan, who was in charge of education / propaganda in the commune, acted fairly based on his principles and no other interference existed in the process of selecting the best candidate. Whatever the case might be is up to everyone's guess.

Whatever happened in that process, Dai-shan got the job, a job many people would have dreamed of at that time in that rural area. He was just the lucky one!

31. Rural Mobile Movie Showing 农村流动电影放映 (nongcun liudong *diànyǐng fàngyìng*)

On the next day in the afternoon, a little while after lunch, Dai-shan headed down the hill to the Commune complex to report to Mayor Tan for the job. After he found Mayor Tan, he was taken to another room, where the film projection equipment was stored and there was a bed as a temporary sleeping place.

An older, skinny man in his late 40s or early 50s, greeted them. The mayor introduced the older man, "This is *Gong shifu* 弓师父 (Master, referring to someone with skills in a trade) and this is Dai-shan, the replacement for the outgoing zhingqing". They both said "Hi" to each other.

The mayor then turned to Dai-shan, "Gong *shifu* is an experienced master. He was a film projectionist when he served in the army, and you should humbly learn the film projection skills from him".

About that time another young man, the outgoing *zhiqing*, came in. His surname was Nan and people called him zhiqing Nan. Dai-shan was introduced to him.

He said, "Welcome to the Team" and shook Dai-shan's hands.

"Thank you", Dai-shan replied. The mayor left.

The first day on the job 第一天上班 (diyitian shangban)

Gong then said to Dai-shan, "Now that you are here, we need to start working. We will show a movie tonight here outside in the school yard. We will start setting up everything before supper time and test the equipment. "

Dai-shan started his on-the-job training right away. "What can I do to help, Gong *shifu*?" he asked.

"You can start by cleaning the equipment and getting prepared. "

"I will show you what to do. Just follow me", zhiqing Nan said and started moving the equipment out of the room to the covered courtyard. Dai-shan followed and lent him a hand to move a portable power generator, a 50 lb gasoline tank, a film projector, a slide projector and other accessories.

They used rags to wipe the equipment surfaces and dust. The generator was powered by a two-stroke gas engine, the two units being directly connected. They needed to fill up the engine tank with gasoline. To do that, one end of a hose was inserted into the gasoline tank and the other end was left outside. The first step was to induce flow in the hose by deeply sucking the open end of the hose with mouth, sealing the end immediately with a thumb once the gas gets into the hose, and inserting it into the filling port on the engine tank. As soon as the hose end was open by removing the thumb, gasoline was supposed to

235

flow by gravity if the gas level in the tank was maintained at higher elevation than that of the engine. If the tank was full, no sucking would be necessary. When the engine tank was nearly full, the hose was pulled out of the gas tank to stop the flow, and both tanks were then tightly capped.

The trick in the process was to suck the gasoline into the hose, but not into your mouth. If gas did get into your mouth, don't swallow it, just blow it out and rinse your mouth with clean water. If the gas tank is full, no sucking is necessary. You just put one end of the hose into the tank, keep another end outside, cover the open end with thumb and quickly pull the hose out the tank with the thumb-covered end below the gas level in the tank, and the gas would start to flow by gravity once your thumb is released.

The next thing to do was to check the projectors and lubricate all the moving parts. During the process, Gong was there supervising, pointing out this and that.

"Once the preparation is complete, we need to test the equipment to make sure they all function properly", zhiqing Nan explained.

"Before we do that, we should take all the gears out and set them up on the site", Gong added.

In an open film "theatre", anyone could go to watch free of charge, and some people came from far away, sometimes over 10 kilometers from the mountainous area of the neighboring county, which didn't have a mobile film team like this. The courtyard would be too small for the crowd and unsafe at the beginning and the end because there were only two small exits. Movies were usually shown in the playground of Hongxing Junior high, where Dai-shan was a student two years ago.

Dai-shan helped move the equipment and other things to the site except the gasoline tank. On the playground, two wooden poles were previously planted at the far end and there was a cross bar on the top. This is the place to hang the screen. He helped zhiqing Nan get things set up. Nan tossed a rope up onto the cross bar at one end and said, "You try another rope to that end."

They then tied the two corners of a large white fabric, pulled it up and tied the other two corners of the fabric at the bottom onto the two poles. The screen was ready. Then a load speaker was hung on the pole and connected to the projector via a cable.

Dai-shan helped take two desks out of one classroom and put them side-by-side in the middle of the playground. The film projector and slide projector would sit on the top.

They placed the generator at the far edge of the ground to minimize noise and ran a long (>50 m) electric cord to the desks. Oh, remember that the whole commune did not have electricity yet. So, wherever the film team went to show movies, they had to bring the generator with them.

"Let's try the generator first", zhiqing Nan said and started demonstrating how to start the generator engine. It's just like starting a gas chainsaw today. Dai-shan tried pulling the string. The engine coughed a couple of times and then started. After a few seconds, the engine sounded normal. That was what zhiqing Nan told him anyway.

"How can you tell if the sound is normal?" Dai-shan asked.

"After some time, you will be able to tell the sound difference. It sounds normal right now. "

They then walked to the desks. Nan switched on the power panel and the lights lit up immediately.

"The engine and the generator seem fine" , zhiqing Nan announced.

"The engine probably needs major maintenance very soon" , Gong came over and added.

"Gong *shifu*, how often do we need to do major maintenance and what is involved?" Dai-shan asked.

"We take apart all parts of the engine and do a thorough clean and replace worn parts. Usually, we do it after completing one round of shows to all Dadui in the commune. So, we do it about twice a month" .

"The generator too?" Dai-shan asked.

"No, we don't touch the generator except to clean the electric brushes. It has to be sent to the repair shop in the county when it has a problem. "

Dai-shan was going to ask more questions. Then Gong said, "You seem to have lots of questions. You will learn a bit at a time and there will be plenty of time ahead. "

Then zhiqing Nan started testing the film projector and Gong tested the slide projector. Dai-shan was instructed not to touch anything on the desk but to watch. Of course, the most important step was to make sure the video and audio systems function normally. Music from the loudspeaker could be heard from far away, a signal of a movie night to nearby villagers. Once everything was ready, they headed back to the complex to get supper.

A note about accommodations, this was the only place different from all other sites in the commune. In rural areas, there were no restaurants or food facilities around the village. Usually, the crew would go to a host family designated by the local Dadui to have supper. However, this site at the commune complex was the geographic center of the *Alliance Dai-dui*. It was also the base for the film team, and they had their own room and a place to eat. No arrangement on accommodations and eating place was therefore required for them. They would go to the shi-tang where all commune officials got their food. A few years ago, when the junior high was still under construction, all the teachers had their food there too.

Supper for Dai-shan at home was normally after dusk. It would not be suitable for him to go home for supper and then back to work. On that day he would need to buy food in the shi-tang. It was his first day and he hadn't prepared anything for eating there. He purchased food and vegetable tickets and borrowed a bowl for his food.

Normally there were only a few people eating in the shi-tang since some officials were often in the countryside and couldn't get back. They simply went back to their homes if nearby or stayed with a host family. Therefore, if more people than normal wanted to eat there, they needed to inform the chef in advance to prepare more food. Otherwise, he would have to cook a second time. That was what he had to do that day because suddenly three extra people from the movie team showed up to eat.

After supper, Gong went to their room, while zhiqing Nan and Dai-shan went directly to the movie site.

"Nan *shifu*, do you normally have a place to stay here?" Dai-shan asked. It was a custom to call someone *shifu* 师父 if that person had more knowledge or skill on something than yourself.

"Yes, I normally stay in that room, and Gong *shifu* would go back home which is about 4 kilometers away. But now I have packed all my stuff away", he replied.

"When are you leaving?"

"I'm leaving in 2 days. Tonight is my last day on the job. Let me show you how to use the projector".

Zhiqing Nan took out one film reel from a metal box.

"Oh, it's so narrow. Are all films the same size?" Dai-shan asked.

"This film is 8.75mm wide for our projector, the narrowest. There are two wider ones. The widest one is 32 mm and normally used in theatres".

Zhiqing Nan started getting the film ready, at the same time he gave explanations. It took him less than one minute to assemble the film reels on the projector and get them ready to show. "You are so fast", Dai-shan praised.

"The standard time for changing film reels is 45 seconds from the time the light goes off to the time the light goes on again, without lighting. There is not much to it. Just practice. Do you want to try it?" zhiqing Nan asked him.

"Yes, I'd love to".

Then zhiqing Nan took off everything he had just put on and started to teach him.

"Pull out the two arms on the projector, one in the front and another in the rear.

"Put the reel with films on the front arm and lock it.

"Put an empty reel on the rear arm and lock it.

"Find the film end on the front reel and pull the film out long enough to reach the rear reel.

"Insert the film end into the slot on the rear reel and turn the reel a few rounds to hold the film in place.

"Hold the film, try not to touch the images, and look for the start symbol or the first image on the film. Use your pointers and middle fingers of both hands to hold the film straight and place it onto the teeth behind the lens tube. Slightly move the film up and down to engage the teeth.

"Then run the film to the magnetic drum and engage it onto the teeth.

"Run the film through all other pulleys, guides, etc. turn the rear reel again to slightly tighten the film". Zhiqing Nan finished his instruction, and Dai-shan completed all the steps in less than 10 minutes.

"Not bad for your first try," zhiqing Nan commented.

"If every step is done correctly, it should be ready to go. You just turn the switch to 'RUN', the projector will work by itself with video and audio", he added.

At that point, Gong arrived and saw what they were doing, and said,

"The first thing to learn is the generator, cleaning and maintenance. Once you have mastered that, you need to learn how to make slides. We need to show slides at the beginning of each show".

"Sure, I will do my best to learn. Will I be able to learn how to use the film projector later too?" Dai-shan asked.

"You need formal training before you can operate the projector. It's delicate work. In about two-months time, the County will start a training program for all new crew members. You can go to the training class", Gong replied.

As dusk approached, some people had started arriving, mostly small kids with their benches and stools, trying

241

to find a good spot to sit. About half an hour after dark, many people had arrived, and the show started. Gong turned on the slide projector and made an announcement. That was the time when local officials would normally cut in to say something, make an announcement or educate peasants on government policies, etc.

However, Uncle Hua as the CP branch secretary did not make a speech that night. Actually, he seldom did. Then zhiqing Nan started the film projector, first to show a documentary then the planned movie.

Dai-shan was instructed to check on the generator from time to time and patrol around, keeping an eye on things. Other times he sat beside the desk watching the movie and zhiqing Nan at work. The show lasted about two hours and went well.

When the show was over, Dai-shan helped take down the fabric screen, pack up the power cord and the generator, and then move all the equipment back to their room inside the complex. Some villagers gave a helping hand too. They needed to take down everything they had just put up before the show. The after-show work would take almost 30 minutes to finish. Before they left for home, Gong told Dai-shan that they would take a few days off and there was no show during that time. However, he wanted to talk to Dai-shan about a few things the next day and to prepare for shows later because the two of them would have to work together to get the shows going.

By the time Dai-shan got home, his siblings were already asleep, but his parents were still awake, waiting for him to come home. Could you imagine, their son had become a movie projectionist. They sure had a lot on their minds, just like Dai-shan.

"You are back. Have you had supper? I kept some food for you in the kitchen", his mother said to him.

"I had some food there. Don't need any now".

"You are probably tired after a whole day. Go to get some sleep now", she continued.

Indeed, he was tired. But could he sleep after a day full of excitement, a day totally different from the past, a day he had never known he could experience? He tried to sleep but his brain was going through the day's events, and he thought more about tomorrow and the day after.

Basics on motion pictures 影片常识 *(yingpian changshi)*

It is necessary at this point to provide a little bit of knowledge on motion pictures before the digital era. This was how things worked then.

To take a photo, you needed a reel of film, normally 12, 24 and 36 exposure, one exposure recording one image. That is one picture. The exposed film needed to be processed in a dark room and the processed film was called a negative, showing the opposite of an image. A photo could be printed many times from the negative in a specialty store.

A movie would consist of a large number of images on negatives, all on a long reel of film. How did the still images become a motion picture? When the light went through the film and projected onto a white screen, the image on the film became visible on the screen. If a series of similar images passed in front of our eyes, the still pictures became alive - the motion pictures. The proper moving speed is 24 images per second for the human eye. If there were more than 24, the motion would be too fast. If less, the motion would be too slow.

A film projector was designed to show 24 images per second. The light beam on a projector had very strong power and would burn the film immediately if the film stayed under the light beam for more than a second. During a show, each picture would only be under the light beam for one 24th (1/24) of a second.

The film came in three sizes: 8.75mm, 16mm and 32mm in width and each could only be played on a proper film projector. The first two were much smaller and normally used in mobile movie shows.

A movie film had images and a soundtrack on one side. The images would be made visible through the lens and light beam. The soundtrack would be converted to an audible sound by a magnetic drum on the projector. The images and sound were not recorded at the same spot on the film but staggered and they were synchronized on the projector.

There were two rows of equally spaced holes on both sides of the film. The teeth on the projector would engage in the holes and pull the film down one image at a time. The pulling mechanism would complete four actions to move one image: the teeth moving forward to engage the film, pull down the film, retreat from the film and move up to the original position. It would move 24 images per second, discretely and the film would move and stop, in a repetitive pattern at the lens location. When the film was being pulled down, a piece of metal would shade the light beam and move away once the film was in place. Without the shade action, we would not be able to see clear pictures but only traces of moving light.

A 90-minute movie would have approximately 129,600 images on the film. Normally a movie film would be cut into sections, not more than 30 minutes per section, each section being wound onto one reel. A two-hour movie would have four reels.

On each reel of film, there was a mark for the beginning, to be placed right at the lens and a mark for the ending at another end, a sign for switching off the light beam. When there are two film projectors working together, like in a theatre, those two marks were used by the projectionists to synchronize their actions. When the light of one projector was off, another must be turned on immediately. If they collaborated well, the viewers would not be able to notice the switch from one projector to another.

If only one projector was used in the show, when one reel of film was finished it was necessary to stop the projector and change to the next reel. The audience would notice the interruption, and some become anxious while waiting.

After a show, all reels had to be rewound back before the next show.

A movie film could be duplicated to make many copies. Each copy was called a *kaobei* 拷贝.

Starting as an apprentice 当学徒 *(dang xuetu)*

Now back to Dai-shan. After his first day on the job, he sure had lots to think about and plenty to learn. When there was a show away from his village, where would he sleep and eat? How long would it take for him to walk home? When he was away, how could he help his parents? More importantly, how could he do a good job?

The next day after breakfast, he went to the film team's office/storage room in the commune complex to see Gong *shifu*. Gong stayed there overnight after the show the night before and was there waiting for him.

"You are here now", Gong greeted.

"You stayed here last night, Gong *shifu*?" Dai-shan responded.

"Now that zhiqing Nan has left, this film team will only be you and me from now on. We need to work as a team. Since you have just started and don't know much about it, and I have been showing movies since I was in the army, I will be your master to teach you, and you will do as I tell you. Is that understood?"

"Yes, understood. I will surely be happy to learn. Whatever needs to be done, please just tell me and show me how, and I will try my best. " Dai-shan really appreciated the opportunity and his attitude was sincere.

"There are nine Dadui in our commune. When we pick up a new *kaobei* of film from the Jindian County Film Management Station 京甸县电影管理站 (*Jindian xian dianying guanli zhan*), we will show the movie to all of them before exchanging to another movie. In general, each Dadui has a pre-determined central village for the show. However, Alliance Dadui is very long and has two sites, so we will alternate between the two sites.

"At present, I will operate the film projector, and you will focus on the generator and assist on the slide shows, of which we need to make our own with local news. Do you have any questions so far?"

"I am listening now and will ask them later".

"For the next two days, we will take a break. After that, I will go to the Management Station to exchange *kaobei* and we will start showing a new movie".

"What will it be?"

"I won't know until I have picked it up. It's normally assigned by the Management Station".

"Where do we stay at night after the show, do we go back home?"

"It depends. If it's close to my home, I usually go home. If it's too far away, I would stay with a host family. Sometimes, hygiene may not be good, just keep that in mind".

"What about food?"

"Most of the time, the host family prepares food for us. We will pay the host family a per diem rate (a predetermined amount of money). Currently the per diem rate is 15 fens per meal per person and 25 fens if there is meat."

"Is that sufficient to pay for the cost of materials and labor?" Dai-shan wondered.

"Not really. That is why each Dadui is supposed to subsidize the host family", Gong replied and then continued with financial information.

"We are operating on a self-supported basis. I have been the treasurer, and zhiqing Nan was doing the accounting when he was here. Since you are new, I will be doing both for the time being. We must keep all details on income and expenses and report it to the Commune accounting staff every month. The film team has its own bank account.

"Our revenue is very simple. At present, the only income source is the fee of ¥15 per month charged to each Dadui, which is another on-going task for us to collect the fees. Our salaries and all costs of material, supplies and the fee for the Management Station will come from that revenue. There is no subsidy from the commune or upper levels of government.

"Talking about salary, since you are new and lack the required skills, the decision for your starting salary is ¥25 per month starting yesterday, prorated this month. For your information, I'm paid ¥29.5 a month. All commune officials including the CP secretary in our commune are paid less than ¥35 a month. We may be able to increase our salary later when we can generate more revenue, but it cannot be more than other officials."

"Do you have any questions?"

"Not really."

"We have lots of work ahead. Here is a key to this room. You can come here to read instructions on the equipment and get your self familiar with it." Gong continued.

"I will go to pick up a new film *kaobei* in the morning two days from tomorrow and meet you here a little after lunch."

"Where will we start the first show next round?"

"From *Dongba* 东坝 dadui and move up towards the mountain area".

"How do we get the equipment there?" Dai-shan wondered.

"The Commune officials are trying to get us to carry them ourselves. They are quite heavy and not easy on the mountain trails. So far, we have been asking each Dadui to send two people to pick them up.

"I will contact Dongba Dadui to pick up the equipment. So, you need to be here a little earlier to wait for them on that day. We will then go to the village."

From that day, Dai-shan was solely responsible for the generator. He read the engine manual and the generator's instructions. It was a good thing that he learned about the internal combustion engine in high school and there was not much difficulty for him to follow the instructions. He just needed more time to become familiar with all components and practice on maintenance.

He found some information on how to make slides and show them on the slide projector. It was a primitive process to make slides using transparent paper, handwriting or carving on it. He also spent time to become familiar with the geography of Hongxing commune to see what challenges lay ahead.

There were nine Dadui, stretching a long distance. Six of them were in the mountainous area:

- *Baba* Dadui,
- Star Dadui,
- Bright Dadui,
- Big-step Dadui,
- Alliance Dadui, the largest Dadui with 12 production Groups and near the commune center,
- Happy Dadui.

The other three Dadui were on the flat terrain at the downstream of *Hongxing* Reservoir 红星水库（*shuiku*）:

- *Advance* Dadui,
- *Dongba* Dadui,
- *Qiqi* Dadui.

The first-movie showing 放第一部电影（*fang diyibu dianying*）

Two days later, Dai-shan went to the complex as scheduled. He went to the room and got the equipment prepared: the gasoline tank and the generator each in one 箩筐（*luokuang*）, the film projector in one and the rest in

249

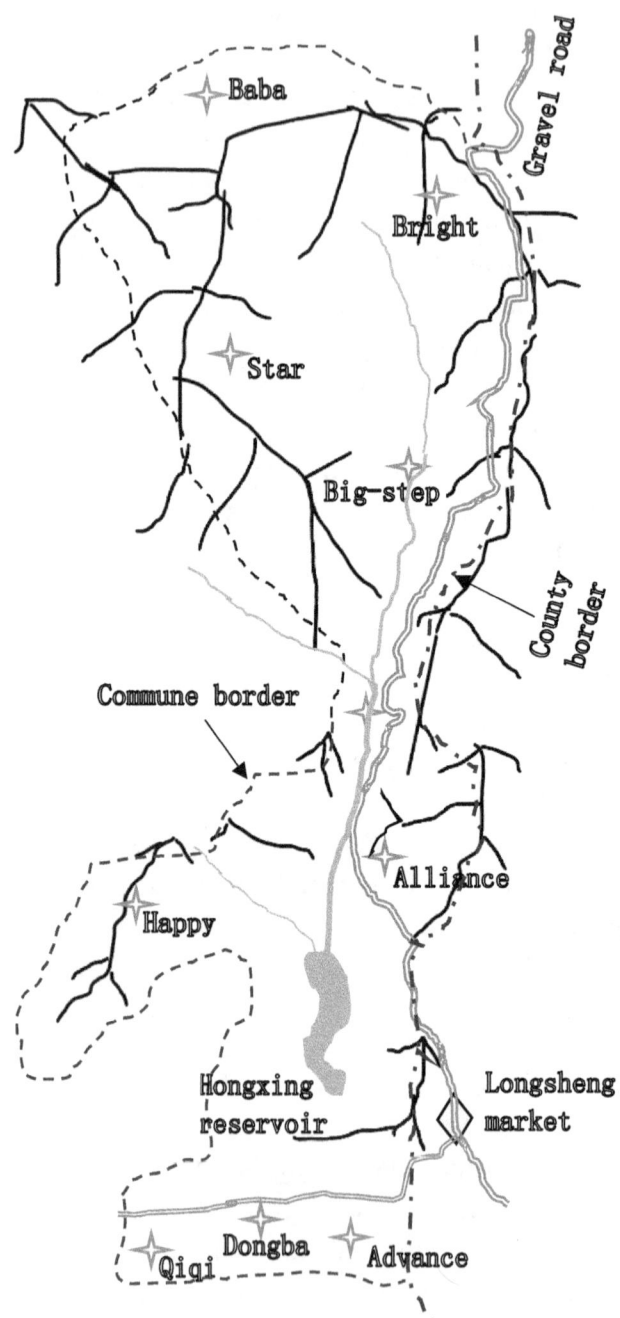

Hongxing Commune geography and 9 Dadui

another one. He didn't see anyone around and waited for someone to come.

One hour later, Gong arrived with a metal box in his hand.

"Gong *shifu*, you are back. What movie do you have?" Dai-shan greeted.

"*Chunmiao*春苗 (meaning, spring seedlings, implying something new). The kaobei is in the metal box. Has anyone come yet?" Gong asked.

"I have been waiting for over one hour and haven't seen anyone yet".

At that time, someone came and knocked on the door. "Is Gong *shifu* here?" he asked.

Dai-shan opened the door, "Yes, he just came back".

"We are from Dongba Dadui. Gong *shifu* wanted us to pick up the movie equipment."

"Oh, yes. Come in, please. they are all here", Gong greeted.

The two men used their *biandan*扁担 and carried the four *luokuang*s on their shoulders and went on their way.

Dai-shan and Gong followed them but couldn't keep up with their pace. "Let them go first. We will find our way." Gong said.

By the time they got to the destination, the equipment was already there, and the two men had left. It was in Dongba elementary school. Classes were over and most students had already gone home, except a few local kids. There were only two teachers who lived on the school campus and the rest were from the local area and had gone home already. After Gong had introduced Dai-shan to the teachers on site, they immediately started unpacking everything.

251

"The first thing we need to do is to hang the screen to let people know we are here", Gong instructed.

Dai-shan remembered how they did it last time and worked together with Gong. In a few minutes, they raised the screen on the two poles which were already planted in the ground and hung the loudspeaker too.

"Now I'm going to rewind the kaobei and check on the film projector. You can set the generator on another side of the classroom to reduce noise and get it prepared. Do you remember how to do it?" Gong asked.

"I think so. I will come to ask you if I need help". Dai-shan replied.

As usual, there were some kids around watching. One big kid helped him move the generator. He then started refilling the engine, checking the lubrication oil level, etc. Afterwards, he ran the power cord from the generator to the desk at the centre of the playground. Gong was about to finish rewinding the kaobei.

"Gong *shifu*, I completed checking the generator. When do you want me to test it?" Dai-shan asked.

"I'm almost done rewinding. You can start it to test the lights now", Gong replied.

Dai-shan went back to the generator and pulled a couple of times on the starting cord. The engine started. At the same time, Gong had put the power panel on the desk and the light lit up as soon as it was plugged in. In a few minutes, he also set up the film projector. When the loudspeaker was plugged into the projector and the switch turned on, there was a static noise sound from the speaker. Gong tried the microphone. It was loud and clear in the speaker. Then he mounted a documentary film kaobei and switched the projector on. There! The show was on. It could be heard from far away. That was the signal to all nearby villagers that there was a movie that night.

"Everything looks fine. We are now all set for tonight", Gong said.

About that time, the CP branch secretary of Dongba Dadui came.

"Gong *shifu, ni-hao*. What is the movie tonight", he asked.

"*Chunmiao* 春苗, a story about a rural barefoot doctor[56]. It's a new movie". Gong answered. Then he turned to Dai-shan "This is Xiang *zhishu* 支书 (CP branch secretary) of *Dongba Dadui*".

"Em, it is good for us, and we need barefoot doctors", Xiang *zhishu* responded.

"Oh, you have an apprentice. Where is Nan *shifu*?"

"That zhiqing has returned to *Zhongdu-fu*. This is Dai-shan, a local new graduate from high school and he is taking over the job from zhiqing Nan."

"Welcome, young man. Follow Gong *shifu* to learn", Xiang *zhishu* told Dai-shan. Then he took out a pack of cigarettes from his pocket and offered one to Gong "Gong *shifu*, have one cigarette?"

Gong took one and put it on his left ear.

The *zhishu* then turned to Dai-shan, "smoke?"

"No, thank you. I have never smoked before". Dai-shan replied.

The *zhishu* then lit up a cigarette himself and continued,

"Supper should be ready soon. You can go there when you are finished here. I will see you tonight." Then he left.

---

[56] See next subsection for the meaning.

"Gong *shifu*, do you smoke too?" Dai-shan asked.

"Not really. But sometimes our hosts are very hospitable. I will just accept it to be polite. Otherwise, they don't feel comfortable.

"Let's go for supper now. Our host family is just in the nearby village, a short walking distance."

Dai-shan followed Gong and in less than 10 minutes they arrived. The hostess was a middle-aged woman. She greeted Gong and Dai-shan, and said,

"Supper is ready, please sit down and I'll get the food right away". Dai-shan and Gong sat down beside a square table. He whispered to Gong,

"Is anyone else in the family going to join us?"

"They are probably still busy in the field. We will start eating as soon as the food is ready. The family don't usually join us at the dining table. We can't wait as we have our work to do".

The meal was ordinary family food: Yam *xifan* 稀饭, fried vegetables, plus pickles. After supper, they left 15 fen cash each on the table, thanked the hostess for serving the meal and went on their way back to the movie site.

Gong told Dai-shan, "Most of the time we have supper like this. In some places, some officials in the Dadui may join us for supper. In that case, there may be some meat. Sometimes there is liquor too if the meal is after the show.

"Once in a while, we may be invited to show movies in other places outside our commune. In that case, we would be treated as VIP guests".

They soon returned to the movie site. There was already a crowd on the ground, mostly on benches and some kids simply sitting on the ground in the front. The children were so happy to see them return.

It was almost dusk, time to turn the light on. Without delay, Dai-shan went to the generator and checked its condition to make sure everything was in order. A bunch of kids followed him.

"Eh, he is new. Where is Nan *shifu*"? One noticed.

"Who is he?" Another asked.

"Nan *shifu* has gone. This is Yao *shifu*". Dai-shan heard someone speaking behind him and turned around. An adult was coming over and said "Yao *shifu, nihao* 你好". He introduced himself and reminded the kids not to touch anything.

Dai-shan started the generator and immediately the light came on. The children shouted, "*Haola* 好啦 (Okay), we are going to watch a movie now".

When the power was on, Dai-shan walked to the desk to see if Gong *shifu* needed a hand.

"Gong *shifu*, can I help with anything"?

"Everything looks fine. We could play some music, but we don't have a turntable player 唱片机 (*changpian ji*). For now, we just need to wait for Xiang *zhishu* to come.

"Meanwhile, you need to walk around to keep an eye on the generator and the screen and watch out for the kids".

About the barefoot doctor 有关赤脚医生 (*youguang chijiao yisheng*)

Let's pause for a second here.

During those years, medical services were in very short supply in rural areas. Hospitals were only in cities and the county capital. There were two medical clinics in Hongxing commune, which had a population of over ten thousand people. One was at the commune complex site, and

255

another was at the Advance *dadui*. Most of the time, people would just seek family recipes and herbs for a cure when they were sick. One reason was they were poor and couldn't afford to see a doctor and buy medicine. Another reason was the difficulty getting to the medical clinic in the rural areas. Usually, people had to walk on foot for several kilometers through the mountains. If someone couldn't walk, the others had to carry the patient on a simple handmade stretcher or whatever they could use to get to the clinic.

In an effort to ease the problem of access to medical services, the government came up with an idea: training one or two health assistants in each Dadui to provide light health care duties, such as for headache, flu, temperature and blood pressure checks, and first aid. They could be full-time or part-time, depending on how many people needed help, but they were not equipped nor paid like a doctor or a nurse in a hospital. At the beginning, they were basically like other peasants, earning *Gongfen* for the work. At later time, they received stipend. Since they were still part of the village and were available on short notice, they were labeled as barefoot doctors. They sure wore shoes too.

Now let's get back to the movie. Soon, Xiang *zhishu* arrived. By that time, the field was filled with many people, men and women, young and old.

"It is about time to start. Xiang *zhishu*, do you want to say something first?" Gong asked. The *zhishu* picked up the microphone and spoke for a few minutes about routine activities in the *Dadui*. Then Gong *shifu* announced the movie name and started the projector.

It was routine to first show a short documentary before the movie. Those documentaries were mostly about the central CP government activities and state events, like showing Chairman *Mao* 毛主席 (*Mao zhuxi*) meeting a foreign country's president, Premier *Zhou* 周总理 (*Zhou zongli*) welcoming foreign guests, some central government leader 某中央领导 (*mou Zhongyang lingdao*) visiting a factory or a foreign country, etc, all the good news across the nation. That was how ordinary people got educated and informed about the good things that happened in China.

The documentary film was about 20 to 30 minutes long. They only had one film projector and after finishing one reel of film, the projector must be stopped, often the light turned on too, to change to a new reel of film. It was a short interruption during the show, which you would not have noticed in a theatre where there were two film projectors operating side by side.

Then the movie started. Like the audience, Dai-shan paid full attention to the movie while patrolling around. He followed the story, tried to understand the theme and the implications, and paid attention to the main characters. Although he knew that the movie was a made-up story, he chose to believe the story. After all, he was born and grew up in that environment, how could he not believe it?

Two hours later, the show finished. The audience started leaving. Dai-shan headed to the screen to lower it. With help from some enthusiastic villagers, he got it packed up in less than 15 minutes. Then he helped Gong pack up the projector and other stuff and move them to a classroom to store overnight. The last thing to do was to stop the generator and move it to the same storage place.

After the show, Gong shifu went to his home which was not far and Dai-shan stayed in the school with a teacher before walking home the next morning.

The second night's show was in the nearby *Qiqi Dadui*, also in the local elementary school nearby. Dai-shan walked there in the afternoon as planned. The show went well.

Reconnecting with classmates during the movie showing tour 巡回放映同学重逢 *(xunhui fangying tongxue chongfeng)*

The show on the third night was to be in *Advance Dadui*. This time it was not in the local school but in the #2 group village.

Xin-kun, one of his high school classmates, as a returning *zhiqing* also lived in that village. Xin-kun was a hard-working student. In memorizing English vocabulary, he would read out the same word loudly over and over many times until he got it. That was his way to memorize something. He tried hard on other subjects too, but somehow it seemed not very effective during the examinations. He had a buddy from the next village in the same class and the two were always together. Some people joked "they're
seemingly wearing the same pair of pants[57]" .

That buddy of Xin-kun was a potential competitor for Dai-shan's job as mentioned earlier, since his older brother was the vice CP secretary at the higher level of government above Hongxing Commune. Dai-shan got along with them fine in school. Both were good Chinese chess players and sometimes played chess with Dai-shan but often considered Dai-shan not up to their level.

---

[57] It implies that the two people were together wherever they were.

When Xin-kun heard that Dai-shan was coming to show movies, he was happy and tried to get Dai-shan to eat at his home and stay with him. After Dai-shan explained that their *Dadui* had already arranged to have food in a host family in their village, he then insisted Dai-shan stay overnight with him after the show, to which he agreed.

Once the show was over and everything was packed, Dai-shan and Xin-kun went to his home, which was very close to the show's site, only a few minutes walk. They shared the same bed and talked a lot. You can imagine, they would discuss more than just the movie. They never had the chance to talk and share like that while they were in school. But it was a new reality and a new relationship. Their discussions would include what the future would be like, what lay ahead of their generation, etc. Somehow, they both believed that universities would eventually resume. They got to do this twice a month when Dai-shan returned to show movies. Xin-kun was the eldest with four younger siblings. His parents welcomed Dai-shan and were happy to see their son have a friend like him.

The show the next night after *Advance Dadui* would be at *Happy Dadui*. From then on, they were going to the mountainous areas. The show in *Happy Dadui* was also in the playground of the local elementary school. Unlike the previous shows, the audience would walk to the school from quite far away on mountain trails, some with very steep steps, not easy to walk. They often held flashlights or kerosene lamps on their way back after the show. It was the big event for many villagers.

Dai-mang, a returning zhiqing who graduated from the same Yangjia high school one year earlier than Dai-shan, lived in *Happy Dadui*. He was considered a distant cousin of Dai-shan but they didn't know each other well. He had heard about Dai-shan in high school through his previous teacher and was certainly happy to see Dai-shan. Dai-mang was helping their Dai-dui in doing something: He was in charge of building a masonry bridge for a main road and had a good relationship with their CP branch secretary. He designed the bridge, the size and shape of the stone blocks and was supervising the construction.

When Dai-shan got to the school site that afternoon, Dai-mang soon came by with their CP branch secretary. As usual, Gong *shifu* introduced Dai-shan to them. *Dai-mang* acted like a very close cousin and asked Dai-shan to go to his home for supper. However, his home was in another village. Dai-shan told him they had a prearranged host family.

The host family was actually the CP branch secretary's family. He was the only one among all the Dai-dui who invited the film crew to his own home. Apparently, he served better meals than they usually had and sometimes served the meal with some drinks, fried peanuts and meat.

After supper on the way back to the school, Dai-shan asked Gong shifu, "How could that little money we paid him be enough for the meal?"

"It was definitely not enough. He treated us well as his guests, but we don't know how much subsidies he may receive later. "

Back to the movie site, the audience was smaller in the mountainous areas. One reason was the smaller population, and another reason was that many older people couldn't walk there at night.

After the show, the branch secretary also invited the crew to stay at his home overnight as usual. Dai-mang told the *zhishu* he wanted to take Dai-shan to his home because they had lots to catch up on. They would then walk more than 15 minutes to Dai-mang's home. They shared the bed and again they had lots to talk about, beyond the movie itself. They talked very late.

The next morning, before they got up, Dai-mang's mother had already made breakfast and it was waiting for them, a fried egg on top of a bowl of noodle. That was a feast for Dai-shan. By that time Dai-mang's brother and his father had gone to the field to do their morning work. Only the two of them sat there eating. From then, every time Dai-shan was there to show movies, Dai-mang invited him home.

It should be mentioned that the CP council secretary of the Hongxing Commune 公社党委书记 (*gongshe dangwei shuji*) lived in *Happy dadui* too. However, he usually stayed in the commune complex and occasionally went home. His son was one of Dai-shan's junior high school classmates, another potential competitor for Dai-shan's job.

Dai-shan was not sure whether he saw that classmate that night at the movie, but he was invited to his home at another time later. Dai-shan remembered that the home of the CP council secretary was not much different from other families. They lived in a small clay-made bungalow up on the hill, with a few shabby pieces of furniture. His classmate was the oldest in the family with a few younger siblings.

The route of the movie tour was based on the geography of the area. The next show would be back to the *Alliance Dadui*, which had two alternating sites for movies. Since the last show in this *Dadui* was in the commune complex, near Dai-shan's home village, this time it would be in another site called *Guanyin* bridge 观音桥 (*Guanyin qiao* –

the Bodhisattva of Compassion), about 2 kilometers deeper into the gulley at the foot of the mountain.

Two girls in his class from junior high to high school lived in that village too, and one of them was *Yufang*, the girl he had had a crush on. She was second in the family and had two younger siblings. The other girl was around the average in the class but pretty. She had a privileged family status because her older brother was serving in the military as a regimental officer 副团级 (*fu tuan ji*). The two girls were often together at school.

Dai-shan had mixed feelings. On the one hand, he was hoping to see them, particularly *Yufang,* and to have a chat with her. On the other hand, he still felt he was not in the right position to get too close to her. Although his situation was much better now than before, his mind was not there, and he continued focusing on a much bigger picture and far in the future. He kept his feelings to himself and behaved as if nothing were in his mind.

After they set up for the show in the courtyard just beside the other girl's home, many villagers started setting up their benches and stools in the yard hoping to have a better spot to watch the movie. Then he saw that girl and a little later, Yufang came too. Dai-shan said hello to both and asked how they were doing. They replied the same and nothing more than that.

In those days, people were very sensitive to a scene of boys and girls talking. Whenever they saw a boy talking to a girl, they would whisper behind their back, talking nonsense 嚼舌根 (*jiao shegen*), speculating things. Sometimes that could ruin someone's reputation. Dai-shan was very aware of that and left the two girls alone and went on with his work.

He did not get to talk to them during the show. By the time the show was over, and the crowd dissipated, they had left the site too. After they cleaned up the site, Gong *shifu* said to Dai-shan "We will take a couple of days off to do some other things, then go to the next Dai-dui on the maintains two days later.

Dai-shan walked back home with neighbors from his village that night.

Despite being very cautious, there were still rumors flying around: Dai-shan and Yufang appeared to be in a relationship. Dai-shan knew very well that he liked her, but he had no idea what was on her mind. They had never talked to each other about anything in that direction at all. How could people come up with something like that? Well, they did, and they were creative.

A few months later, one day his mother said to him,

"Someone came to me and asked if she could introduce a girl to you".

His father overheard it and cut in, "That is very good then".

"Mama, you know I am not interested in that yet".

"Well, that's what I replied. But she wanted to make sure whether or not you and that girl in your school are 耍朋友(*shua pengyou*)[58]. Aren't you?"

"We were classmates, but nothing like that. I'm currently focusing on my job and my career", Dai-shan replied.

The next show would be in *Big-step Dadui*, at the deep end of the gully, which covered the mountains on both sides. However, the school was located at the bottom.

---

[58] meaning: dating. literally, "playing as friends".

Villagers would walk down the hills to the school to watch the show. Though the trails were difficult, they seemed to be used to it since they went to the Longsheng market, a few kilometers away, on those trails all the time.

Zhan-hui, a classmate during Hongxing junior high and Yaojia high school who was considered by their teachers to be an academic competitor to Dai-shan, lived there. Zhan-hui was an optimistic person, often with a smile on his face as if nothing bothered him. On the news that Dai-shan was coming on the movie tour, he was certainly happy to see him. They discussed many things and often went together to see Teacher Ye and his younger brother Ye-zhong, another classmate.

Zhan-hui invited Dai-shan to stay at his home, but his home was further into the gulley. Instead, Dai-shan and Gong *shifu* had their meal with a host family, where Gong would stay over night.

There was a local youth, named *Mao-wang*, who seemed to be related to the local CP branch secretary, was very social and often went to the different markets here and there doing some buying and selling. He lived close to the school just down the trail.

He came early that afternoon and chatted with Dai-shan while giving him a helping hand whenever he could. He seemed friendly and easy to get along with. He was familiar with Gong *shifu* too. They chatted about where to stay that night.

"Well, I will stay in the same place as I have stayed before, but the host has only one space. We will probably need to find another space for him", Gong shifu said.

"In that case, Dai-shan can come to stay with me tonight. I live by myself, and my brother has his own room", he responded.

"That might work", Gong shifu said "why don't you go to take a look. It's not far, is it?"

"No, just a few minutes away".

Dai-shan walked to his home with him. It was a small but new clay-made bungalow, with simple furniture, but looks clean. Dai-shan decided to give it a try that night. In fact, he stayed at this place often afterwards, for the convenience and its cleanliness. There were a few times he stayed with his classmate Zhan-hui too when the next destination was up the hill toward where he lived.

The remaining three Dadui were located on the top of the mountains. They were a little too far to walk home after a show. The movie crew would go to the new site after breakfast with the host family and they usually had to stay with host families until the show was completed.

Bright *Dadui*, was above *Big-step Dadui* up on the mountain. The show was in the school. Less than five minutes walk away from the school, there was a family home. Logically, that was their host family. The family consisted of a middle-aged woman with two grown-up sons and a daughter, both boys still single. She seemed to be a capable lady, she did all the house chores, kept the home clean and often went to help in the field too.

The school had two resident teachers, one was old, and another was young, a zhiqing. The other teachers were locals and did not stay at the school.

The family treated the two teachers well, often providing them with dry wood for cooking, sometimes their home produce too. When Dai-shan and Gong *shifu* showed up, the family made them feel welcome. Their bed was clean. The older teacher was nice and kind, and the young teacher was talkative and helpful. Dai-shan liked being around them. Needless to say, the show in that place went well and Dai-shan liked being there too.

Surprisingly, despite the high elevation, there was plenty of spring water for the village and it was not far from their host's home and the school.

The unpleasant sleepovers 难以忍受的夜宿 (nanyi renshou de yesu)

However, the experience in the last two Dai-dui, *Star* and *Baba*, weren't as pleasant as the others. They were at about the same elevation as *Bright* dadui but located on different mountains nearby which were connected by mountain ridges. Being on the top of the mountains, water shortage was the first thing to notice. As a result, it became a big problem for villagers to wash clothes. They got drinking water from wells but most of the time washed their clothes in dug pits, where water accumulated during the raining season, which was no longer fresh after some time.

In rural areas, peasants didn't have the luxury to take baths or showers at home. Instead, they poured boiled hot water in a basin, mixed it with cold water and used a towel to wipe their body. It was hard to say how often the peasants in that area could even do that.

The shows were in the local schools too, and the movie crew stayed with host families in these two locations. The food they had was typical for those days: corn porridge cooked with yam, pickles and sometimes stir-fried vegetables. Gong warned Dai-shan, "Water shortage is obvious around here and home hygiene is a problem".

"What problem?" Dai-asked.

"Well, you will see soon".

Dai-shan's worst home-staying experience was the last place, *Baba Dadui*. The host was a teacher at the school and his wife was a distant relative of Gong *shifu*. He was hospitable and often would bring out his liquor to share, apparently because of Gong *shifu*.

After the show that night, Dai-shan and Gong *shifu* were both supposed to stay with the host family. They didn't have a spare bed, however. His oldest son was a grown-up. When the movie crew were there, his son would find a place elsewhere in the village to sleep. That night, only Dai-shan and Gong *shifu* were there, sharing the bed.

Just as Dai-shan was ready to get into the bed, he heard "Wait a second", Gong warned, took out his flashlight, and looking for something on the bed very carefully. He opened the quilt and examined the seamlines and all around the bed.

"What are you looking for, Gong *shifu*?" Dai-shan asked.

"Can you see this?" Gong whispered and pointed to a large fat little bug with many feet. Dai-shan got close and saw it crawling.

"Ai ya 哎呀, it's a louse 是个虱子 (*shige shizi*)! So big and fat". Dai-shan exclaimed and felt a chill and itching on his back.

"Oh, another one", ⋯ they found quite a few lice lying there sleeping or waiting for humans to come. Although they were tired, they couldn't sleep in the quilt anymore after they saw the lice. Instead, they moved the quilt aside and tried to sleep with their own clothes on for the whole night. It was unlikely they got any sleep at all that night. The next morning, at dawn, before the others got up, they got out the bed.

"Let's go home now. I can't stay any longer." Gong suggested.

"Me neither. What about our movie gear?" Dai-shan asked.

"We will keep all the equipment here in the school and our next movie will start here. Take the film *kaobei* with us and we will go to exchange it for another one in a few days."

At that moment, the host teacher woke up and came out of his room, asking "It's barely daybreak. Are you leaving now without breakfast?"

"Oh, we have an early meeting today and we have to go now. Thanks for your hospitality." Gong said.

"Thank you and bye now". Dai-shan followed.

It took about two hours to walk back to the commune complex and there were no shops or stores on the way. Dai-shan went back home just in time for breakfast because peasants usually do early shift work in the field before breakfast.

"Dai-shan, you came back early today. Have you eaten anything yet?" his mother asked.

"Not yet. Mama, the last host family was not very clean, and they had lice on the bed. So, we left early." Dai-shan replied.

"Oh, quick, take off all your clothes and I will boil some water to soak them and kill the lice", his mother instructed. The boiling water is supposed to kill the lice eggs too.

The first round of movie shows was completed in 12 days. Dai-shan was so dedicated to the job and paid full attention to his work and the show itself. After the movie tour, he could remember most of the songs from the movie.

They took two days break before the next show to catch up on other things. During the break, Gong would go to the neighboring Dadui to collect the movie fees if they had not paid yet. In some cases, the CP branch secretary would get it prepared and pay Gong when they were on site for the movie show. Gong would write a receipt. In other cases, the crew had to go back there to collect. Even then, the payment may still be delayed because the fees had not been collected by the dadui and the peasants were really poor and had a hard time coming up with the cash.

Dai-shan would take the time off to do other things, such as collecting local news, learning to make slides, etc. He was given the partial responsibility to collect the fees in some Dadui at a much later time.

Two days later, Dai-shan met Gong *shifu* at the pre-arranged time in the commune complex. There was only one telephone in the whole commune at the commune complex. It was primarily used for the officials to connect with upper levels of the government.

The broadcasting station was still in place to reach every village and family, three times a day. Any announcement on the broadcasting network would be heard by the entire commune of over 10,000 people. The broadcasting station was basically for public interest and the movie team seldom used it. For them, communication would usually be by other means. The most common way was by word of mouth. It was very effective, especially on a market day.

When they met, Gong discussed a few things relevant to their work and added,

"The commune official has reminded us again that we need to carry the movie equipment ourselves. On the flat terrain, it is less of a problem if we get a wagon to pull ourselves. But on the mountain trails, it would not be possible.

"I just want you to be prepared. We will try to delay it as long as we can. I have told them we cannot do so at present since there is no road for a transporting wagon and everything relies on our shoulders. We would need one more person because many movie teams in other communes have three people and some teams are equipped with a pull wagon on flat terrains. Our situation just does not allow us to do that.

"I have heard that the training program may start next month. I will go to exchange the film *kaobei* tomorrow in the county and will confirm when it will start."

"I guess we will start the next show at Baba *Dadui*." Dai-shan wondered.

"Yes, I will meet you here the day after tomorrow and we will see if we can hitch hike a tractor up the hill."

When Gong *shifu* came back two days later, he confirmed that the training would be one month long taking place the next month in the county Film Management Station.

He also said, "Many teams have upgraded their equipment to a 16mm projector, and we will also upgrade ours and will use it in our training. Because it's a different machine, I will be in the training too".

That got Da-shan excited, official training to be a movie projectionist and a new larger machine!

This round of movie showing followed the same route but in the reverse order. Except for the lice encounter, things went quite well.

Each time when they needed to have the equipment transported to the next stop, they would inform the person in charge, which was often the CP branch secretary of the next Dadui, to send two male laborers. They had to make sure the message got to the branch secretary. If someone from the next show place came to the show place, they would ask this person to pass the message on. Sometimes they would pass a message onto a villager on the way. If it **was** on a market day, there would always be someone in the market who knew the movie crew and would relay the message to the person in charge. The most reliable spot to find someone at the market was the post stop. That was the place where the mailman would pick up mail and news papers in the morning and deliver them whenever he spotted someone from the relevant villages.

There would be no problem to ask someone to pass on a message to their branch secretary that the movie showing would be in their area the next day and two people were needed to carry the equipment.

After two weeks, the second round of shows was finished. By that time, Dai-shan had been on the job for over one month.

The first pay 第一次发工资 (di yici fa gongzi)

The next day, Dai-shan met Gong *shifu* in the commune complex. Gong went to the local branch of the rural credit agency 农村信用社 (*nongcun xin-yong-she*), which was similar to a bank and withdrew some cash.

"It's payment time", he told Dai-shan.

"Oh, that's good".

"As I said at the beginning, your salary is ¥25 per month. In addition, you get ¥0.10 per night subsidy 补助 (*buzhu*) when working away from our home base, except here at Alliance dai-dui, which is considered our base.

"The subsidy would be (9 - 1) x 2 x 0.1 = ¥1.6. So, your total pay for the last month is ¥26.6."

Gong counted the cash plus coins and handed it over to Dai-shan, "Here you go."

Dai-shan He took it and put in his pocket.

"Don't put in your pocket yet. Count it first to make sure it's correct." Gong warned him.

Dai-shan took it out and counted "correct. Thank you."

"There will be no show next week. We need to get prepared for the training in the county. I will see you here in three days in the morning." Gong *shifu* reminded.

"*Hao* 好, see you then."

Dai-shan was very excited. This was the first time he earned a salary, real cash. Unlike many people who might spend their first payment treating themselves to a feast or nice clothing, he was thinking how he could use this to help his family. He estimated his expenses and family needs and recognized he must help his family. He decided to give ¥10 to his parents to help the family, to save ¥10 for himself for future use (though he was not sure for what yet) and the rest for his daily expenditure. The remaining money was not much but he would try hard to save as much as he could and only buy things he absolutely needed. He might not be able to save anything right away due to the up-coming training in the county which would cost money, but he planned to start saving thereafter.

32. Professional Training 专业培训 (*zhuanye peixun*)

The training was in the county's capital, *Jingdian-zhen* 京甸镇, a small town (though not really small in population when compared to western countries), with nearly half a million people, approximately 20 kilometers away. It was on the other side of the mountain where Dai-shan had his movie showing in *Baba Dadui*.

272

Hotels would be too expensive. They were arranged to stay in a dormitory. Each person brought their own quilt, washing basin, towel and other personal things. That was the first time Dai-shan had gone away from home after high school. His mother helped him prepare personal belongings to take with him. Before he left, she asked,

"You are going to stay there that long. Do you need to bring any food?"

"Mama, I'm going there as part of my work now. There is a *shitang* 食堂 to buy food. You don't need to worry about me anymore."

On the day before the training started, Dai-shan and Gong *shifu* both took a bus with their generator and film projector and arrived at the County Film Management Station, which was located near the town center just beside the main road between two bridges.

Jingdian-zhen sat on a peninsula surrounded by three rivers, which merged into one river here and eventually to the Yangzi 长江 River down stream. The town was a beautiful place. However, flooding was almost an annual event in those days. Whenever there was heavy rain, the rivers rose very high over the banks and often covered the roads and streets. The protection banks that were built many years later eased the problem.

When Dai-shan and Gong arrived at the County Film Management Station, there was a large crowd in front of a window next to the gate to the compound building.

"What are those people doing over there?" Dai-shan asked Gong.

"There is a movie theatre inside the Station. That crowd is there to buy tickets to watch a new movie." Gong replied.

Dai-shan wondered what movie it was to attract that many people. In those days, movie watching at a theatre was still the primary entertainment event, especially when there was a new release. Often a large crowd would be at the ticket window, pushing and squeezing, trying to buy tickets. People often were disappointed when they couldn't watch the first show or to watch it in the first few days. It was common to have multiple showings a day at the theatre, one after another. Most likely there would be multiple crews, taking turns to show the movie.

Dai-shan and Gong got to the gate, where two staff were collecting tickets from people to enter the theatre.

"Do you have tickets?" One asked them.

"Oh, we are not here to watch the movie. We are here for the training program." Gong explained.

"You can go to that side door. Someone will be there to meet you."

They got in through the side door. Inside the compound, they were led to the registration room. Gong seemed to know lots of people inside and greeted everyone on the way:

"Hang *shifu*, *ni hao*,

"Dai *shifu*, *ni hao*."

"Gong *shifu*, is this your new young apprentice? " Some would ask. Gong would then introduce him.

After registration, they were led to a residence room which had four bunk beds. They put their belongings on their assigned beds and prepared to settle in. A little later, two more roommates came in, who were from another commune, also there for the training.

There were more than ten teams in the training, some of which had three crew members. The trainees had a variety of backgrounds. Some served in the military, like *Gong shifu*, but might not have the technical skills and were privileged to have a job like this. Some were youth

274

activists in their communes. Some were *zhiqing* who were city boys/girls but had not had opportunities to return to the cities. There were a few like Dai-shan who were new high school graduates, but he was probably the only one of the few who was not related to a local authority.

In comparison to other trainees, Dai-shan was just a rural boy who had not been exposed much to the outside world and obviously could not easily blend in with the others. He did not feel bad or ashamed of it. Instead, he considered it an opportunity to learn about the outside world.

The training program was divided into four sessions, one week to learn about the 2-stroke gas engine and generator, one week to learn about the film, film repairing and film projector, one week to learn about making slides and propaganda on government policies and local politics. The last week was to be a real-show practice tour to the neighboring communes.

Opening ceremony 开训典礼 (kaixun dianli)

On the first day, there was an opening ceremony in a small auditorium, where the VIP and all staff engaged in the training program were introduced to the class. At the beginning, a tall gentleman wearing a pair of glasses and a smiling face, called the meeting to order in a gentle, soft and clear voice.

"Hello everyone." He paused and waited for the audience to quiet down. The class went quiet, and everyone waited to hear what he was going to say.

He then continued, "Welcome to the second training program. My name is Hu." He gave a friendly smile.

"Is he the leader of the Management Station?" Dai-shan asked Gong quietly.

"He was declared a Stinky NO.9 during the cultural revolution and has now been invited back to help manage the Station. The technical professionals would only listen to him, not the CP secretary." Gong whispered.

"First, let me introduce our CP branch secretary. Please welcome *Lang shuji* to give us instructions." Hu continued and smiled.

The person sitting next to him waved his hands and started speaking, like a typical politician.

"Not much instruction, but here to welcome you." What he spoke thereafter was mostly about policies and not much related to the training. What looked strange to Dai-shan was that none of the professionals at the front row seemed to be listening to what he was saying and there was whispering in the room.

"People don't seem to pay attention to him. Why?" Dai-shan hoped Gong would know something.

"He is completely an outsider, a politician who knows nothing in this field. He was appointed as the CP Branch secretary by the County CP Council. He is just a figurehead and will rely on Hu to manage the Station." Gong explained.

The good thing was that this *Lang shuji* was self aware, knowing his position in the minds of the professionals and cut his speech short, saying he was busy and had to go back to a meeting in the County CP Council. He left the meeting right away.

Hu continued with an explanation of the agenda and schedule of the training program, followed by introductions of the technical professionals one by one.

The training sessions 培训 *(peixun)*

The first week of training was on the 2-stroke engine and generator. *Hang shifu,* a graduate from the old school,

276

was the instructor. He was an expert on the engine and was able to take the machine apart into pieces and put them back together again. He was the one who provided major engine and generator maintenance services to all the teams across the county.

The class started with lectures on the design and components of engine and generator. The focus was on the engine. Huang *shifu* made it sound easy:

"There are three things you need to check: the fuel, air and spark. The carburetor controls the fuel and air, and the spark plug generates sparks to light up." He explained.

He brought real components to the class to demonstrate. He also taught where to check if any of the three elements didn't work as expected. After lectures, he started demonstrating how to do regular services and small maintenance on engine. All the teams followed by working on their own engines and practiced until he was satisfied.

Regular services included cleaning the piston top after being used around 20 times. The primary reason was that the gasoline had high content of impurities in those days. After some time, a thick black deposit accumulated in the combustion chamber, mostly on the piston top. This kind of service is no longer needed for cars these days as the gasoline is cleaner.

The generator was directly connected to the engine through a shaft. Once the engine was started, the generator would produce power. However, the generator itself was basically self contained and needed no services except for regularly cleaning of the carbon electric brushes.

Dai-shan listened carefully and watched every step of the maintenance process. He was quick to grasp the know-how because he had been on the job for over one month and did regular service to the engine already. At the end, he passed the tests without any problem.

The second week was on films and the film projector. A female instructor first gave instructions on care and maintenance of the films, including repairs. The mechanical action on the projector eventually would tear and damage the two rows of holes on both sides of the film. In that case, the damaged holes were repaired, sometimes the part of film was cutoff, and the remainders were reconnected using glue. That would reduce a few images, but no one would be able to notice it during the show.

Dai *shifu* came on the 3rd day to give instructions on the film projector. Dai-shan thought he looked familiar and told Gong "I think I have seen him somewhere before. "

"Before we had our movie team, he used to go to our commune to show movies once or twice a year. "

"Yes, now I remember. Kids used to call him *duyang long*独眼龙（cyclops）*shifu*, because one of his eyes didn't seem normal. "

"Shu⋯. That didn't affect his work at all" . Gong cut Dai-shan off.

The training included the design, components and the moving mechanism of the film projector.

"The projector was designed to move the film 24 images per second in a stop-move repetitive pattern. " Dai shifu explained.

"The sound and images are not recorded at the same location on the film, but all parts are synchronized so that sound and images are displayed simultaneously.

"During a show, a projectionist should pay attention to the sound and light (images) systems. " Dai *shifu* also demonstrated how to mount a film correctly and handle the machine properly.

Since they had already ordered a 16mm projector, Dai-shan and Gong practiced on a brand-new machine. Although Gong had handled different machines when he was in the military, this machine was a new design, and he also needed to practice on it.

Up to this point, Gong had been good to Dai-shan in couching him, though sometimes he tried to hold back some details or tricks. When it came to manipulating the films on the projector, he seemed to lag a little behind and his fingers were less dexterous. The standard time to change a reel of film during a show was 45 seconds, but it would take him 2 to 3 minutes. His fingers just didn't move that fast anymore, perhaps because of his age? Meanwhile, Dai-shan was quick to master the tricks and with a few times of practice he was able to pass the test. That was probably the first time Gong realized that he was no longer "the best" and this young apprentice could surpass his skills. He became more cautious thereafter.

After the two weeks of training, Dai-shan and Gong both were qualified to handle the engine/generator and the film projector.

The third week was on how to use the opportunity of the show time to help governments educate citizens on their policies, how to make slides using film and glass paper which were to be stuck onto small square glasses.

"Since you have the highest education level on our team, you should pay more attention to this part of training. We will rely on you to do the propaganda work later." Gong told Dai-shan.

Training on the propaganda work was dry and boring and Dai-shan managed to get it over with. But the part focused on making their own slides was interesting. Overall, with lots of technical skills to learn, three weeks went by quickly. Dai-shan had learned many new things and was very happy to be in the training.

The first beer 第一口啤酒 (diyikou pijiu)

After three weeks of intense training, the whole class of trainees seemed to be relaxed. Many wanted to go to restaurants to give themselves a treat.

The training was short and intense and technical training was the primary goal for all. But some would also try to do something else, like making social connections or dating despite the small chance of success. There was a female zhiqing, a city girl, who was obviously attracted to a young veteran by his experience and looks and often seemed to tag along with him. Another rural boy, who seemed to have things under his control back in his hometown, was openly chasing that city girl, who was pretty but from another team and geographically far away. Apparently, they were up to something more than social connections. Dai-shan couldn't understand what was in their minds. On an occasion like this, they would certainly go out to have fun and celebrate together.

Dai-shan wasn't planning to go with them, nothing much in common and too expensive anyway. Another young guy saw him and asked, "are you not going to treat yourself?"

"I'm not that interested, and I don't know them very well. I will just go for a walk outside." Dai-shan replied.

"I'm not going with them either. Why don't we walk around to see if there is anything we can have for the two of us?"

"That sounds good to me." Dai-shan responded.

The two boys walked out of the Station compound, crossed the Peace Bridge and came to a pedestrian street. There were quite a few small restaurants with a variety of foods. They stopped at a bar style place, which was very busy, where some customers were sitting around on street-side tables, drinking beers, eating snack foods, etc.

"This place may be good with so many customers. They have beers and appetizers. Do you want to try this?" The boy asked.

"Okay, let's try this." Dai-shan agreed.

Some customers had just left and a small table on the street side became available. They sat down themselves and a waitress came by, cleaned the table and handed a menu to them. There were beers, appetizers and meals too.

"We can order two bottles of beers, one dish of pork liver and one dish of boiled peanuts. We can split the costs." The boy suggested.

"Sounds good to me."

"What kind of beer do you want?" The boy asked.

"What? There are different beers?" Dai-shan wondered since he had never had beer before, although he had tried liquor before at his cousin's wedding and got drunk his first time drinking, only a small amount, about 100 grams.

"Yes, a few different brands to choose from."

"Well, to tell you the truth, I have never had beer before and I'm not sure if I will like it. Just get me the same one as yours." Dai-shan decided to give it a try.

So, the order was placed. The beer was ¥1.00 per bottle (750 ml) and the appetizers were ¥1.50 each dish. Soon came two bottles of local beer and two dishes of appetizers. That boy started drinking and seemed to enjoy it. Dai-shan followed with a sip from his own bottle. It smelled and tasted like the a-few-days-old dish-washing waste liquid that had gone sour. He quickly spit it out.

"Yuck. Are you sure the beer is supposed to taste like this?" Dai-shan asked.

"Yes, this is what beer tastes like. You just have to get used to the flavor." The boy said. "Try more. You will have to do this often in the future."

Dai-shan tried the second sip. No, that was a terrible taste. He gave up and said, "I don't really like it. You can drink my bottle too."

"In that case, I will drink both bottles." The boy was so happy to "help" and drank them all by himself before you noticed.

Group movie showing tour 组队巡回放映电影 (zudui xunhui fangying dianying)

Now it had come to the last week of the training program. They were divided into groups, with two teams in each group. A person from the Management Station was assigned to supervise a group on the tour. Dai-shan and Gong were with another team and Hu was their supervisor. There was a total of six people in the group.

They set out to the assigned commune and made five shows in a row in five different villages in the surrounding area. The two teams had two projectors, and the show would be like in a theatre. The goal was to complete a show with no interruption during *kaobei* change without any light. The two teams must cooperate and synchronize their actions. Many of these villages in that area had electric power and generators were not used in that case.

Dai-shan and Gong both took turns to practice on their film projector. As they had practiced already in class, they both did well on the tour. Dai-shan did what he was supposed to. Gong as a veteran did well without a doubt. The only thing with him was that his fingers weren't as flexible as he wanted them to be. Since there were two projectors in action, no one would have noticed how long it took him to change a *kaobei*.

"The normal process of showing the movie was not a problem. We just need to learn how to handle emergency situations if it occurs during the show", Hu told them. "Like power interruption, film breaking, film getting caught on the machine, projector breakdown, etc." The tour and the show went quite well, except some small issues. The audience apparently liked it because they didn't notice any interruption until the show was finished.

The crew stayed with host families after each show. With that many people on the tour, accommodation was somewhat of a challenge to the host village. They generally split into two or more families with two people sharing a bed. Food was up to the hosts. In one village, the crew stayed with a group of *zhiqing*, who were still in that village. For breakfast the next morning, they had green bean xifan (porridge). When Dai-shan got to the table, everyone was already eating, including the hostess, a female zhiqing. She got up and said, "Please sit here" and went to the kitchen. Dai-shan sat down at the table where she was sitting and picked up the bowl of xifan in front of him and started eating. One boy looked at him and gave him a strange looking smile. The others looked at him but didn't say anything. That was weird, Dai-shan thought. A little later, the girl came back with another bowl of xifan, but she sat down at another seat to eat since Dai-shan was in her spot.

Dai-shan asked that boy after breakfast, "Why were you smiling like that on the table? What was funny?"

"Nothing".

"You must know something. Tell me."

"Nothing much really. Just that the bowl of xifan you were eating was the one the girl was eating".

"Why didn't you tell me then?"

On the tour, the biggest challenge was the toilet first thing in the morning. It was not the style, smell or cleanliness. They were used to it. The problem was that there were too many people and often only one toilet. Some did their business fast, but some took a long time. If someone was in a hurry, he/she just had to hold it.

Professional film projectionist 专业放映员 *(zhuanye fangying yuan)*

After completing the training, they all went back to their hometowns to continue with their normal shows. So did Dai-shan and Gong. Now Dai-shan was a trained professional projectionist.

Villagers were certainly happy to see them back and to see a bigger brand-new machine. The screen was bigger than before, and the speaker was louder. Everything seemed be better than before.

Gong continued operating the projector during the first round of shows. He knew that he should give the opportunity for Dai-shan to operate the film projector because he was also a trained professional. One reason was that the Hongxing commune officials wanted both people to be able to handle all equipment and not to rely on one person only. Another reason was that sometimes if one person couldn't go to work for whatever reason on a short notice, the other person should be able to continue with the planned show.

In the second round of shows, Gong let Dai-shan operate the projector, while he looked after the generator. From then on, they often took turns handling the generator and the projector.

Perhaps, Gong felt regret for that. His fingers were not as flexible as before anymore. He would need 2 to 3 minutes to change a *kaobei*, even with the light on, while Dai-shan was able to change it in 45 seconds or less without light. That time difference did not seem to be much but during a show, it felt like ages. No one knew the difference until there was a comparison. Now the audience saw a completely different performance.

Gong's slow actions often made people very impatient, particularly young people. Plus, he needed the light on to change a *kaobei* every time.

"Hurry up, Gong *shifu*", some would shout at him politely.

"Let Dai-shan *shifu* operate the machine. He is much faster", others might add.

The worst time was when some people even threw things at him and told him "Go get Dai-shan *shifu* to help".

That sure made Gong uncomfortable and humiliated. He couldn't blame Dai-shan directly for that and couldn't say anything to him either. But he felt jealous and gradually started behaving unreasonably towards Dai-shan.

"You should continue with the generator and focus on making efforts for the propaganda work ahead of a show", Gong told Dai-shan one day and was reluctant to let Dai-shan operate the projector.

For Dai-shan, it did not matter much. He knew that the other people and the commune officials knew his skills.

Besides, the generator or the film projector was not the destination of his career. In his mind, there were things more important in his life. However, he was not sure what it was yet. He only knew that he needed to learn more, read more books and gain more knowledge. Therefore, he didn't mind whatever work it was he was doing now.

A new addition 一个新成员 *(yige xin chengyuan)*

Not long after, the mobile movie team hired another veteran named Wang-jin, who served in the military too and returned home not long ago. One reason for having three on the crew was to have the film team transport all equipment by themselves, according to the commune officials.

Wang-jin didn't have much education but had strength. He was assigned to handle the generator. The crew did try to carry the equipment by themselves for the three communes on the flat terrain, where they had roads accessible by motor vehicles and wagons. They loaded all equipment on the wagon and pulled the wagon by themselves from village to village.

But they gave up in the mountainous areas. There was no road and trails were not good. There was no transportation equipment, and so all relied on their shoulders and backs. It was just too hard for them.

Wang-jin did not go through the training program and was taught about the generator on the job. He was happy with that job and liked to talk to Dai-shan about almost everything on the job. The two got along very well.

Some travails 几点小事 (jidian xiaoshi)

In those days when everything was scarce, it was very difficult to buy things that were needed. Sometimes, even if someone had the money, there was no, or very short supply of the goods needed. Dai-shan remembered clearly, gasoline was not sold freely in the store to everyone. There was no gas station around. Tractors ran on diesel which was sold in specialty stores. Kerosene was sold in stores and was used for lighting at home. People often used lighters for lighting up cigarettes as well as a lighting source, and it was cheaper than matches. Lighters needed gasoline and could be refilled when the gas ran out. The problem was that there was no place to buy gasoline around the area. A number of commune officials and local village people in charge often came to see Dai-shan with empty bottles and asked for gasoline, which was for the generator. At the beginning, Dai-shan didn't know how to respond. Gong told him it was hard to refuse them. Dai-shan would fill some in their bottle and they would take it away secretly. That became an open secret.

After graduating from high school, Dai-shan tried to maintain connections with some of his high school classmates. The only venue for communication was writing a letter or visiting in person. Due to his job, he could often meet his friends in the same commune during the movie shows, but there was not much opportunity to visit anyone outside the commune.

One day, he went to Yangjia commune to visit the movie team on work related purpose. On the way, he dropped by the nearby Yangjia high school which he attended. He went to see his friend *Yue-dong*, but he was not back home yet.

His mother, Teacher Lu was home. She told Dai-shan that Yu-fang was at the school teaching as a substitute and unfortunately, she was sick. Dai-shan dropped by to see her, just a few doors away. She was lying on her bed, looking exhausted, but it was not serious, just a cold. They greeted each other and had a short chat. Somehow Dai-shan felt that the atmosphere was not like when they were in school and after a while he returned to his friend's home. Teacher Lu asked with a big smile as usual, "How did it go? You two know each other well, right? What a nice couple. "

"Oh, no. Nothing like that, Teacher Lu. We were just classmates. If you didn't tell me, I would not even know she has been teaching here", Dai-shan clarified quickly.

As they were talking, his friend *Yue-dong* came back and added, "As far as I know, she has been teaching here about two months now because one teacher has been away". Then *Yue-dong* and Dai-shan had a chat, catching up on their days since graduation.

That was probably the last time Dai-shan saw Yu-fang. There didn't seem to be any opportunity or need for them to meet each other afterwards.

33. Building a New Bungalow 增建住房 (*zengjian zhufang*)

It had been over one year since Dai-shan became a movie team member in the commune. At that time, there were 5 siblings in his family including himself. Two younger brothers were still in school. The whole family of 7 lived in a three-room clay bungalow. There was one bedroom for his parents. Dai-shan was the oldest, living in the main room 堂屋 (*tang-wu*) on a simple home-made "stretcher bed", just beside the old shrine. The bed was made of mud bricks, a few wooden sticks, bamboo lattice, wheat straw and a bamboo mat. The other siblings were jammed in the other room – the old kitchen. The original kitchen had been moved out to the front porch and Dai-shan was the one to build the earth stove. When he was away for high school, the problem of space was not so bad. Now that he had returned home, it has become more serious. They were in desperate need for more living space.

But how could they afford to build a new house? Both of his parents worked every day for the whole year and by the end they were still in debt. What they earned in working in the farming group was not enough to pay for what they had been allocated during harvest. They didn't have extra food left and just barely had enough to feed everyone. His family was not alone. Many other families were in the same situation.

The poor land didn't produce much. The inefficient management system didn't increase productivity. Many families could barely make ends meet. The only way for them to have a little cash to buy necessities like cooking oil, salt, etc. was to raise pigs, rabbits and goats and sell them. Larger animals were sold at the end of the year.

Fortunately, his parents were good at saving money and never spent anything unless it was absolutely necessary. His father was barefoot most of the time in the year or wearing straw hoes made by himself. His mother made shoes for his father, but he seldom wore them unless it was very cold in the winter. His father couldn't earn much, but he knew how to save.

His father was a simple-minded person. In his mind, there were only two numbers: one and half. When he went to the market to buy something and asked for the price, he would always say "that's too expensive, half more than the others. " Sometimes, the price difference was two or many times in comparison, he would still say "too expensive by more than half. " If you tried to correct him "That was two times, not half", he would just look at you and smiled, as if he were saying "why has to be so accurate".

One evening, his mother said at supper time, "Our children are growing bigger and Dai-shan is back home. We need more living space and need to build a house somewhere. "

"Yes, we do. I have been saving for that. " Father replied.

"For the past one and a half years, I have saved all the money Dai-shan gave me. We have over ¥150 now.

"We may not have enough money to build a good house, but it should be almost enough to build one using more bamboo rather than wooden boards. "

Another problem was to find a building lot. Their three-room bungalow was sandwiched in the middle of other houses. The front was a small yard, and the rear was the neighbor's yard. There was no space around it to add anything onto it. The only solution was to find a space away from the existing house. Building a house on a new lot required approval from the captain of the production team and upper levels. It was a complicated process and not transparent. To get approval, it had been customary to invite the person in charge to your home first and feed him with a good meal of meat and liquor. If he drank a lot and became drunk, he would agree to anything. Otherwise, he might hesitate because he didn't drink enough yet.

His parents decided to invite the captain home for a meal and to discuss the issue. Perhaps because of Dai-shan's position, he did come and seemed to be happy to help. After drinking enough, he said, "The current policy does not allow anyone to build on the public land[59]. You can only build on your own *ziliudi* 自留地 – the small pieces of land（2分 - *2 feng*, per person, approximately 1437 square feet）. That was the land allocated for private use on the basis of the number of people in a family and it was supposed to be used to grow vegetables for their own consumption. If it was used to build a house, there would be less land for growing vegetables. His parents faced a dilemma and eventually decided to build on their own vegetable land about 50 meters away from the existing house.

After discussing with his parents the needs and budget, Dai-shan sketched a plan for a clay bungalow with three rooms. To increase the space use efficiency and save on materials, he designed the rooms larger front-to-rear dimension than usual and added a clay wall in the middle of each room to separate it into front and rear rooms. That made 6 six rooms out of a 3-room plan. They were small rooms but would serve the purpose.

A clay house was built with clay walls, which was constructed by compacting properly moistened soil on site all the way up to the roof line in a pitched shape. The walls were reinforced by bamboo strip loops inside. On the top of the walls, wood logs would be placed across a room as the load bearing frame. Then wooden boards would be nailed on the logs before ceramic tiles were laid on the top to complete the roof. There was no lumber mill around. Wood boards would be made of logs by manually sawing them to split the logs. It would be stronger but

---

[59] The policy changed from time to time. Many families built on public land a few years later.

cost a lot more. In lieu of wooden boards, they used two bamboos tied side-by-side and wrapped with rice straw to prevent tile slippage.

To make ceramic roof tiles, they hired a mason professional to make clay tiles on site a few months in advance. After formed, the clay tiles must be dried without exposing to direct sunlight and be heated up to 1200°C in a kiln, constructed in the ground, to produce a ceramic tile. The kilning process would take a few days. Tile making was a highly skilled profession and the heating process must be properly controlled.

Since other families were doing the same thing in their village, a kiln was already built and was ready for use by any family. They bought bushes and tree branches as fuel for the kiln. It took more than three months from forming to kilning the tiles. The kilning process would take about one week.

Then his father bought small wood logs, bamboo and rice straw on the market. A wood log suitable for building a bungalow would be 5" to 6" in diameter and cost ¥3 – ¥4 each.

There were two brothers in the village who inherited house-building skills from their father. They were hired to build the bungalow and paid ¥2 a day each. The other required laborers were assistants to mix clay, transport and lift it up to the wall as the wall went up, and later to help lift other material and the ceramic tiles to the roof.

Since Dai-shan had to work and his siblings were still small, most labor helpers were hired from the village. Some relatives outside the village also came to help. His mother had to cook food for all two meals a day. By the end the savings they had was not enough unfortunately.

His parents had to sell their pig and goats before the animals grew old enough for more cash. Dai-shan also took some of his personal savings out to help. Eventually they had the bungalow completed.

Although it was simple and small, it was a new bungalow house for the family, and it provided the much-needed extra space for the growing family. Dai-shan's two brothers (second and third oldest) moved into the new home as soon as it was finished. Dai-shan continued to stay on his home-made stretcher bed and his sister and youngest brother also stayed in the old house with their parents. A few years later the two middle bothers settled down in the new bungalow after they got married.

Chapter 7

The later Stage of the Cultural Revolution - Gaokao Resumption 文革后期 - 恢复高考 *(wenge houqi - huifu gaokao)*

34. An Eventful Year 多事的一年 (*duoshi de yinian*)

It was just after the new year in 1976, when suddenly funeral music was played on the national radio network. Soon it became clear that Prime Minister Zhou had passed away. Many people felt like a national disaster suddenly occurred in China. "Our most respected Prime Minister Zhou has left us", was the general feeling among many ordinary people. However, for some unknown reasons there was no big memorial event, and it was said that before his death, Zhou had instructed others not to bury him in the usual burial yard in *Babaoshan* 八宝山 where the past high ranking revolutionary leaders were supposed to be laid to rest, but to spray his ash in the rivers. It was meant to leave no trace on the land.

That was still during the cultural revolution and the revolutionary committees on every level of governments and organizations were calling the shots. No big events, no memorial ceremonials. It was something very hard for ordinary people to understand. It had to do with the people struggling those days. Interested readers should find other sources for more detail.

Holding vigil for Chairman Mao 为毛主席守灵 (*wei maozhuxi shouling*)

A few months had passed. It appeared quiet for a while in the whole nation. Dai-shan and the movie team continued with their movie show tour in the rural areas.

One evening in September that year, the movie team went to the Alliance Dadui, Dai-shan's home Dadui, to show a movie. This time was supposed to be at the village of *Guanyin* bridge 观音桥 (*Guanyin*) according to the rotating sequence schedule, not at the commune complex. The crew went there by foot early in the afternoon and started preparing for the show as soon as they arrived. The screen was up, table was in place, and they were about to test the equipment.

Suddenly, the small speakers of the broadcasting network in the commune on the nearby house in the village came on earlier than usual, in the mid afternoon. There was a loud announcement to every village in the commune, the voice of the CP Council secretary of Hongxing commune,

"Attention please, comrades 社员同志们 (*sheyuan Tongzhi men*). There will be no movie show tonight.

"Movie team crew, when you hear this message please come back to the commune complex immediately for new tasks.

"If anyone see them, please inform them right away."

The movie site was just beside a house and the crew heard the message loud and clear and their names and the message were repeated several times.

A few minutes later, local villagers came by and repeated the same message to the crew.

"What is going on? Why did they cancel the movie show tonight? What is the new task?" The movie team crew had many questions like that, but no one had the answers. Everyone was wondering. This had never happened before. The villagers asked the same questions. At that moment, there was no news on the national news network yet. Perhaps, something in their commune needed their help, the crew thought.

They packed up what they had just set up, left the equipment in a storage room and started walking back to the complex. It was less than 3 kilometers away and they arrived one hour later by foot to report for the new task.

As soon as they set their foot into the complex door, one person came to them and said,

"You are all back now. Please go inside to help set up the stage. "

"What happened? " the crew asked.

"We have been informed by the upper government to prepare for an important event today. It will be announced at 4pm on the national radio this afternoon. You are all required to help. "

"Actually, there was a pre-announcement on the radio for an important news at that time" , someone added.

As they were chatting and wondering what was going on, while waiting for further instructions, they turned on the radio. The time of 4 o'clock approached quickly. First there was a few seconds of silence on the radio. Then a heavy male voice began, reading the following lengthy announcement word by word very slowly:

"The Central Committee of the Communist Party of China, the Standing Committee of the National People's Congress of the People's Republic of China, the State Council of the People's Republic of China and the Military Commission of the Central Committee of the Communist Party of China announce with deepest grief to the whole party, the whole army and the people of all nationalities throughout the country:

Comrade Mao Zedong, the esteemed and beloved great leader of our party, our army and the people of all nationalities of our country, the great teacher of the international proletariat and the oppressed nations and oppressed people, Chairman of the Central Committee of the Communist Party of China, Chairman of the Military Commission of the Central Committee of the Communist Party of China, and Honorary Chairman of the National Committee of the Chinese People's Political Consultative Conference, passed away at 00:10 hours, Sept. 9, 1976, in Peking, because of the worsening of his illness and despite all treatment, although meticulous medical care was given to him in every way after he fell ill. ......"

"Oh, that was why!" Someone exclaimed.

That was giant news. Suddenly, the whole nation turned into funeral mode. Funeral music played on the national radio reaching every corner of the land. Many people felt Mao's passing like the loss of their most respected and beloved family members. No more movies, celebrations, and even the routine radio agenda was completely cancelled and all dedicated to the grieving and the funeral. It felt like the whole world had stopped at that moment.

In those days, when an elder passed away, the family would set up a memorial table beside the coffin with the corpse inside, light up an oil lamp, play funeral music and give family members and relatives the chance to say goodbye and allow them to grieve their loss. Crying out loud was a common custom. The harder, the louder and the more heart-breaking one cried, the more it showed his/her love to the deceased. If any of the direct family members didn't cry out or grieve, people would shake their head and look down upon him/her. After all, that was one of the few opportunities in one's life to cry out like that in public.

That would continue for a few days until the burial day, which would be selected on a "good day". During the process, it was very important to keep the oil lamp on all the time to allow the dead to find its way back home in another dark world. Someone, particularly one of the children must be present at night. This process is called *shouling* 守灵 (holding a vigil).

At the same time, other relatives and/or family members at a far away place who couldn't get back home may also set up a memorial table, with an oil lamp, a portrait, name and birth and death dates of the deceased, and proceed in the same way.

The movie team crew and other commune officials in the complex did just that. They set up a memorial table on the stage of the auditorium, placed a large portrait of Chairman Mao beside the table and lit up a lamp. They also made a huge wreath. During the process, everyone was careful and spoke quietly, seemingly trying not to disturb the dead and give him peace.

Not sure if there were any specific requirements from the upper levels of government, Dai-shan just followed the others to help with the set up. One person came by and passed everyone a black sleeve band to wear on one arm. There were quite a few people around and it didn't take long before the setting was completed.

"Thank you everyone for the work. Now we need to have two people on duty to be beside the memorial table all the times until we hear from the upper government. We are going to take turns, two hours each shift." The CP secretary said.

Dai-shan took a late shift that night with another commune cadre 公社干部 (*gongshe ganbu*). One cadre brought out a bamboo chair to allow anyone on duty to sit on. They were quiet, not doing much other than sitting down or pacing around. Other than the funeral music, there was no other sounds. Not sure what people were doing in the big cities and Beijing, but that was what Dai-shan and his comrades did that night in the vigil for Chairman Mao. It continued for more than two days.

For a few days, the most talked about topics were what Mao's funeral would be like in Beijing, what the new central government would be like, who would be the supreme leader with real power in the country. In the bigger picture, what will the future of China be like? Although

Hua Guofeng was the designated successor to Chairman Mao, somehow people were still a little worried.

Hua led the central government and called for party unity. They all seemed to have focused on Mao's funeral affairs. Instead of cremation, they decided to preserve Mao's corpse and build a Memorial Hall (which took nearly one year to complete) right in the middle of the Tiananmen Square, where people can go to view his body.

For a short period of time, the nation seemed to be peaceful, focusing on the funeral. At least that was the impression to ordinary people, like Dai-shan.

In fact, it was not as peaceful as it had appeared. In just about one month after Mao's passing, the "Gang-of-four", as defined by the CP government, including Mao's widow and her three political alliances, were arrested. That was probably the official ending of the Cultural Revolution. It stirred up a nation-wide celebration. However, in the rural areas, there was not much celebration, but everyone seemed to feel a kind of relief, looking forward to a new era to begin, hoping life will get better with no more people struggling with each other to get by.

35. Keep Learning No Matter the Situation 不管环境如何，学习不能丢 (buguan huanjing ruhe, xuexi buneng diu)

When all schools resumed after a few years of chaos in the education system at the early stages of the cultural revolution, people started changing their views on knowledge and education. Although it was common sense that there must be knowledge and people with knowledge to make something, to build something or to do anything, the once-believed "knowledge was useless" remained in society, particularly in rural areas. One simple reason was that many educated young people in the cities were sent to the rural areas, and they were stuck there. The educated youth like Dai-shan in the local areas had to return home to do the same farming work as the other peasants who had no education at all. At the time, it was really hard to see any hope of change and to see the usefulness of knowledge. As a result, many young people had intentionally or unintentionally given up on learning during that time.

For Dai-shan, that kind of thinking came to his mind often too. However, based on his personal and family situation and the situation of his village, he understood that if he didn't learn anything, the answer was clear that he would live a life just like his parents, his ancestors and many other peasants, being poor and unable to make ends meet no matter how hard they worked. He would never know what the outside world was like.

On the other hand, if he learned some knowledge, there would be some hope, even if it was just a glimpse of hope, that he could do better in his life than otherwise.

His mother planted two walnut trees in their front yard years ago and there had been fruits on the tree for some years. As a child, he liked eating walnuts. When it was ripe, he helped his mother pick up the walnuts when she beat them off the tree. After removing the crust, there was a hard shell, like an eggshell around the nut. To get the nut, the shell must be cracked first. Some walnuts were easy to open but some were not and required a stone, a hammer or a wooden stick to 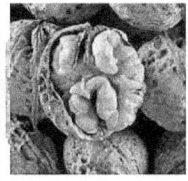 break. He remembered that once he had difficulty opening the nutshell and was not happy with a nut-in-shell walnut in his hands.

His mother asked, "you have a walnut now, why are you still not happy?"

"I don't have anything to open it with", he replied.

"You silly son 傻儿子 (*sha er-zi*), you have a walnut and are still worried about having nothing to crack it with 有了核桃 (*you le hetao*) 还愁没有棒棒敲 (*hai chou meiyou bangbang qiao*)?" His mother picked up a small stone and took the nutshell from his hands, gently beating on the nutshell and it opened.

From then, he understood, if he wanted to eat walnuts, he must have walnuts first. When he had walnut in possession, there was no need to worry about finding something to open it with 有了核桃 (*you le hetao*) 不愁没有棒棒敲 (*bu chou meiyou bangbang qiao*). That became his Motto 座右铭 (*zuo-you-ming*) in life.

When he grew older, he remembered that. If he wanted to change his life, he must have some knowledge first. Once he has knowledge, there must be a place or an opportunity to use it later in the long term. But first, he must learn to gain knowledge. He did just that, no matter what the others were thinking about knowledge at the time.

That motto was what kept Dai-shan energized and motivated all the time, even at the most unfavourable time during the cultural revolution. After finishing high school, he went back to his village, but he did not give up on learning. After he joined the movie team, he spent more time learning things, not only those topics related to his work, but everything which seemed useful.

He tried to learn more on radio waves and attempted to assemble a TV set himself. However, he couldn't do it because of the high cost of buying the necessary components. He tried to learn the movie making techniques, but that did not seem to be something an amateur could accomplish. From time to time, he took out his old high school textbooks to review, just to keep himself refreshed on what he learned before. Wherever he went, there was always a book in his bag. Whenever he had spare time, he would read.

You can imagine, in those days how people would respond when they saw someone having a book in their hands so often. His teachers were happy to see him doing that, although they didn't even know what the future would hold. Peasants would think it would be better to spend time working in the farm field, while some others thought it was just a waste of time. In the movie team crew, his co-worker, Wang-jin, a veteran supported him, while Gong *shifu* was different. At the beginning, he didn't care much. But he behaved strangely, especially after they completed the training and Dai-shan became a favored projectionist in the eyes of the public. He would say something to discourage Dai-shan or become sarcastic. But that made no difference to Dai-shan. He continued with what he believed.

36. Resumption of Entrance Examination to Higher Education Institutions 恢复高考 (*huifu gaokao*)

Time went by fast and shortly another year had passed. It was already in late summer of 1977. One day, there was a rumor that universities would start recruiting new students through entrance examinations. It would be different from the previous three years when students were recommended by local authorities primarily based on "personal behavior" and loyalty to the CP and the government. This time, it would be primarily based on academic merit of the candidates, proved through examinations, which would be held at a specific period of time for a region.

That was great news to Dai-shan. He tried to confirm the news from various sources. It was eventually announced in newspapers and national radios in the month thereafter. The entrance examination 高考 (*Gaokao*) system to enter university, which had been stopped for ten years, would officially resume that year. That moment has been the most important time for many youths in China ever since.

The group of youth, the *zhiqing* from the cities, were most excited apparently. That may end their lives in the rural areas and start their new lives. Dai-shan too was exited. This was the opportunity he had been waiting for.

Wait, it was October already. Weren't schools supposed to start in early September usually? How could it be possible to complete the complex process that year after 10 years of interruption? Those were the questions running in the minds of many people including Dai-shan.

The process would take time. The decision made by the government was to postpone the starting time until after the Chinese New Year in early 1978, though that year's students were still labeled as class 77 (1977 entrance). When the exam schedule was announced, there was one and half month time to prepare for the exams.

The urgency mounted up for all parties involved. The exam questions, the selection criteria, the protocols, the exam schedule and locations, etc. all had to be worked out within the short period of time.

For the candidates, the big question was, "are you ready? "

Everyone with equivalent high school graduate studies including those in the current high school graduating class were eligible to take the exams. That was the cumulative 13 years of high school graduates in total. A total of over 5.7 million candidates registered for the exams. The university capacity in that year for the whole country was however only a little over 0.2 million. The average acceptance rate was 4.8%, the lowest in Chinese education history. Due to the difference in education quality, bigger cities would have a higher success rate and rural areas where education was not as good, would have a much lower success rate[60]. Every candidate was aware that they were facing the toughest competition.

Nevertheless, this was an opportunity. Once the exam was scheduled for the one week at the end of November that year, the clock started ticking. All candidates were busy preparing for the challenge of a lifetime.

The government propaganda systems called for all levels of government to provide convenience for the qualified youths to prepare for the exams. In some places, like in the cities, there were organized classes for candidates to learn and prepare, while in other places like in the rural areas, there wasn't such opportunities provided.

For those *zhiqing* who had a solid background with adequate knowledge, they were totally focused on the preparation. Some even took a "leave of absence" to prepare with 100% of their time dedicated. At that time, the local authorities in the rural areas seemed to be supportive, as instructed by the upper governments. After all, the nation needed knowledge and the best people for its future. However, there were also some *zhiqing* who were depressed and regretted because they did not have a solid background, having wasted their time during those years.

---

[60] The actual success rate was less than 1% outside the major cities.

No doubt, some regretted not having learned enough to catch the lifetime opportunity.

For Dai-shan, there was no catch-up classes to go to nor any organized help. It was all on himself. However, there was no obstacles to prevent him from the exams. Dai-shan wasted no time and started reviewing his high school books and assignments. Believe it or not, after reviewing them, he thought there was not much in them. There was no library where he could borrow books. There was no bookstore where he could buy any textbooks.

He went to see his middle school teachers near his village. You can imagine, the teachers were happy to see him asking for more materials and encouraged him. When he went to see his physics teacher, the teacher picked a tough question in his old book and asked him to try to solve it on the spot. Dai-shan finished the question in about 20 minutes and handed it back to his teacher. The teacher looked at it and smiled to his wife who was making lunch, and then turned to Dai-shan, "You have a good chance to get into university. Let me find my old books for you". That made Dai-shan feel good inside and increased his confidence. The teacher then fetched his old books used prior to the cultural revolution and lent them to him.

Unlike other *zhiqing*, Dai-shan did not leave his job. He continued with his daily work in the movie team, completing his duty as usual and tried to spend more time to read his books and working on solving questions whenever he had spare time. His co-worker Wang-jin was supportive and tried to provide him convenience when possible. On the contrary, Gong *shifu* was not quite the same. He seemed to be jealous of someone who could do something that he was not able to. Although he could not stop Dai-shan from preparing for the exams on his own time, he would gossip, "He thinks he can pass the exams? How many people in our commune have got into university in the history? None! Even in the whole county, there has not been more than a handful."

Well, Gong was not wrong on the statistics. No one had heard of anyone they knew in the commune or nearby areas who got into a university. They had only heard people in the cities did but not anyone in the rural areas. Many ordinary people just thought universities were for people in the cities, like those *zhiqing*, but not for anyone in the rural areas. That was actually true given the history of the education systems and the differential resources available.

Dai-shan was aware of the history and the statistics, but he was not discouraged. He put all those rumors aside and focused on his preparation. Somehow but not sure why, he had so much confidence in himself. "If I can't get into a university, no one else around here can". That might sound naive but that was what he believed. It was not because he was arrogant, but because he knew himself and how much he had studied and prepared and was aware of the education quality in the rural areas in those days.

However, he took the examinations very seriously. He knew he was not good on every subject at school. The key was how to allocate his time appropriately in order to achieve the best overall outcome.

There was a saying around those days, "do well in math, physics and chemistry with sound knowledge 学好数理化 (*xuehao shu-li-hua*), there is nothing to be afraid of wherever you go around the world 走遍天下都不怕(*zou pian tianxai dou bupa*)". Luckily, those subjects just fit Dai-shan's interest.

It was also common sense, "3 feet of ice 冰冻三尺 (*bingdong sanchi*), is not formed in a single cold day 非一日之寒(*fei yiri zhihan*)". It meant to him that in the short period of time (only approximately one and half months), it was not possible to cram for the examination if he didn't already have solid background in a subject.

It was announced that the examination would separate into two categories: 1) liberal arts, and 2) science and engineering.

Dai-shan liked math and physics and liked analyzing and reasoning, and he did well on those subjects in school. But he did not like politics and was not interested in literature, which he did poorly in school. In fact, he hated memorizing things, or someone's speeches and flattering people. That might be why he couldn't make much progress in his political status. He knew that kind of personality might not be the best for his future, but he was exploring life one step a time.

He was not good in describing and elaborating on things. He couldn't understand why some people would make a long speech and say things in different ways back and forth, inside and out, when it could simply be summarized in a few words. That might explain why he didn't do well in literature in school.

Well, it was what it was. He couldn't change the past nor the current situation. In selecting his choices in the examination registration forms, he considered the above aspects carefully and chose the science and engineering category. The exam was intended to test the overall knowledge and potential of the candidates in several aspects, which required four subjects in the exam: Politics, Chinese literature, Mathematics, physics and chemistry (combined). The full marks were 100 for each subject with a total of 400 full marks in the whole exam.

The situation did not look good in his favor. Out of the four subjects, he knew he couldn't compete with others in politics and literature, and he had to maximize his potential and do better than the other candidates in the remaining two subjects (math, physics and chemistry) to bring his overall marks up.

He thus arranged his time and priority to prepare for the exam in a way to achieve the best overall outcome. He spent time first on math, physics and chemistry, and made sure he fully understood the contents in the books. Then he did as much as he could without wasting too much time on politics and literature.

On his movie tour, many times the movie show took place on the local school campus. The teachers obviously noticed him reading books often. Older teachers encouraged him. Some *zhiqing* substitute teachers however appeared disappointed in the conversations and tried to avoid the subject of *gaokao*. Perhaps they did not think they had the sufficient knowledge for the challenge at that time.

Many of his high school classmates were also preparing for the exam. There were eight of them in the same commune, including *Ye-zhong*, down the village, *Zhan-hui, Dai-mang, and Xin-kun* in the neighboring *Daduis*. During those days, Ye-zhong, Zhan-hui and Dai-shan often gathered together, particularly on the market days to discuss things in Ye-zhong's home, which was just beside the commune complex. Often, Teacher Ye, Ye-zhong's older brother, joined their conversations, analyzed the situations and suggested what type of universities or colleges to select based on individuals' strength. Sometimes Dai-mang joined them too. Xin-kun was a little further away but Dai-shan would meet him when the movie show was in his village. It had become routine that Dai-shan shared Xin-kun's bed every movie night there. They often discussed practice problems on the bed late into the night.

Dai-shan and his classmates were preparing for the *Gaokao* just like that. There were no school organized classes to help. Everyone was on his own. They were busier and had more pressure than when they were in school. Before they noticed, one and half months passed by very quickly. *Gaokao* time was quickly approaching.

The examination time 高考开始了 (*gaokao kaishi le*)

Ready or not, the time is here. It was the end of November. The weather cooled down and *gaokao* time had arrived. All the candidates in the local five communes were required to write the exams in the school of the *Xingxing* commune, the location of the *Qu* 区 government, which administered the five communes. The exam would be completed in two consecutive days. Two subjects per day, at the same time in the whole county and perhaps across many counties in the province.

Some candidates might be cramming on the last day hoping to learn something. Dai-shan took the last day off to do nothing related to the *gaokao*. He needed a rest to clear his mind and to recharge his brain. He asked for two days off from his work to write the exam.

The exam was scheduled to start at nine o'clock in the morning for the first subject for three hours, with a one-hour break at lunch time before the second subject. Candidates were required to arrange their own accommodations. Those who came from far away and couldn't go home would have to find a place to stay overnight.

It was about 10 kilometers distance from Dai-shan's home to the exam site. There were very few buses as public transportation and the buses did not work on the schedule of the exam. As a result, like most candidates, Dai-shan and his buddies relied on their own feet, walking to the exam site. Some candidates in the mountains would have to walk twice as far. The lucky ones might be able to get a ride on a hand-held tractor trailer 手扶拖拉机 (*shoufu tuo-la-ji*). No one seemed to complain about that. They simply followed the instructions to arrive at the exam site early.

On the first day, Dai-shan got up early, around five o'clock. He had to arrive before 7am for registration. His mother got up early too, cooked two eggs and made *momo* 馍馍 (hand-made thick pan cake from corn flour) for his lunch. He took a water bottle and filled it with boiled water. With everything needed in a bag, on the way he went.

Dai-shan walked down the hill to meet *Ye-zhong* and *Zhan-hui* had arrived there already. The three of them immediately went on their way. They passed the Longsheng market, seeing no one in the market yet. Soon they passed another small town and gradually saw other young people walking on the road. No doubt, they were also on the way to the exam. Before they reached the exam site, they were no longer alone and many other candidates from the neighboring areas were arriving too.

They registered at the registration desk with their exam notice. No one had a photo ID in those days and that notice with their names on it seemed sufficient.

Not sure exactly how many candidates were writing the exam that day at that location. They occupied five classrooms. Each candidate was given a number and went to their designated room. There were 25 or so desks in a room, each candidate would sit at a pre-numbered desk.

On the first day, the subject was physics/chemistry in the morning and Chinese literature in the afternoon. On the next day was math in the morning and politics in the afternoon. It was a closed book exam for all four subjects. No reference materials were allowed and only tools were allowed on the desk. Calculators were unheard of. There were a number of invigilators patrolling the exam rooms. Some may be local schoolteachers, and some were from the county education bureau office.

It was still half an hour before the exam time, everyone who arrived in time was already sitting at their desks, quietly, waiting for the school bell to ring. Meanwhile, the invigilator distributed the exam sheets on each deck, but no one was allowed to peek. Then the invigilator announced the rules, "… if anyone is caught violating the rules, he/she will be required to leave the exam room immediately and will not be allowed to continue writing further exams this year."

"Ding …, ding …", the bell rang. It was 9 o'clock.

"Now, you may start writing your exam." The invigilator announced.

Immediately, everyone opened their exam sheets and started reading and writing. No one was supposed to talk. It was so quiet that you could hear dropping a pen on the floor. The only sound heard was that of moving papers, pens, and writing if they knew what to write. However, there were some candidates sitting there chewing their pencils. Maybe, they didn't know where to start or were just thinking.

Dai-shan quickly glanced through all the questions on the exam sheet. Some were within his knowledge, and some were more difficult than he expected. He did the easier questions first before tackling the difficult ones. He managed to finish them all in time, though it was very tight. In an exam like that, he would never want to be the first person to hand in his work even if he had finished early. He would check and check again his answers if there was time. This time, he barely had much time to double check the answers. Overall, he completed all the questions and felt good about the exam.

"Time is up", the chief invigilator announced.

After handing over his answering sheet, Dai-shan went out the classroom to get some fresh air. Soon other candidates came out too, but they did not try to compare their answers. They knew they had to move on. Well, once it was done, it was done. He had no time to think about whether what he did was right or wrong in the morning as he had to move on to the next subject in the afternoon.

He took out his *momo* and water bottle and had his lunch in the school yard. The lunch time passed quickly and soon the next exam would start.

The exam in the afternoon was Chinese literature, which was not Dai-shan's favorite subject, although he tried to catch up as much as he could. There were questions related to grammar and comprehension, but the major component was to write an essay on a provided subject. Dai-shan did what he could and handed over his answer sheet in time. He didn't feel as good as the exam in the morning, but he was prepared to accept the outcome.

When Dai-shan came out of the exam room, many other students were out there too. He was just looking around to find his buddies who came with him in the morning and was planning to walk home before dark.

"Hi, Dai-shan". Someone called to him from behind. He turned around and saw another high school classmate. It was *yue-ben*, the class committee member in charge of physical exercises (体育委员 *tiyu weiyuan*) in high school.

"Hi, Yue-ben". He walked up to him, and they chatted about the exams.

"Where are you going now, Dai-shan", Yue-ben asked.

"Oh, I was just looking for my friends we came together this morning and are planning to go home soon."

"You will have to walk back here again tomorrow morning. If you don't have a place nearby to stay overnight, why don't you come to my place? My home is only about 15 minutes' walk from here."

"Ah, ⋯", Dai-shan didn't plan for this. It would be nice and would save lots of time, but he wasn't sure if that was appropriate since he had never been to his home before. He then answered, "Thanks for the invitation but it is not convenient to you and your family."

"Don't worry. There are only my younger brother and my mother at home. Besides, we can discuss the math for tomorrow. I will prepare some lunch for us too." Yue-ben insisted Dai-shan go with him.

As they were talking, *Ye-zhong* and *Zhan-hui came* by. Later, *Xin-kun* too. When they understood what was happening, they told Dai-shan, "why don't go with Yue-ben. We will see you tomorrow."

Dai-shan often did not stay at home when he was on movie show tours and his mother would not be worried

314

about him in this situation. He walked with Yue-ben through the flat field and soon arrived at Yue-ben's home. The rural homes were quite similar in construction, with chickens and ducks around the yard. Dai-shan was used to the environment. They went into Yue-ben's room, which had an unpainted clay wall and floor but was clean with a table beside the bed. Apparently, this was the place where Yue-ben had been preparing for his exams. The two hadn't seen each other since graduation from high school. They had lots to catch up on. However, their conversation was primarily focused on the math exam the next day. They talked until supper time.

Yue-ben's mother prepared the supper. She was an elder woman who looked thin and tired but otherwise healthy. She had a smiling and kind face and welcomed Dai-shan to the home. From the conditions of the home and the wrinkles on her face, it was not difficult to imagine that this family was in hardship too.

Yue-ben came out of the kitchen with two large bowls of *xifan* with green beans in it. His mother followed with some pickles on the table. When she saw that big bowl of *xifan* in front of Dai-shan, she said, "that is too much for a young man." and went to get another empty bowl to take some xifan out. Yue-ben saw that, felt embarrassed and hurried to his mother, "Ma, what are you doing?" trying to stop his mother from what she was about to do. Dai-shan saw this and quickly told Yue-ben, "It's Okay. I understand."

Dai-shan learned later that *Yue-ben*'s mother had been supporting the two boys to go to school on her own and *Yue-ben* had been the laborer to help his mother support the family since graduation. Like many families, their lives had not been easy.

The next morning, they woke up early and after breakfast walked to the exam site. It was the math exam in the morning.

The exam started. Dai-shan opened the exam sheet and glanced through the questions. He knew what to do with most of the questions except one, which he decided to leave for the end.

For analytical geometry questions, he would first understand the question, then analyze it, plus a drawing if necessary to arrive at the answers. For calculation questions, he would analyze and calculate manually. Calculators were not heard of at the time. Somehow the time seemed to go by faster than usual. By the time he finished the rest of the questions and was about to tackle that last question, there were only 15 minutes of time remaining.

He looked at the seemingly difficult question: to draw a circle of zero radius with given coordinates of its center. It was worth 10 points, 10% of the marks.

What the heck? "I can find its center, but how could it be possible to draw a circle with zero radius?" He tried hard to understand the question. He drew the x and y coordinate axes but couldn't figure out a way to draw a zero sized circle. He thought, no matter how small a circle he drew on the paper, it would have a size. Even the pencil itself had a size, not zero. He continued thinking.

"Ding…, ding…" the bell rang, and the time was up. He had only drawn the two axes but hadn't been able to draw that zero sized circle!

If he tried to do it in two steps: first mark the location of the centre and then use compass to draw a tiny circle around it, he could have gotten partial mark, couldn't he? But he hadn't drawn any circle.

He handed over his answer sheet with disappointment on that question.

After the exam, he went to ask his math teacher about that question. He was told, "it's just a dot", a special case of circle. In that case the question was too simple!

At first, he felt bad losing the easy mark and somewhat resentment towards his high school math teacher who didn't explain special situations like that. Then he thought it more and came to the conclusion that a dot should not be the right answer either because its size was not zero. Instead, a plain paper with nothing on it should be the correct answer. His reasoning was, a circle of zero radius meant that the circle did not even exist, and drawing of any non-existing thing would have no trace on the paper.

That was his reasoning. What do you think?

The exam in the afternoon was politics. Dai-shan managed to answer the questions, just trying to earn some marks.

The Gaokao was finished. Whatever they did was what they would get. There was no more chance to do anything differently or make any corrections.

What was the correct answer for that math question had become a mystery forever. Dai-shan never knew what mark he earned on that question, and no one saw their exam scores afterwards.

If they passed the exams, they would have an opportunity to go to a university. Otherwise, they may try it again the next year (the Gaokao for the following year was actually held in July 1978, only a few months away), or just give up the hope and look for something else in life.

It is worth to mention that during the two days of exams, Dai-shan didn't remember seeing his chess master friend, *Guang-cai* who helped him build the biogas chamber two years ago. He learned later from other classmates that *Guang-cai* got married to a *zhiqing* in his village the same year he graduated from high school, probably shortly after he went back home from Dai-shan's place, and they already had a daughter. He wasn't prepared for the exam that year[61]. A number of Dai-shan's other high school classmates did not show up in the exam either, including Hu-chou, the CYL secretary, his other friends: Yue-dong, Gong-hua, and Yu-fang. Some of them, Dai-shan had never heard from since graduating from high school.

After the exam, like other candidates, Dai-shan went

---

[61] Dai-shan learned a few years later that *Guang-cai* took the exam in the following year and was accepted into a normal college, becoming a high school teacher, specializing in Marxism-Leninism.

home, back to reality and continued his job as a movie show crew member. How well he did in the exam was unknown. None of the candidates knew because no final marks were released to the public in that year. At least that was the case in the rural areas.

The minimum entrance mark set by each university was not publicised in that year either and no one knew where they stood on the list. They just had to wait and see the outcome, hopefully within one month or two.

For those candidates in the cities, they might be able to see if they made it on the accepted list in a large red poster in their schools or in their communities. For the candidates in rural areas, there was no such poster and there was no way for them to find out much information about the outcome of the exam. All they could do was to wait for a something from somewhere. No news meant "not good news".

Perhaps someday something would come in the mail, directly from the university which had picked the student. No mail would probably mean no luck. For now, Dai-shan, like the others, just had to wait. The best way to get by and pass time was to forget about it and focus on work and life. Expect the best but prepare for the worst. Dai-shan was trying to do just like that. But was that easy to do?

www.ingramcontent.com/pod-product-compliance
Lightning Source LLC
Chambersburg PA
CBHW072100020726
47501CB00003B/653